"I loved this trip down Route 66....

... Kris Neri keeps the action rolling with a tight plot, a cast of loveable loonies, and a nostalgic tour of Americana."

— Elaine Viets, author of *Final Sail: A Dead-End Job Mystery*

"Outrageously Funny"

"There's a reason why Kris Neri is a three-time finalist for the Lefty Award – her books are outrageously funny. She's the Carl Hiaasen of the desert. This 4th Tracy Eaton Mystery is a zany trip down Route 66 with characters as bizarre and entertaining as the kitsch the Mother Road is famous for. Neri is a master plotter, weaving together the Eaton family history and Route 66 lore into a murder that will have you guessing to the last page but hoping you don't get there because you don't want it to end. *Revenge on Route 66* busted my guffaw meter."

— J. Michael Orenduff, author of *The Pot Thief Who Studied D. H. Lawrence*

"Adventure, Unpredictability, and Fun"

"Kris Neri has done it again! *Revenge on Route 66* delivers just as much adventure, unpredictability, and fun as the Mother Road itself. Tracy Eaton's fans will delight in this entertaining trip with enough bumps and kitsch to please the highway's devotees and enough danger and secrets to satisfy mystery enthusiasts everywhere."

— Pari Noskin Taichert, author of *The Belen Hitch*

"Buckle up!"

"Kris Neri's Lefty Award nominated Tracy Eaton is back, this time on a wild ride along the famed cross-country road in *Revenge on Route 66*. Forget the scenery—there are murders to investigate! If you're looking for laughs, hairpin turns, and whiplash plot twists, you won't want to miss this madcap adventure. Buckle up!"

— Julie Hyzy, *New York Times* Bestselling author of the White House Chef Mysteries and the Manor House Mystery series

"Quirky, Evolving Characters"

"Past and present crimes merge in *Revenge on Route 66* to provide an enjoyable mystery full of quirky, evolving characters."

— Linda O. Johnston, author of *Oodles of Poodles*, a Pet Rescue Mystery

"Entertains from Beginning to End"

"*Revenge on Route 66* has as many twists and turns as the road it's named after. With an endearingly snarky, engaging heroine and a colorful cast of supporting characters, this book entertains from beginning to end. A very satisfying ride!"

—Jess Lourey, author of the Lefty nominated Murder-by-Month series

"Action-Packed"

"Get ready for an action-packed detour through a twisty mystery with more laughs and quirky characters than the real Route 66. Sign me up for the next road trip with Tracy and Drew!"

— Laura DiSilverio, author of the Lefty finalist *Swift Justice* and the Mall Cop mysteries

"Vivid, Funny"

"There's a funky rhythm to Route 66—that loopy, swoopy highway connecting the past to the present—and Kris Neri totally gets it. She also understands the passion of the folks who travel the Mother Road and captures it in vivid, funny prose."

— Roger Naylor, author of *Arizona Kicks on Route 66*

A TRACY EATON MYSTERY

REVENGE
ON ROUTE 66

Kris Neri

Cherokee McGhee

Williamsburg, Virginia

ISBN 978-1-937556-02-0

First Edition 2013

Cover by Braxton McGhee

Published by:
Cherokee McGhee, L.L.C.
Williamsburg, Virginia

Find us on the World Wide Web at:
WWW.CHEROKEEMCGHEE.COM

Printed in the United States of America

For Sherry, who always asks when Tracy will return
in a new book,
and
for Ada for GNO.

Author Notes

I've taken a few liberties with Route 66. Some of the places I mentioned in this novel do exist, and if you're planning a Route 66 trek, you might want to include a few of them among your stops. Other places, such as Tecos, New Mexico, the Tecos caves, and Hinky Dill's Biker Bunny Bin, are figments of my imagination, though I've tried to bring a Route 66 spirit to them and all the other places and the characters I've created for this adventure. I hope you'll think I succeeded in that.

I've cruised Route 66 many times, and I've drawn on my own experiences to capture its unique combination of quirkiness and innocence, and the special way it takes us back in time. I've also relied on a number of other sources. My favorite Route 66 guides are: *Route 66: The Mother Road 75th Anniversary Edition* by Michael Wallis, *Route 66: Spirit of the Mother Road* by Bob Moore, and *Arizona Kicks on Route 66* by Roger Naylor with photographs by Larry Lindahl, but you'll find great insights and direction in most of the other guides as well. Any errors of fact are mine alone.

REVENGE

ON ROUTE 66

Kris Neri

CHAPTER ONE

Which is worse, secrets or lies? I could scarcely remember the first time Dad asked me to keep something from Mother. He never encouraged me to lie, of course. Not outright, anyway. But sometimes the only way to keep the truth under wraps is by telling a big fat whopper. Maybe they both become worse when they're joined together. More unstable, too. Is a secret really safe when it's propped up by something that can be shown to be a lie? I learned that on my last trip along Route 66. I also discovered that when you throw chance into the mix—well, then they make dynamite.

* * *

The strains of a disco beat, as cheerful as a pack of chipmunks and as relentless as the dentist's drill, wafted into my dream. My feet, in their glitter socks and platform wedgies, began to tap along to the rhythm. Given the tunes and the duds, I guessed my dream took place in the eighties. Despite the depth of my sleep state, though, and the fact that I really bought into the storyline, I always knew that it was a dream.

Well, what else could it have been? In the early eighties my parents hadn't moved that far beyond their one and only stab at procreation. I hadn't even started school yet, so I could not have been the fully-grown woman I saw in my mind's eye. But mostly, slob that I am, I knew it had to be a dream because I looked too well dressed for it to be real.

If anyone could describe the clothes from that era in those terms, that is. My dream hair wasn't any blonder than in actual life, though I wore it so big and puffy, I looked like one of the stars of the nighttime soaps that were that era's version of reality TV. My bod was stuffed into a pair of Jordache Jeans, so tight they could have doubled as a tourniquet. Topping them was a Hang Ten satin jacket the color of an Orange Julius, whose towering shoulder pads rose higher than the walls of the Grand Canyon. See what I mean about "well dressed" being a relative term? The only good thing I could say about the whole get-up was that encased within those tight jeans were a trimmer pair of thighs than I'd see in the bathroom mirror when I awoke in the morning. Ah, dreams do come true, as long as you never wake up.

More bizarre than my dream wardrobe were my actions. I stood at the open door of a commercial jet hovering in the air, holding hands with a guy I'd never met in real life as far as I knew. Certainly not the one who was probably snoring softly at my side, if I'd had any awareness of anything outside of my nighttime reverie. And in the odd way we have of sensing the conditions that rule our dreams—or maybe from the gun he carelessly waved about—I knew that man had hijacked the flight on which I was a passenger and had fallen hopelessly in love with me. Obviously, we were about to jump off into the sunset together.

Now I understood the cause of the dream. The prior night I'd watched a TV special on the thirtieth anniversary of the still-mysterious hijacking of an airliner by the notorious T.K. Mann, who, after he leaped from that plane, never surfaced again. And neither had even one cent of the ten million dollars in marked bills he'd collected as a ransom. I'd found that news special riveting, partly because my dad and I used to visit the very place where it's said T.K. Mann landed when he jumped from the hijacked plane. But I watched it too late, and it must have sparked something squirrelly in my brain. Or maybe I should blame Loco Pepe's Kitchen Sink Burrito, so named because it contained everything but the...well, you get it. That concoction had been known to produce some loopy dreams, too. Maybe it was the combination that did me in—I'd found that TV special so compelling, the only moments I missed were the ones I spent at the door with Loco Pepe's deliveryman.

T.K. tightened his grip on my dream-self's hand. "You're sure about this, Tracy?"

It didn't seem to trouble me that I really couldn't see what he looked like. According to the news special, the real T.K. Mann had covered his face during the skyjacking. Different passengers provided varying descriptions, as did the witnesses on the ground, who had claimed he'd ridden off on a motorcycle hidden at his landing spot. My dream-mind had simply whipped together lots of nothing and came up with a guy who was charmingly vague.

People had also reported that he'd worn a black stretchy garment, though the descriptions of the bod below the suit varied enough to be useless, from small and wiry, to big and bony. In my dream, T.K.'s duds looked more like something they might wear on Star Trek, which always made me wonder why in the future we won't need pockets. Won't we ever need to carry a tissue to blow our noses?

My T.K. covered his head with an oversized motorcycle helmet, which hid the color of his hair, while its darkened windshield obscured his eyes. All I could see of him was a squarish jaw and the impossibly artic teeth of the toothpaste ads that were all the rage today, thirty years into the future.

T.K. threw his arm around my waist and pulled me toward him. As close as I could get anyway, with all he wore. He flashed me the grin that the guys in the disco flicks always seemed to give their girls, as if to say, "Ain't it great to be young, stupid, and unemployed?"

With my return smile, I conveyed, "It sure is, baby." Long as we had the loot.

Obviously, the pesky laws of physics don't govern dreams. Not only was there no apparent danger that we'd be sucked through the open jet door, the plane was so steady, we didn't even need to hold on. Neither did we seem troubled that the passengers or crew might rush us from behind, though I did hear some resentful grumbling from the cabin, probably because we looked so impossibly good.

"This will work, won't it, T.K?" I asked.

I didn't know whether my dream-self was asking whether we'd get away with the crime without being apprehended—or if we'd land alive. I hoped I had enough sense to question the latter. Even in a dream, you can't be too careful. T.K. wore nothing more than a skimpy secondary parachute strapped to his chest, the kind that most jumpers regard as a backup in case the main deal fails. He had to wear the chute there because covering his flipside was a backpack the size that people often carry when they hitchhike through Europe, for five or six years, and don't expect to have access to a Laundromat. He obviously hadn't yet shared his booty with me. I, on the other hand, carried nothing more to slow my descent than the tiny denim purse embroidered with pink flowers, which I'd thrown over one shoulder. Sure, that would help. I hoped my dream-self had enough sense to grab one of those under-the-seat floatation devices before she jumped. Maybe it could float on air.

"They haven't caught me yet, and it's thirty years later," T.K. bragged. "You're not bothered that we're taking the money, are you?"

I didn't feel bothered. "Can we give a few bucks to charity?"

His anachronistic teeth gleamed extra brightly. "Sure thing, sweetheart."

What a guy. Was it any wonder I was willing to leave behind my luggage, and what must have been a really cool wardrobe, for him?

From somewhere nearby, a buzzing sound began to wail.

"T.K., your cell phone is ringing." I didn't see it on him, so it must have been small. "You wanna answer it before we jump?"

He shook his helmeted head. "Not mine, honey. Smart phones won't be invented for while yet, and as soon as I hit the ground, I'm going splat."

I admired the good cheer he brought to that remark.

Then...*someone* shattered my dream, by giving my real life self a nudge in the side and muttering, "Tracy...alarm."

In that moment, the dream vanished. While I wasn't fully awake, I wasn't asleep anymore, either. I knew I lay at home in my own bed, with my husband Drew at my side, while he prodded me to turn off the alarm clock that howled beside my ear.

"That's T.K. Mann's cell phone," I said. Until someone disproved it, I refused to give up that theory. Besides, he wasn't there to deny it.

"Noooo," Drew said, his voice now more awake. "You just had to eat that burrito. They always give you crazy dreams."

"The TV special did it." Though burrito fumes still burned in my esophagus, I'd never admit it.

"Every time you eat Loco Pepe's..." He sighed. "Turn off the alarm, Trace."

"You turn it off." Where is it written that, simply because you're grown, you have to stop behaving like a child? My parents were so old, they knew Adam and Eve in high school, and they had yet to give up their infantile ways. Why break a family tradition?

"It's on your side of the bed."

Right. We'd originally put the alarm clock on his side back when he worked as a lawyer. After he gave up that pursuit—a source of some tension between us—he moved it to mine. Just another step in his campaign to nudge me into assuming the primary adult role in this household, which I was resisting with everything I had.

Since the clock's buzzer wasn't getting that message, I finally smacked it off.

This was the morning when we planned to take off after my father and Drew's uncle, to join our vacation to theirs on Route 66. Though Dad was an aging Hollywood hunk, he'd always liked to take road trips along Route 66, convincing himself, when he moved through the bizarre hoi polloi you find on the Mother Road, as those of us who know it call Route 66, that he was really a regular person, deep down. Traveling with him this time was Drew's Uncle Philly, who had to rise up a ways to reach "regular person."

Was it really time to get up already? The early morning light creeping around the sides of the heavy drapes at the window said it was. How was that possible? I felt like I'd never slept. How long had my encounter with T.K. Mann lasted?

This wasn't the way I wanted to start a vacation I'd been planning for weeks, the last one I was likely to have for a while if *someone* didn't go back to the law. While what I really wanted now was to roll over and sleep for another few hours, with a groan, I dragged myself from bed.

If I had any idea how many juicy secrets I would turn up along Route 66, I would cheerfully have run all the way.

CHAPTER TWO

Curiosity rules my life. I mean it—if Nosiness were a country, they'd make me queen. While I brewed coffee, which I'd desperately need if I had to begin this trip without enough sleep, I thought about how odd it was that T.K. Mann stole into my dreams last night, rather than Dad's old friend, Lucy Crier. Whenever I thought about Tecos, New Mexico, a rustic little town between Grants and Albuquerque, which Dad regarded as his other home and where we were headed, it was Lucy who always captured my imagination. Even if that was also where T.K. Mann was said to have landed when he jumped from that plane.

Lucy wasn't anywhere near as notorious as the country's most infamous hijacker. Other than painting some pretty, if forgettable, scenes on the lunch pails decorating a diner that specialized in meals that would make a gourmet yawn, the most daring act she'd ever taken was to plug her married honey, Billy Rob Royce, which had happened during my second trip along the Mother Road. It earned her a lifetime residency in the home for Women who Love Unwisely and Get Pissed-Off too Easily.

It occurred to me for the first time in thirty years of visiting it that Tecos produced a helluva lot of crime for a sleepy little town that most travelers forgot as soon as they blew past it. Had Tecos' felony wave influenced my own direction in life, as a mystery author and determined amateur sleuth? Or, even as a kid, had my own innate interest in crime set in motion everything that happened there? Tracy Eaton—crime prodigy. Ridiculous as the idea was, I loved it.

I'd intended to start the trip from our home in the northern part of Los Angeles with a little speech, something about the excitement of hitting the open road, taking a step back in time and seeing the country as it once existed, from the vantage point of America's most famed big-ass highway. But the caffeine hadn't fully hit yet, so I limited my opening remarks to a grunt and snarl, pausing only long enough to make sure the lunch pail that Lucy Crier had given me decades earlier was packed with our luggage in the backseat of Drew's cinnamon-colored Volvo sedan.

This pail depicted a charming artistic rendering of the Hollywood sign on hill that was a brighter green than anything the Golden State had ever seen. And, sure, Lucy had spelled "Hollywood" wrong, with only one "l," making it "Holywood," which gave it a vaguely religious quality that *really* didn't describe the place where I grew up. Still, I felt such a sentimental attachment to that lunchbox, I never cruised Route 66 without it.

This time we might need its contents—I didn't mean the heavy thermos, but a sizeable stash I'd kept in there for most of my life. Though the idea of dipping into it pained me, considering our looming financial crisis, thanks to Drew's unemployment, I could no longer rule it out. Before leaving, I took another look into my wallet, to make sure I actually had cobbled together enough cash to get us through the next several days, after which Dad's largesse could take over.

Drew seemed grateful when I climbed behind the wheel, offering to take the first leg. Probably thought he'd snooze in the car. Maybe he'd take up the adventure of T.K. Mann and me, so he could tell me how it ended. But his gratitude went sour when, after less than a half-hour, I bid the freeway farewell, exiting into a questionable San Gabriel Valley neighborhood and parked in the shadowy lot of a public park.

"Where…?" Drew sputtered, still groggy.

I tried explaining all this to him when we planned the trip. I'd told him a jaunt down America's Main Street would be nothing but stops and side excursions. If you don't pull over and savor every tacky bit of it, you might as well fly. But, okay, maybe I could understand his anxiety. In this neighborhood, the park's darkness had less to do with an attempt to save on electricity than the fact that all the streetlamps must have been shot out. But Dad and I regarded this stop as the most essential of all. When it comes to Route 66, tradition is everything.

"Uh...Trace, do you think a service station would be better?" Drew asked, not budging from the car.

"I'm not a toddler. I used the bathroom before we left the house."

For all the good it would do. I'd also brought along a commuter coffee cup as big as a missile silo. To make it more than another few miles, I'd probably need a salt lick to guarantee bloating.

"Besides, a public restroom in a gangland park wouldn't be my first choice," I added. In the distance, I heard the thickita-thickita sounds of Rain Birds irrigating the park's patchy stretches of grass.

"Then why are we here?" he called from the car when I walked off. "If you know this is gang territory—"

"Drew, even gang members sleep-in." I felt sure every sensible person but us had slept late this morning, though it did occur to me belatedly that gang-banging was probably not the wisest of career paths. "Bring the flashlight, okay?" I shouted, pressing on. "It's not bright enough yet to read out here."

"We're reading?" he asked. I didn't bother answering.

Finally, over the noise of the Rain Birds, I heard a sigh, and at last, the slamming of a car door.

I smiled to myself. Not merely because Drew fell in with my plans—he usually did eventually. It was just a question of how hard he made me work for it. I smiled because he sounded like the old Drew, the stodgy one that I used to try to change. The Drew I wasn't wise enough to appreciate when I had him.

Drew was "evolving," to use his word. After years of my struggling to bring that about, it stunned me to discover my own wish had come back to bite me.

Not that long ago, he had been moving up the ladder of the cutthroat law firm of Slaughter, Cohen, Rather, Word & Dragger— or as Mother referred to it, SCREWED—when he made the pesky mistake of bloodying the nose of one of the senior partners. When that partner was found floating face down in our swimming pool, deader than disco, that not only put Drew in Dutch with the law, it put the kibosh on whatever future he'd once had at SCREWED.

But, hell, Drew was a good lawyer. I wasn't worried. I mean, *if*

it ain't broke, don't be an idiot and break it—that's my motto. He
initially applied for a job at the L.A. County District Attorney's
office. They had now offered him, not one, but three positions, and
Drew had turned them all down.

Don't ask me why. Seems he didn't know himself. He wasn't
sure if he wanted to practice law anymore. Too bad he didn't have
any other ideas. Not good ones, anyway. The guy who had probably
mapped out his entire future, from birth to death, in the first few
moments of life—was now trying to find himself.

He was waiting, he insisted, for the universe to show him what
he should be doing. Too New Agish for me. Yeah, I was a native
Angeleno, and we're all flakes, but I was also too superficial to be
that cosmic.

"And what if the universe doesn't show you?" I'd asked.

Drew shrugged. "I don't know, farm or something. We have
enough land."

Farm? Hello! It was true that we did have some acreage
surrounding the old wreck of a house that Mother gave us, in the
Northwest San Fernando Valley in Los Angeles. But if you scrape
more than an inch below the surface, you hit solid sandstone rock. If
formerly New York-Boy wanted to become Farmer-Guy, he'd better
learn rocks don't produce the best crops.

That meant that it fell to me to keep the boat afloat. Sure, I
pulled in some decent coin as a mystery author, but it ran through
my fingers faster than water. I'd squandered my last advance on so
many doo-dads and whatnots for our house, the place now looked
like a gift shop. Even worse, I suspected that Drew's metamorphosis
meant I had to take over as the designated adult in our household,
a role I was not fit to play. No fair. If I stomped my foot, would he
get that?

I'd always believed the glue that held us together was the fact
that I provided his fun, and he served as my rock. If he suddenly
started making his own fun, would he still need me? Even worse,
would I be rock-less?

"Oh, for the love of…" I heard from behind me. "The ground is
saturated. My shoes are getting soaked."

I bit my lip to keep from laughing. What did Farmer Drew think was making that thickita-thickita sound? Rattlers? Fortunately, my clunky leather sneakers were watertight. I stomped on the soppy ground, splashing him.

"Hey, watch it, Trace," Drew shouted. "Why are we out here anyway? I thought you were so eager to get to New Mexico."

"Drew, there are rituals to observe when you set out on the Mother Road." Not to mention an errand my father expected us to perform for him along the way. "We're there," I said, stopping. "Gimme the flashlight."

I took it from where it dangled at the end of his fingers and pointed it toward the large brass plaque on the ground before us. Since the sun was low in the sky, it cast long shadows over the plaque, but the flashlight allowed us to read it.

"On this day..." Drew read, rattling off a date when I was six years old, during my third Route 66 jaunt. Right after Lucy went up the river. "Actor Alec Grainger and Mayor Randall Josephson designated this spot as the end of America's Main Street, Route 66." With a huffy little snort, Drew said, "That's not right. Route 66 ends in Santa Monica. I read that online. They have a plaque there that—"

"*A* plaque. This is *the* plaque. Lots of people think Route 66 ends right here," I insisted.

"And everyone else knows it ends in Santa Monica."

I shined the flashlight into his eyes to make him shut up. Then I directed it back to the plaque, where they'd printed lots more. It was quite a plaque. It described how they'd buried a time capsule on that day, and listed everyone in attendance. Almost everyone—I'd been there, and my name wasn't on it. Little kids don't count?

Not employees either, apparently. Drew took the flashlight from my hand and directed it to a modification someone had made to the plaque. "What's that?" he asked, shining the light to where someone had scratched, after Dad's name, the words "and companion."

"Companion?" Drew asked. "Was he with some floozy?"

"Nah, he and Mother were cozy there for a while." My parents made a bigger production of marrying and divorcing each other than any of their movies. Besides, there was only one floozy associated with Route 66, and she had just entered the big house at that point. "He picked up some gopher-type assistant that we'd known in New Mexico, some young guy named Terry Kennedy, who was slick like spit."

Drew continued moving the flashlight's beam across the plaque. "That's not like Alec. He's never surrounded himself with an entourage like everyone else in Hollywood."

No, he never had. He'd always seen himself as an ordinary guy, who got lucky before the cameras. But he wasn't, really. Not ordinary, I mean—he sure had been lucky. "Months earlier he'd promised the organizers of that event that he would build and fill the time capsule himself, and he forgot about it. Turns out that wasn't something he enjoyed doing."

"Ah," Drew said. "If he likes it, your dad has great sticking power. Look at all the carpentry he's done at our place. But if he doesn't, he shucks it off onto somebody else."

Maybe we weren't being fair to Dad. Sure, that was the way things usually worked with him. But back then, one of his dearest friends had just pled guilty to a crime he never thought she committed, and began serving a life sentence. How could he focus on such meaningless things as a time capsule? I explained all that to Drew.

"So Dad forgot about it, and then he couldn't deal with it, but we were down to the wire. The nasty assistant was the one who came up with the capsule design, such as it was, and was responsible for filling it. Obviously, Dad hogged all the credit. I guess that explains the little post-plaque etching Terry must have added at some point."

Since the ground was mushy, I couldn't kneel before the plaque as I had at other times. Instead, I squatted low and placed my hand on it, as was our ritual. After a moment Drew squatted next to me and placed his hand beside mine. He might have become an aimless universe-watcher, but sometimes he understands things like nobody else. I tilted my head against his shoulder.

"Why did you call the assistant nasty?" he asked.

"He always did rotten things to me. The day of the commemoration, he stood behind me when we gathered before the hole where they placed the time capsule, and he kneed my back during the ceremony. Naturally, I fell into it and started crying. The mayor acted like I ruined the dignity of the occasion on purpose." Probably why my name didn't end up on the plaque. "But I was a little kid, and I'd fallen on an old Army trunk filled with junk."

"An Army trunk? That was the time capsule?"

"The assistant wasn't any more interested in constructing something creative than Dad. I think the choice disappointed the committee, but it was too late to do anything about it by then."

"What did you put into the trunk?"

"Oh, lots of cool stuff. Magazines and newspapers of the time, clothing catalogs that showed the way people dressed, money, eight-track tapes, and movies on Betamax."

"Money? Why?"

I shrugged. "I can't remember why that seemed important. In case they changed it, I guess. And they have changed it, so it was a good choice. Who would have predicted our tens would look like they were soaked in mud, and our fives would resemble something a counterfeiter made with a purple marker?"

We'd actually put lots of currency into the trunk. I vaguely recalled whole packets of twenties, fifties and hundreds. That had to be my memory playing tricks on me. Dad had delegated the filling of the trunk to Terry, but after a while, he shucked it off onto Lucy's son Woody and me. Since Woody was more scattered than usual then, given that he was losing his mom and going to live with his grandmother, mostly, it had fallen to me. Someday when they dug it up, people were going to be pretty disappointed that the time-frozen look at Americana reflected the perspective of a six-year-old. But there couldn't have been as much cash in it as I thought. Where would I have gotten it? That was an awful time for me as well, what with Dad riding an emotional roller coaster, so my memory was pretty fuzzy, too.

"We also put in loads of Route 66 memorabilia, of course—Dad had a collection of the stuff, and he donated some of it. Or maybe I just took it," I said, moving on. "And Pet Rocks and other fad stuff. Toys, too. I donated one of my Barbie dolls. I mean who'd believe a gal with her wasp waist and gynormous chest would still be popular?"

"Who'd believe she wouldn't be?" Drew said with a snort. "So what happened to this assistant?"

I shrugged. "Got me. Back in L.A., he lived in our guesthouse for a short time, and then one day, he was just gone. He's probably in some rat hole now, dispensing worldwide spam. He was that smarmy."

That's an important lesson to learn about the Mother Road. Almost every stranger becomes your friend…except for the odd guy you never want to turn your back to. The trick is picking that guy out. They aren't always as obvious as Dad's old bootlicker.

CHAPTER THREE

MEMORIES OF ROUTE 66
TRACY

T*hree weeks past my April 1ˢᵗ birthday: I had just turned six years old. For the second year in a row, my birthday present was a trip with Dad along Route 66.*

Mother could never imagine roughing it like we did. Of course, she refused to acknowledge a world existed beyond the Beverly Hills city limits, unless you counted Paris, London, and Milan. Still, she never seemed to question why he escaped down the Mother Road every year or so. Maybe she thought he was still promoting his old movie, Revenge on Route 66. Or maybe she knew why he left and didn't choose to acknowledge it. But I'd always wanted to understand why that road took him away from us.

Last year before my first trip, he'd promised that once he introduced me to his favorite haunts, I would understand its appeal. Even at that young age, I totally got it, and my love for Route 66 deepened again this time, and would continue to with every subsequent trip I made. Yet I still failed to grasp its hold on Dad, since he never venerated the kind of kitschiness you saw along the Mother Road, like I came to.

Now, we were headed home, cruising down the concrete highway in Dad's Lincoln Continental. One of his hands hung over the big white steering wheel, while the other elbow peeked out the open window.

I sat beside him, my little patent leather Mary Janes barely stretching beyond the deep bench seat. On my lap I held a lunch pail—the kind with the dome lid that workmen carry—beautifully painted, but with a misspelled Hollywood sign on an artificially green hill.

Dad beamed down at me. "It was nice of Lucy to give you one of her precious lunch pails for your birthday, wasn't it, Tracy? I've never known her to part with one of them for anyone. She couldn't very well give away all her decorative lunch buckets and still call her restaurant the Lunch Pail Café."

I discovered the clasp at the front and began popping it. "Daddy, why do the people in Tecos call Lucy Crier Lucy Liar?"

Dad's photogenic features twisted into a sick frown. "People are nasty sometimes, honey. You're old enough to know that."

"Is it true?"

He ran his fingers through the longish shock of dark hair that fell over his forehead. "You sure do ask the questions, sweetheart." He sighed heavily. "Some people along the Mother Road think they have the best of lives. The whole world comes to them. But others feel stuck, like everyone else gets to go somewhere except for them. Lucy's one of those."

"That makes her lie?"

"It's not lying...exactly, Tracy. Lucy's one of those twitchy types, like your mother. But Martha has a chance to use all that drama on the screen. Lucy doesn't have that outlet. So...sometimes she fibs a bit, to make her life seem grander. Understand, sweetheart?"

I shrugged my little shoulder. "I guess." I continued to flip the clasp. "Why did those policemen keep coming to see Lucy?"

Dad hesitated. "That was because of her friend Billy Rob. You remember him from when you met him last year, right? Well, something bad happened to him the first night we were there, when all the police cars came and woke us up. Remember that, Tracy?"

I remembered his trying to distract me from the reason why all those police cars showed up that night.

"You see, honey, Billy Rob went to heaven. The policemen wanted to talk to Lucy about that. That's why they kept coming back."

Went to heaven. Sheesh! I was six, not stupid. I knew all about death—I had goldfish. We were always having toilet bowl funerals for them. I did wonder, though, where they would find a big enough toilet to flush Billy Rob.

"You didn't like Billy Rob, did you, Tracy?"

I didn't. Despite his hearty laugh and funny walk, he hadn't been a nice man. Mostly, though, I hadn't liked him because I sensed my dad didn't. Because I thought he wanted me to agree with him. But I also didn't like Billy Rob's friend Terry, and Daddy thought Terry was great. Terry knew how to play all the grown-ups.

We rode for a while in silence. Then I asked, "Do you think Lucy is pretty?"

Dad smiled at me. "Do you?"

Another shrug. I moved on to opening the top of the lunch pail. Did I think she was pretty? Not likely. "Pretty" to my young eyes meant soft and sweet. The image of Lucy still burned in my mind was anything but. She was all angles and curves, flat where it counted and full where that mattered more, with natural white-blonde waves that tumbled past her shoulders.

Dad sighed softly. "After your mom, I think she's the most beautiful woman I've ever seen."

Viewing the memory with adult eyes, I had no doubts of that. If looks were all that mattered, Lucy could have made it to the top of the modeling game. Her dark, hooded eyes and the beauty mark placed at the most photogenic point on her upper lip, along with her strong cheekbones and full lips, would have captivated the camera. But modeling is a career that calls for drive and organization, skills Lucy sorely lacked.

"But pretty...?" Dad continued musing. "No, Lucy isn't happy enough for that. She's had a hard life."

None of us knew it then, but her life was about to get a lot harder. Lucy would soon confess to murdering Billy Rob, and within weeks, she'd begin serving a life sentence, and Dad and I would be back in Tecos to close down her restaurant.

But Lucy was always her own worst enemy, what with the stupid yarns that she would defend to the death, not to mention the married men she gravitated to. Now don't get me wrong—I appreciate a good fib as much as anyone. I've actually come to regard myself a master of artful prevarication. But there's smart lying for a good reason, and the dumb, pointless kind. Those were the ones Lucy specialized in, the ones any idiot could see through. I remembered wondering then whether the policemen knew that Lucy lied a lot.

I continued to pop the clasp, opening and closing the lunch pail, until Dad frowned at me. "Tracy, if you keep doing that, you're going to break the clasp. When someone gives you a precious gift, you should treasure it."

I'd snapped the lid of the lunch pail closed. "Daddy, Lucy didn't just give me the lunch pail, she gave me money, too."

While staring through the windshield, he shook his head. "Now why would she do that? She knows she can't afford it. The lunchbox was enough. How much did she give you?"

"Five..."

"Five dollars? That's too much."

"No, Daddy, it's—" I broke off suddenly, making an instantaneous choice not to correct him. The rush of keeping that first secret gave me a lifelong love of them.

He didn't seem to notice, misunderstanding my remark. "Now, you stop it right there, you privileged brat," he said with stern affection. "Just because we lavish you with everything doesn't mean five dollars is not a lot of money to some people. When someone who doesn't have it gives you that much, you owe it to her to show that gift the respect it deserves. You should put that lunch pail and the money away so that every time you take them out, you'll think of Lucy and appreciate her generosity."

We drove for miles in silence. Then Dad said, "Uh...Tracy, if you tell your mother about Lucy's gifts, it might make her feel bad that... well, that she didn't get to come along with us. Maybe this should be our little secret."

"Yours, mine, and Lucy's?"

"...Right. Understand?"

That was the first of many things he would ask me to keep from Mother. Jeez, if I had a dollar for every secret my parents foisted on me and insisted I keep from the other—well, I wouldn't care that today, Drew wanted to become a kept man. But looking back, I could see that many of Dad's secrets were associated with Route 66.

Dad suddenly pointed out the window to a rickety wooden tower, scarcely twenty-feet high, plopped in the middle of an open sandy field. "Look, Tracy, the Wonder View Tower. 'If you don't climb the tower, you'll wonder what you'd see,'" he read hastily from a hand-painted sign. "Let's stop and climb it."

Even as young as I was, I knew Dad wanted to distract me from the secret he'd sworn me to keep. Didn't matter. He didn't know that I had a secret of my own.

CHAPTER FOUR

These days, it's impossible to follow the whole length of the Mother Road actually on Route 66. Long sections of the old road still exist, mostly through the centers of towns. But those stretches are just threads that fray off of the ribbon of the interstate. Don't get me wrong, interstates have done lots of good for this country. Like the railroads before them, they moved people and goods fast. But we gave up something for them, too. We traded the adventure of discovery for the comfort of sameness. Now we no longer question that they take us from Anytown, USA, to Everytown, and it all looks the same. We've traded unique Americana for the same big box stores, same fast food stops, same chain motels with their free HBO and WiFi. Unless you take those detours off the interstates, you forget how much individuality rocks. Besides, where else can you read Burma Shave ads?

So...maybe I was a bit over the top with my detours. But who knew how much longer it would last?

We'd spent hours at the Route 66 Museum in Kingman, Arizona, with its photos, old cars, and murals, and we'd spread our lunch out over three down home cafés. Now we were finally coming up on Flagstaff, a mere four hundred-plus miles in just over thirty-three hours. Drew said the old pioneers were laughing at us.

Unlike all the stops I'd insisted we make to show Drew how to fully experience the Mother Road, we were on our way to a chore my dad had asked us to perform. I'd jotted the address on a Post-it that I'd stuck to the dash, which Drew struggled to read.

We continued on along Route 66 until we reached a driveway in an industrial area, which was guarded by two giant plywood figures of cartoon rabbits from a place you'd never want to see. The bearded bunny on the left had eyes that pinched together into a disgusting leer. And the hairless one on the right displayed yellowed, rotting teeth. They were both outfitted in black leather, with loads of studs and chains. In the warmth of the car, I shivered.

"What is this place?" Drew asked, sounding aghast.

Despite the revulsion I felt, I presented a confident pose. "It's the Biker Bunny Bin. What's the matter, Drew? Haven't you ever seen a self-storage yard?"

"Not one that looks like Disneyland on acid."

"Yeah, well, I think the owner, Hinky Dill, was shooting for..."

"Absolute terror?"

"Terror" hit a little close to home. The first time I saw those horrible rabbits, during my third Route 66 trip, after Lucy went to prison, they caused one of the worst nightmares I'd ever experienced. Those bunnies chased me in my sleep, ripping gouges out of my hide with their ugly yellow teeth whenever I didn't run fast enough. I couldn't explain how they affected me. I was a show biz brat, after all. Reality to me was having so many notes sent home from school, the principal put a messenger service on retainer—plywood and paint were the stuff of movie make-believe. But those wretched bunnies still felt real enough to me now that I watched them in the rearview mirror, to make sure they weren't coming after us.

"I was gonna say *whimsy,*" I said, "but I don't think Hinky would know whimsy if a Biker Bunny bit him on the ass."

"So why are we here?" Drew asked, when I drove to the office in the center of the storage yard. "This chamber of horrors doesn't seem to capture the same sense of fun as the rest of the oddball places you've dragged me to."

He *was* starting to get the Road. "Dad wants us to clean his storage unit," I said sourly. "And don't ask me why because I have no idea."

Since I hadn't intended to spend my vacation cleaning, I'd balked at that. Dad was insistent, though, yet oddly evasive about the reason why it mattered to him. I could never understand why he kept that awful storage unit after all these years.

"Dad, you know they've built one or maybe a million of those self-storage places closer to home," I'd said. And those joints weren't guarded by awful hellish creatures. "Do you think it might be time to move the stuff you have stashed there?"

"We don't have any in Beverly Hills," he had said. "Not up in the hills, anyway."

Gee, they didn't build anyplace to store garage sale rejects in some of the priciest real estate in the country. Go figure.

"I'd still have to take out the car to check on those things, even if I moved it all back to California."

Maybe so, but he wouldn't have to take the car out for thirty-three hours.

"Anyhoo, Trace, I can't pull the business away from Hinky. He's got a little gambling problem. He needs every cent he can get. Besides, everything in that storage unit belongs there on Route 66."

I suspected we'd gotten to the real reason why Dad wouldn't move to a more convenient storage center, and it had nothing to do with the Route 66 connection. He had a soft spot for people down on their luck, even if they'd caused it themselves.

Apart from the grim, disgusting cartoon figures that loomed over us at the gate and other choice spots around the place, the Biker Bunny Bin was a pretty ordinary storage facility, made up of five or six buildings filled with different sized units, all with padlocked doors.

Hinky's little cottage rested in the middle of the yard. Paint, in Pepto-Bismol-pink, peeled from its clapboard sides. Small planting areas had been cut in the pavement surrounding the cottage, but the dirt within them had fossilized to stone. Instead of landscaping, Hinky filled them with plywood cutouts painted to look like dead plants. To say the guy's standards were unusual was the understatement of this or any century.

I rapped on the front door, only to have yucky pink paint flake off on my knuckles.

"Come on in," someone called from inside, in the style of a game show host.

I pushed the rotting door open. A giant slot machine filled the space beyond it. Poised before it was a small, hairless man, whose pink and puckered skin looked as shiny as Saran Wrap. He stood before the one-armed bandit, with his scarred hands ready at his sides, like an old West gunslinger. Without warning, one hand flew out and he grabbed the slot handle and gave it a sudden yank. Jeez, taking a machine by surprise—there was a winning tactic. After a few more pulls, he turned to us.

In case I thought there might have been loads of pink and puckered creatures in the area, the head-on look confirmed that he was Hinky, all right. I hadn't seen him in years, but I could never forget the impression he made. He didn't look a day older than he had when we'd set up this unit, nor a bit more normal. His scarring was extensive, but it didn't make him look outright grotesque, just peculiar. That his big brown lashless eyes seemed to pop out at you, like a 3-D movie, only seemed strange the first hundred or so times.

"The machine don't have no money," he indicated with a toss of his odd-looking head. "I use it to stay in shape."

"Like a home gym?" I asked.

"Right!" He must have liked that idea—his eyes popped about a foot closer.

I explained who I was.

"Oh, yeah, Alec's kid. Haven't seen you in ages. You were the most annoying little brat. Always asking questions."

"She hasn't changed," Drew said, and then immediately asked about the cause of Hinky's scarring. He throws out lots of questions, too, like all lawyers. And he believed he could leave the law behind.

"Got caught in a fire. I guess it's getting better if you can't tell," the hairless man said.

Right. *Dream on, Hinky.*

"I'd been in a poker game in the back room of a lumber yard, when a pile o' rags some dipshit had soaked in linseed oil exploded." While he spoke, Hinky lovingly caressed the slot machine.

"And you were trapped in there?" Drew asked.

"Nah, the door was right behind me. But I had a good hand, you know. I figured we'd keep on playing, only the rest of them wusses chickened out and ran. They didn't get burned, but I took the pot. Whatta they got today that I don't?"

"Fingerprints?" I suggested.

"Turns out you don't need 'em."

Law enforcement would be happy to learn that.

I couldn't remember the way to Dad's storage unit, so, after a wistful glance at his one-armed bandit, Hinky led us there. "Alec comes to check on his unit every coupla years, but I haven't been in that thing since he filled it."

Why would he? Wasn't privacy the point of those lockers?

"Alec built all them shelves in there himself, you know? Who would of thought a big star like him would know how to do that?"

I took the remark as rhetorical. People were always impressed when Dad did ordinary things like building shelves, and annoyed when he dropped the ball, as he had with that piss-poor Route 66 time capsule. He'd recently grown bored with the remodeling he had been doing around our place, so he subcontracted the project to Drew's Uncle Philly. Knowing the house would never survive Philly's inept handiwork, we'd hired a handyman to re-do all of his projects. Something we could ill afford now that our household's major breadwinner wasn't winning any bread.

When we reached the door, I pulled a key from my pocket and stuffed it into the heavy padlock. Dad had left an extra key with me years ago, but I hadn't been back here until now. The lock felt so stiff at first, it refused to budge. I had to twist the key really hard before it finally moved. We pushed the door open and walked inside.

Dad had taken one of the larger units, which must have been around twelve feet square. Lining all the sides were unpretentious floor-to-ceiling shelves that had been painted white. And filling all those shelves were the hundreds of lunch pails, with their rustic hand-paintings, which had once adorned Lucy Crier's Lunch Pail Café on Route 66 in Tecos, New Mexico. Seeing them all gathered together here, I realized what a good artist Lucy had been, as well as how incredibly obsessive.

"*Anything worth doing is worth overdoing*—that's always been my motto," I said. "And apparently, it was also Lucy's."

"No kidding," Drew said.

The room was dusty, though not as bad as I'd feared, thanks to the door's tight fit. Drew went back to the car for the broom and dust cloths we'd included with our mountain of luggage in deference to Dad's demand that we clean this place.

I stood in the doorway, stalling. How clean did he expect us to make it? It was late afternoon now—a good job could take us all night.

As luck would have it, my cell phone rang, allowing me to put off the dreaded task a bit longer.

"What the hell have you been doing?" my father shouted into my ear. After a lifetime of using phones, he still seemed to think it was the volume that pushed the voice into the other phone.

I didn't bother to answer. He taught me how to do the Mother Road. He should know.

"Where are you?" After I told him we were at Hinky's, he asked, "So you've finished cleaning?"

"…Right." What was one more secret? On the spot, I made the choice not to clean the freakin' joint, after all.

"Good. But now, honey, you kids have got to put the pedal to the metal and get here as fast as you can."

Give the dated slang a rest already. "How come?" I asked.

"Things are really hopping here," Dad said. In the background, I could hear the muttered sounds of Philly's voice, egging him on. "Baby, you remember my old friend, Lucy Crier, right? Well, sure you do. You've just cleaned her lunch pails." He took a deep breath, and then spit out, "Folks around here have been spotting her lately, running between cars on the highway."

Huh? Surely, that wasn't how prison worked in New Mexico. "Dad, isn't Lucy serving a life sentence in the hoosegow for murder? You didn't bust her out, did you?"

With a hearty chuckle he said, still at full volume, "Tracy, your daddy's getting a little old for jail breaks."

Note that he had no objection to the idea in theory. And people wonder about me.

"Besides, I called the warden. Lucy's been there, in the women's prison in Grants, in her cell, this whole time. But people have seen her here, too."

"How is that possible?"

With exaggerated patience, he said, "Honey, that's why you should be here. It's right up your alley." He slowed his speech even more, and spoke as if to the simple-minded. "You see, baby, that's why they call it a mystery."

While Dad went on, providing more details of Lucy's nighttime hijinks, I rattled his little conundrum around in my noggin. How could a woman safely tucked away in her cell also be traffic dodging along Route 66? Lucy had never struck me as ambitious enough to pull off a magic act like that.

Nah, it couldn't have been true. Dad had to believe it, though. Like Mother and me, and even Lucy, he was no stranger to fibbing, but his style leaned toward evasions, rather than outright falsehoods. Unlike us, though, he'd never become comfortable enough to snip the honesty cord. We, of course, had burned ours.

I finally got him off the line with a promise to rush to Tecos, a promise I had no intention of keeping. In addition to well-placed fibs, I also refused to take the concept of swearing seriously. I mean, if we were meant to stick to things, why would we have the ability to change our minds? That's my motto anyway.

Drew still stood there, holding the broom and dust cloths. "Cleaning or not?"

"Not. Put 'em back in the car."

"Great. Alec changed his mind?"

"...Right." Okay, another secret.

Hinky came up beside me. "I remember when Alec brought all them lunch buckets here. He's keeping them for that lady who went to prison, right? Till she gets out?"

Despite her supposed appearances along Route 66, Lucy was never going to get out. She'd gotten life without the possibility of parole. "He was keeping them for her son, Woody." Too bad Woody never wanted them. When he reopened Lucy's café, he'd redecorated, according to Dad, using that word as loosely as Lucy had held the truth. I hadn't seen the café since Woody had taken over, though from what Dad had told me, Hinky's wasn't the only Route 66 business to cause nightmares.

Hinky began playing with the lunch pail's clasp, as I used to. Suddenly, he snapped it closed. "Hey, could I have this one? You know, because it fits the theme o' my place?"

He held that lunch pail out to me, so I could see its painting. Lucy's cute baby bunny, hidden in some tall grass, wasn't in the same universe with Hinky's hellish creatures.

"There's a lot more o' them here?" he went on. "She's never gonna miss one."

I didn't care, but Dad would. I explained that they weren't mine to give away.

"Yeah, I unnerstan," Hinky said, and he placed that pail back on a shelf, even dusting it a bit with his sleeve.

I ushered him out and relocked the padlock and gave it a tug to make sure it was secure. We said goodbye to Hinky back at the cottage, with its fake dead landscaping. Even as we said it, he turned away. Clearly eager to get back to tricking the slot machine, he just tossed us a wave over his shoulder with his shiny fingers.

But as we drove off, I glanced back and thought I saw someone crossing the yard, in the direction Dad's storage locker. I asked Drew if we should go back.

"Have a heart, honey. We've been driving and visiting attractions for hours. I need a meal and a bed. You're seeing shadows."

Sure, that was it. Fortunately, I'm easily distracted. Once we were underway, a great sign called out to me, and I begged Drew to pull in.

"Trace, are you out of your mind?" He drove right past it. "Is there *nothing* you won't stop to see? That sign said, 'New Dead Things.' Who could possibly find any appeal in new dead things?"

Was he kidding? Who wouldn't?

"Why not *'Old* Dead Things'?"

"Drew, that's a museum." What fun was that?

I should have paid more attention. I had no idea how much trouble old dead things can cause.

CHAPTER FIVE

After leaving Hinky's, though it was only late afternoon, Drew wanted to stop for the night. I convinced him to drive on to Winslow, so we could stay at the La Posada Hotel, the jewel of the Mother Road. I figured we'd grab a late dinner in their elegant Turquoise Room. But like I said, I get distracted. Instead of the gourmet dinner I planned, I was seduced by a classic Route 66 diner whose sign read, "Warm beer, lousy food," insisting to Drew that you gotta reward humor like that. Turns out all we rewarded was truth in advertising.

Along the way, I shared with Drew what passed for a mystery in Dad-land, that business about the imprisoned Lucy dashing around Route 66.

"Crazy, I know, but Dad seemed to believe it. Philly maybe, too."

"Consider the sources. An actor and a con artist—which one has the weakest hold on reality?"

Neither. The person with the weakest hold on reality had better be me.

The next day started with a sumptuous breakfast in the La Posada's dining room, as well as side trips to the Homolovi Ruins and the Little Painted Desert Park. And naturally, we couldn't leave without taking photos of ourselves standing on the corner there in Winslow, beside the flatbed Ford—even Drew got a kick out of that one. Then we stopped outside of Winslow to see the world's largest Route 66 map that you'll find anywhere, and I pointed out for Drew everywhere we'd been and were yet to visit. And despite our financial bind, I ran up credit card charges in all the Indian trading posts I plundered along the way. If Drew was right about the universe providing stuff, it might as well provide me with some good jewelry.

Finally crossing the line into New Mexico, in Gallup, we

stopped at the El Rancho Hotel for a quick drink. I always thought its motto—"Charm of yesterday, convenience of tomorrow"— rivaled any of my own. Dad and I had always gone there during our jaunts. In his heyday, it was a popular stomping ground for the Hollywood crowd, and we often ran into some of his cronies there. While Dad always shared some laughs with his cohorts, somehow he also wanted to deny that other celebrities venerated Route 66 as much as he did, and loads of them did in those days. It was like he wanted to believe it was his alone. But that was silly. If there's one Route 66 truth, it's that you're likely to find anyone there, from a cowboy to a king.

When I saw a road sign announcing that we were approaching Grants, without making a conscious thought, I moved over to the right lane.

"Drew, you're licensed in New Mexico, right? As a lawyer, I mean," I asked as casually as possible. "You've argued cases here, haven't you?"

"Yup. Two tough ones. Won them both."

If he felt that proud of his legal accomplishments, why was he leaving them behind? Along with the considerable income they'd provided.

"Why do you care—" Drew started to say. His speech sputtered to a stop when I pulled off at the Grants exit. "No! Tracy, you're not doing what I think you're doing." He gasped. "You are! I saw that sign. I know where you're headed."

Aw, yes. The universal road sign for areas with prisons: "Don't pick up hitchhikers."

"Why don't those signs ever say something more imaginative?" I asked. "Like: 'Don't pick up people in saggy jumpsuits.' Or: 'Don't pick up people with license plate dust on their hands.'"

Or even: "Don't pick up people who look like Lucy Crier."

* * *

I hate jails. I have ever since Drew was tossed in one on trumped up charges, and another prisoner beat the crap outta him. That was so scary, I had to pull a stunt that was wacky even for me to save his life. Now I could never enter one of those joints without feeling pummeled by awful memories.

Though it had to be past visiting hours, it proved to be remarkably easy to get in to see Lucy. With my prodding, Drew reluctantly insisted he was Lucy's lawyer, working on a new appeal. I thought I'd have to prop that claim up with some really clever lies, but they didn't prove necessary, dammit.

They showed us into a room with a utilitarian metal table and chairs where lawyers met with their clients. I'd figured the best way to prove to Dad that Lucy really was here was to visit with her. But now I worried about it. What if she did have a way of slipping out? If she wasn't in her cell when the guards went looking for her, would that spoil everything for her?

Like she could really slip out. Yeah, I had a weak hold on reality, all right.

Still, my anxiety grew. Since Lucy had always been what Dad described as the "twitchy sort," I expected her to show the same jumpiness I felt. But when she appeared at the glass-paneled door and waited for the guard to open it, she surprised me. She radiated a serene, peaceful quality that I never remembered seeing before.

The years in there had served her surprisingly well. Her platinum blonde hair had turned to white, but the color didn't look that different, and while shorter than she used to wear it, it still waved attractively around her haunting face. She had filled out a little, and that fullness reduced the wrinkles I expected her to have at this point. Once she stepped into the room, though she wore a shapeless jumpsuit, Lucy's hips swayed seductively to a runway beat she seemed to have heard all her life.

Lucy immediately pulled me into a big hug. I thought the guard at the door might have objected to that contact, but with only the barest trace of a smile, he turned away. Jeez, was this place, rather than Disneyland, the happiest place on earth? Who knew?

She held me out at arm's length. "Tracy! Look at you. So big."

Well, I was in my thirties now. Being full-sized went with the territory.

When I introduced Drew, though an appreciative gleam rose in her eyes, she didn't turn on the flirtatious charm I remembered her as directing to married men. Instead, she told us what a beautiful couple we were and how happy she was that I found Drew.

"And admit it, Tracy—nobody could have predicted it. You know how it's always your way or the highway."

Hey, I was only a little tot the last time she saw me. Throw one or a dozen tantrums, and you get a reputation.

Still, my sorrow for her must have been evident. Without prompting, she said, "It's not so bad in here, you know. You make friends, work a job…build a life." She flushed with pride. "I'm on the library detail. Me. I scarcely got through a book before I came here, even in high school. Now I read voraciously." With a happy grin, she added, "I'm quite the fan of yours, young lady, I can tell you that. And this thriller you and Martha wrote together—what's it called? *Deadly Shadows,* right? I really can't wait for that one to come out."

She had always dropped Mother's name, as if they were friends, when they had never met. Did anyone do that if she was trying to vamp the other woman's husband?

Lucy amused us with anecdotes about life behind bars, making it sound like a place you wouldn't exactly choose to visit, but which you wouldn't mind too much if you found yourself there. Kinda like a budget fat farm.

"Tracy, I'm glad you and my boy Woody will be reconnecting." Dad had obviously told her we'd be vacationing at her old place. "I've so hoped you would be adult friends, too."

Too? Like we were friends as kids? Not hardly.

"Like Alec and me. Such a loyal friend, all these years." She blinked away the sudden rise of tears.

I made the choice in that moment not to tell her that her loyal friend was spreading a scurrilous rumor about her bumper dodging along Route 66. After a short time more, the guard rapped on the glass panel, and with a tap on his watch crystal, indicated it was time to go.

"Is there anything I should tell Dad for you?" I asked.

She paused at the door, and with a wistful sigh, said, "Tell Alec…

tell him there's pot roast on the menu here tonight."

Surely, it was past dinnertime. I had no idea what that remark meant, but from the sadness of her sigh, I felt certain he wasn't going to like it.

CHAPTER SIX

Now, more than a day after we left Hinky's, we were finally closing in on Tecos, New Mexico. Dad's many calls had grown in frequency today, but I kept ignoring them. Until I could figure out what he was up to, I had no intention of buying into any more of his preposterous fibs.

The darkness surrounding us closed in on me. During the day, the Mother Road, with all its glitter, provides incredible distraction. At night, after so much time staring at nothing more than the elongated half-moons your headlight beams cut into the pitch pavement, the thoughts you took the trip to escape come flooding back. Oh, the odd flash of neon provides an occasional respite. But in the darkness, those unwanted worries always returned.

And that's another lesson about Route 66. Everyone on it is running away from something, to something else. I sure was—what else could explain my taking a trip we could no longer afford. Drew, too, though he wouldn't admit it.

Drew flipped on the radio. In one of the rare spots where we caught a strong signal, we heard an interesting news report.

"In a press conference today, California's Governor Kyle Tandy announced that progress is being made on the planned reopening the Tecos Caves off Route 66, in Tecos, New Mexico."

I remembered playing in those caves when I was a kid, since they stretched behind Lucy's café. But they'd been closed now for decades.

"Governor Tandy went on to remind everyone that he would be donating the property to the states of New Mexico and California to share, once they're ready to reopen."

I guessed that made sense in a cockeyed way. He needed to curry favor in California, but since the caves were actually located in New Mexico, he probably thought that state might claim them by eminent domain if he didn't offer them partial ownership.

Tandy's gravely voice broke in with, "As sure as the sun rises and sets on this great highway, we must never forget the Mother Road's role in our history."

I always thought the guy with that voice should be belting out the blues in some seedy bar. Instead, a whopping eighty-two percent of California voters had sent that man to our governor's mansion.

People either loved or hated Tandy's voice. Me, I was indifferent to it. What made me cringe were my governor's emerald green eyes, which glowed with either the sheen of the fanatically driven or colored contacts. Those eyes never failed to give me the creeps, for reasons that defied my understanding.

"The Caves were closed for safety concerns, after a section collapsed," the announcer returned to say.

I didn't remember any collapsed sections, but it had been a long while since I was small enough to fit through the tiniest passages. I did remember that their closure had hurt the Tecos economy, since it was the small town's biggest tourist attraction.

"Earlier this year, Governor Tandy had formed a committee to raise the necessary capital to reinforce the popular attraction. But after his legal troubles, the committee disbanded, with their efforts falling short of their goals. Now he has promised to contribute the shortfall himself."

Would Tandy really have enough money left after he paid the enormous fine the court levied? Or would he want to contribute it after the people of California kicked him to the curb? Tandy had recently been tried and found guilty of corruption charges and campaign-financing irregularities, though a shrinking minority blamed the misdeeds on an aide of his who'd committed suicide before the trial. Despite his convictions, Tandy got no jail time, being sentenced to house arrest and about a bajillion hours of community service. While our Lieutenant Governor took over his duties, Tandy had asked to serve his sentence in New Mexico, getting the caves ready for their reopening. Though highly irregular, Tandy was a persuasive guy, and people did tend to give him what he wanted. Not always, though—a jury hadn't, and now legions of his former supporters were waging a recall effort to throw him out of office.

The strain didn't seem to be hurting him any, judging by the pictures I saw occasionally on the news. Kyle Tandy was hot, if you like your stud-muffins a bit long in the tooth and edging on impossible perfection. His cheekbones were high and strong, and his chin beautifully chiseled. Those bright green eyes tilted at the slightest angle, giving him a rakish look. He didn't look anywhere near the late fifties he had to be, according to his biography. If he wasn't some plastic surgeon's crowning achievement, nature was doing better work than I'd ever seen before. Unlike most California governors, he was neither an actor nor a body builder before breaking into politics, but a former studio executive.

Since I'm too much of a cynic to trust anyone that charming, I hadn't voted for him. After a lifetime lived behind the curtain of my parents' public personas I knew a performance when I saw it. But some politicians possess such a Teflon coating, not only do the people fall for their cons, even the press gives them a free pass. It was just Tandy's bad luck that the contractor who supposedly bribed him got religion and did such a long and loud *mea culpa*, both the media and law enforcement had to listen.

"The story of how the Tecos Caves came into the governor's possession remains one of the great Route 66 stories," the announcer said. "As a young man working his way across the country, Kyle Tandy won the attraction in a poker game, and through the ups-and-downs of his own financial condition, he's always held onto them. No date has been announced for the actual reopening of the attraction, but Tandy has pledged to do everything in his power to be sure the character of America's Main Street be maintained."

It sounded like he was still campaigning—or trying to influence a jury pool—when those ships had already set out to sea. If he had that much money to throw around, why didn't he lower my state taxes?

Ouch! Talk about hitting too close to home. Money worries kept plaguing me. It wasn't bad enough that I dreamed about hijacking a plane for it, now I wanted to mug our crooked governor for some. That wasn't like me—I'd learned to shape the world to suit my convenience at my mother's knee. But what could I expect? That my life was about to get way too real was what I hoped to outrun on this vacation.

Yet thoughts of our insolvency refused my efforts to avoid them. I remembered an expense waiting for us at home. "Drew, how much do you think Chaz will want for the work he's doing around our place while we're gone?"

Chaz was our neighbor and the handyman we'd hired to re-do the jobs around the house that Philly had mangled. He was actually called Charles Stuart Atherton Barron, or maybe that was Barrington, or Barrymore, or something to that effect. It was such a mouthful, I could never remember it exactly. I did recall the string of snooty names was followed by, "the third." I only remembered that because it's not every contractor who introduces himself in terms of his dynasty.

Chaz had been a trust fund kid earlier on in his life. I never learned what he did to cause the money spigot to dry up. All I knew was that they gave him one of the family homes, a giant old dowager down the road from ours, before booting him out of the clan. He scraped by now by working as a repairman.

I liked having him in the neighborhood. Since his old barn of a house made our wreck look good, the neighbors who worried about property values were more likely to take out their wrath on him than us. We were just thirty years behind on upkeep, while Chaz decided which rooms he'd live in by the parts of the roof that hadn't yet caved in. Big difference.

He was also the one who convinced Drew that a blueblood guy could give that whole achievement route a pass. Now he'd started Drew meditating. Meditating! What was that, just sitting and breathing, right? Something every infant nails before stretching into breathing in motion. Why take a step back? Under Chaz's guidance, Drew began spouting off about bountiful universes and showing way more flexibility than was ever meant to be in his life description. Chaz, that lackadaisical philosopher with a hammer, had a lot to answer for.

In the green glow of the dashboard lights, Drew looked my way.

"Don't worry about it. I already paid him and had plenty left."

"Left from what? You wrote a check?" As lean as our bank account was getting, he should tell me when he did something foolhardy like paying handymen or buying groceries.

"No, I gave him cash."

Ah, he'd used his stash. We'd both always had the habit of squirreling away little hoards of money tucked here and there around the house. I'd blown through all of mine, but then, I'd never kept more on hand than enough to pay for a few pizza deliveries. If Drew was able to pay Chaz for all the work he'd be doing, he had clearly put aside much more than I had. I wished I'd known that. I'd have torn the house apart hunting for it before we left. I'd always rather spend someone else's money.

"Chaz stopped by when I was out gardening the other day, so I paid him. Tracy, stop worrying. What's happened to you? You've been right all these years, babe. I've been way too rigid. Now that I'm loosening up, are you actually moving in the other direction?"

Nooo! Why did he listen to me? Sure, I wanted him to be free, but I wanted him to freely follow the path I laid out for him.

He kept babbling. "I told you, Trace, the universe will send things our way."

"The universe is a collection of gases, for chrissakes, not a traffic cop," I blurted.

"What?"

Oops! Did I say that out loud?

"Tracy, look at me," Drew demanded from the Volvo's driver's seat. With the green glow illuminating the lines of annoyance twisting his face, he looked like some angry alien.

"I'm thinking of writing a travel article," I announced. "About our adventures along Route 66."

Did I say that, too? News to me. It obviously struck the right note with Drew, though, because Angry Alien turned into Happy Green Guy.

"See? Now that's what I mean. The universe does provide."

Huh? The universe? He considered little ol' me as the whole freakin' universe? I had an awful feeling my term as an adult was going to be a life sentence.

Drew rambled on, about what a clever little universe I was. I had to tune him out. I searched for some distraction in the darkness, not expecting to find it. But for once I was pleasantly surprised. With no warning, someone appeared at the side of the road ahead of us, a big-breasted older woman in a long, slinky dress, whose white-blonde hair curled nearly to her waist. If that sounded even remotely sexy, nothing could be farther from the truth. That aging sex goddess was too stout for knit, causing the dress to strain at the seams.

Was this what Dad meant when he said people had been seeing Lucy?

That dress did look familiar. I knew I'd seen Lucy wear something similar. This creature's hair looked something like hers, too—you know, if it had morphed into one of those awful acrylic wigs they sell in the back of women's magazines. In the headlights, when the wind tossed her hair back, I saw that, in the place on her upper lip where Lucy had an exquisite beauty mark, this woman sported a mole the size of a warthog.

With no warning, the woman sprinted into the road.

"Drew! Watch out."

He slammed on his brakes, and after sliding into an S-curve, brought the car to a screeching halt. But the woman had dropped before us.

Calm, ever-in-control Drew totally lost it. "God, no! I killed her. What was she doing running into traffic like that? Please tell me I didn't kill her."

I hated the way we were changing into each other. The way I alone proved to be levelheaded in this situation. I also seemed to be the only one who noticed there had been no thump that would indicate the car and the body had connected. The woman just fell.

While Drew agonized, I stepped from the car and peeked around the fender, which was totally intact. Our victim lay flat on her back before the wheels. As I suspected, there was no sign the tires ever touched her. Her long hair was tossed askew across the pavement, and under the glare of the headlights, her eyes were tightly closed.

Still, close up there was no mistaking the identity of our victim, warthog-mole or not.

Drew stepped from the car, but remained behind the driver's side door, where he couldn't see her. "Tell me she's..." He couldn't seem to finish the sentence.

"She's not dead, Drew."

"You didn't even check for a pulse."

True, but I could see her pudgy belly rising and falling. Corpses don't breathe.

"Check," Drew said. "And then tell me she's not dead."

I picked up a hand with scratchy, rough skin, and gripped its wrist, purely to quiet him. "Not only isn't she dead, Drew." I held out the hand, with its hairy knuckles, for him to see. "She's also your Uncle Philly."

CHAPTER SEVEN

D rew was too shook-up to drive, so I moved the car onto a dirt patch before a fading billboard. I left the headlights on so we could see each other when we talked. Then I zipped around to the front, where Drew and his uncle were already going at it.

"Uncle Philly, are you insane?" Drew demanded. "I could have *killed* you."

Philly tossed off an indifferent shrug that wiggled his big lumpy boobs. "Don't sweat it, kid. I've dodged traffic here loads of times. Tonight I just slipped on a bit of road grease."

"You're the person Alec called us about? The phantom Lucy?" Drew asked.

Drew looked at his uncle like he couldn't fathom who or what Philly was. I regarded this stunt as only a little screwier than some of the things Philly and I had pulled in the past.

I'd first met Drew's black sheep uncle, an aging con man his family never acknowledged, at my mother-in-law's house in New York. He had to be the messiest person I'd ever encountered. With his wiry graying hair that stuck out weirdly all over his head, so it looked as if it had never been combed, and the threadbare suits he always wore, thrift shops across the land should have made him their poster boy. But Philly's childlike grin and his blue-green eyes sparkled with mischief and eternal youth, and that made him my favorite relative.

Despite having almost gone on to meet his ancestors now, Philly's happy-go-lucky grin flickered cheerfully, while Drew chewed him out. But for the first time since I'd known him, the twinkle seemed to have gone out of his eyes.

"Maybe I wouldn't have had to face that oil slick tonight if you two had gotten here faster. Do you know how long I've been dodging cars since Alec called you?"

Philly twisted his wrinkled face in annoyance, causing the warthog-mole to jump around like a beetle in a frying pan. That thing was starting to weird me out.

"But, Philly, on the Mother Road, there are rituals to be observed," I said, while Drew rolled his eyes.

Philly just waved his stubby fingers at me. "Yeah, yeah. Alec told me."

While Drew continued to yammer on, I took a look at where we were. The faded billboard I'd parked before urged motorists to stop at a nearby motel, promising all the modern conveniences. "Color TVs in every room," the aged sign bragged. And "Magic Fingers." Ah, yes, Magic Fingers—the fifties' idea of massage therapy.

I tuned back into their conversation.

"Am I to understand that this whole act was for *our* benefit?" Drew asked.

Philly scratched at the warthog, which came off on his finger. What was that thing?

"Sure. You kids were taking so long, Alec figured to get you here fast, he'd have to entice you with a puzzle. You know what it's like with this one when she sniffs a mystery." He indicated me with a toss of his bewigged head.

It struck me that my father was a better liar than I gave him credit. *Way to go, Dad!* "I can't possibly be that predictable."

Now it was Philly's turn to roll his eyes. Strange, they still looked sad.

"Why was it so important that we be here?" I sensed a contradiction in what he'd told us, but I was too tired and hungry to pursue it.

"Got me." Philly's gaze evaded mine. He absently gave his hand a quick shake, to dislodge the mole-thingie. The revolting object stuck to his fingertip like a growth. "You're gonna have to ask Alec about that."

Once again, a question pressed on my weary brain.

"And I gotta sit somewhere. My feet are killing me." Motor oil streaked gigantic white pumps. "Kids, Alec's waiting for you at the restaurant. What say we head over there?"

Drew sighed in resignation "Need a ride?" he asked. "We'll have to shift the luggage around, but—"

"Nah, I got Alec's wheels." Philly gave his head a toss in the direction of the old billboard. The nose of a silver Bentley peeked out behind it. "Follow me, huh?"

With a sigh of surrender after Philly stomped off in his silly shoes, Drew slipped his arm over my shoulders. "Do you think Alec cares that Philly doesn't have a license?"

I snorted. "Were you under the impression my dad has one? He's always believed that once you get to be his age, they just take them away from you. Don't worry—the car will survive." Other drivers might be a different story, but fortunately, the road was deserted.

We climbed back into the Volvo and tucked in behind the Bentley's taillights.

After a mile or so had zipped by, Drew said, "Do you believe any of that?"

I shrugged. At the moment, all I could say with certainty was—there was more going on here than I once thought.

CHAPTER EIGHT

With Philly at the wheel, I figured the Bentley would meander all over the road, the way he usually drove. But he kept it to a straight line. Some might find it troubling that he carved it down the center of the highway, in the dark yet. But it encouraged me. Once the old coot grasped the idea of lanes, he'd actually know how to drive.

Our little caravan traveled for a few miles within the unrelenting pitch you find under a cloudy sky in the middle of nowhere. But I knew we were nearing our destination when the night air took on the red and white glow of an approaching neon sign. Once the sign itself came into view, I saw the image of a sleeping man with a smiley face, whose nightcap peeked out of one end of a blanket, while his toes popped out the other end. That he wore a big grin in his sleep spoke to the comfort of that bed. The words accompanying the image read, "Rest Ur Head Motel," followed by, "Luxury suites available." Since I knew that would be where we were staying, I looked longingly at the row of Zs that rose up from the sleeper's snore.

"Luxury suites, huh?" Drew said. "Can't come too soon for me. Do you think it'll be as nice as the La Posada, with all those Southwestern antiques?"

I marveled as I often did at the contrast between Drew and his uncle. Philly was a pretty decent con artist, while Drew had to be the world's best mark. He believed whatever he was told, even by a neon sign. Maybe he was right to get out of the law—it was a wonder that he'd survived so long among those sharks.

The Bentley made a sharp right into the parking area of the building next door to the motel. It was a squat two-story structure, whose front half was painted puke green, and the rear part beige, while a two-story ladder resting against the structure marked the line of demarcation between the new paint and old.

The street-side of the building held a café that was where Lucy had once operated her restaurant. Now, one of its two flashing signs identified it as, "The Kontiki Room," with "the" and "room" being either higher or lower than "Kontiki." Alongside the lettering, the hand of a stick figure moved up, allowing the little stick-guy to sip from a martini glass. The sign's style looked like someone's idea of what a big city nightclub might sport, assuming the city was one contained within an *I Love Lucy* episode. Another flashing sign promised, "Pizza and Chinese food."

"Pizza and Chinese," Drew mused. "Strange combination."

Stranger than he knew. See what I mean? Believes everything. "Drew…"

"Decisions, decisions…"

Whatever.

The lone vehicle parked outside the place was an RV. While somewhat smaller than a cruise ship, the compact motor home gleamed so brightly in the glow of the building's neon signs, it must have been spanking new. The personalized license plate read: WDMNSRV. Since Lucy's son had often referred himself as "The Wood-Man," it didn't take a big leap to guess the license plate read, "Wood-Man's RV." Why would Woody have an RV? It certainly hadn't brought him there—Woody had been born and raised there in Tecos, and Dad said he never left it. He sure didn't come to visit us, thankfully.

Since I hadn't made a trip along Route 66 in at least ten years, I hadn't seen this place since Woody redecorated his mom's old luncheonette, though Dad had described it. I pushed through the front door and found more of his oddball stabs at sophistication. When Lucy ran the place, blue banquettes had lined both walls, with tables scattered through the center. The booths were still there, only now they were covered in vinyl leopard skin, a match for the jungle-patterned carpet underfoot. Also gone were the shelves that had once lined all the walls, on which Lucy displayed her lunch pails. Not only had the shelves been removed, irregularly shaped holes had been cut sporadically through those walls. On the walls and in the holes, he had painted something that looked like flat, shapeless bamboo stalks—you know, in a world where perspective and shading never existed. Woody sure hadn't inherited his mother's artistic skills.

Drew draped his arm over my shoulder. "This should be a change from so much Americana," he muttered. "It just shows that not all change is good."

Occasionally, we found ourselves in complete agreement.

Though Philly had turned into the parking area before us, he only wobbled through the door now, wearing one big white pump, while carrying the other. With shoulders so rounded they looked weighed down, he marched over to a table piled high with maps and tourist brochures, and yanked out a chrome leopard-print chair.

"Take a load off," he said. He did as he advised, plopping so heavily into the chair, the dress seams threatened to pop. He pushed aside some of the stacks before him on the table and found a little pouch with his pipe and tobacco, which he set about filing and lighting. I was pretty sure it was illegal to smoke in restaurants in New Mexico, but there were neither cops nor other customers around to complain.

Dad pushed through a swinging door from the kitchen. "Kids! You're here."

Seeing him pass below the dim ceiling lighting, it occurred to me that he truly didn't have a bad angle. Even at his age, he was still as slim as a young man, a fact accentuated by the silk shirt he wore over crisply creased jeans. Though some lines did cut into his face these days, the bones and the killer smile were as engaging now as when they first lit up the screen decades earlier. And though the longish hair hanging over his aqua eyes had turned white, he still tossed it back with his signature rakish ease.

His judgment, on the other hand, was what you'd expect from someone who believed more in movie magic than the real world. It was really a wonder how I turned out as normal as I was.

"Dad, what were you thinking, having Philly dress up like Lucy and dance around the highway? Was this really for our benefit?"

Dad sent Philly a questioning look that I couldn't read. Philly just puffed on his pipe, while pulling off that god-awful wig and letting it drape on the floor.

Finally, Dad said, "Well...sure...I thought it would light a fire under you two. But mostly, we're trying to create a little notice here about Lucy."

"For us?"

"Well, you and the fuzz. Anyone who'll investigate things."

I pinched my eyes closed. See what I mean about his judgment—he believed dated gibberish sounded cool. "Why?"

"So we can reopen her case, attract interest, make people question her conviction. You know, to win her a new trial, or a pardon. Anything to get her out of the slammer."

That must have been why he wanted me to clean her lunch pails, so they'd be ready for her.

Dad sighed deeply. "Lucy has breast cancer, honey, and she deserves better treatment than she'll get in prison."

I sank into a chair, saddened. Though neither her condition nor the effect of the treatment was evident yet, I knew how fast they would come on. I also thought about the way the prison staff had bent the rules for her. They must have grown fond of her. I told Dad that we had stopped to see Lucy and shared that cryptic remark about pot roast.

With a fond smile and a faraway look, he said, "That's Lucy's little joke. It means she wants to stay there. It's what she says every time I talk about getting her out." His expression turned stormy. "But she's served enough time for a crime she didn't commit."

"Dad, if you thought she was really innocent of killing Billy Rob, why didn't you help her all those years ago, instead of merely carting her lunch pails off to Flagstaff?"

"Don't you think I tried?" he exploded. "Lucy wouldn't let me help her then. She pled guilty over my objection. This time we're going to do things my way."

I wondered how serene Lucy would remain if he got his way.

A car horn out on the road played the opening bars of the music from the movie *Jaws*.

"Governor Tandy. His way of saying hi to Woody when he drives past," Dad said, finally taking a seat across from me. "How's the recall effort back home?"

"Building up steam." By now the notes of the musical horn had drifted away. "Was that crazy horn on his limo?"

"No limo, no entourage. Just a guy in a Jeep," Philly said. "Personally, I don't believe the charges against him. That aide who used to work for him...he was living in that house some contractor donated to Tandy. And the aide's suicide before the trial seemed too convenient for me."

Maybe a naïve streak did run in Drew's family, after all.

Drew tapped his fingertips against the black faux-granite tabletop and idly glanced around. "Alec, did you ever meet Tandy back when he was a studio exec?" He shrugged. "Or even here?"

"He never comes in here, just honks in passing." Below his snowy moustache, Dad's lips twitched in annoyance. "I never met him in L.A., either. I was scheduled to take a meeting with him once when he ran the studio, but he cancelled and cast someone else in the part." His shoulder threw off an irritated shrug. "Maybe I met him at some party, but I don't remember. I'm not sure I've ever even seen him on the news after he became governor. Don't watch it much, unless it's about Martha or me."

My parents weren't too self-involved.

"Never watches the news...?" Drew's eyes widened when he looked at me. "I still think Tandy would be a pretty memorable guy. Handsome, charismatic."

"Doesn't matter, son," Dad said with a little laugh that seemed to say his logic should be self-evident. "If I remembered half the people I've met, I wouldn't have any room upstairs for thinking." He gave his temple a little tap with his fingertip.

I stared determinedly down at the table, refusing to meet Drew's gaze. He loves my father, but he still believes Dad's problem is that he has too much unused room upstairs. Did Drew really want him watching the news, and voting?

Dad moved on to talking about our journey to Tecos. "Tell me all about it," he said. "Did you stop at Hinky's?"

Drew groaned.

Before we could answer anything at length, he rushed on with more questions. "How about the plaque? Did you visit the park first? Oh, of course you did—I trained you right. Tell me everything. Don't leave out a thing."

"Dad, you traveled the same way yourself not long ago. You must have stopped at many of these places, too."

"Sure, but you can never get enough of it."

I still wondered about the appeal the Mother Road held for him. With his silk shirt and the dry cleaner crease in his jeans, he looked more Rodeo Drive than Route 66. And though he'd traveled the whole road in his first few jaunts, in all the years I'd gone with him, we rarely went past Tecos.

Drew slowly blew out a controlled breath. He looked like a man who thought that, after being condemned to travel along Route 66, he shouldn't also have to talk about it.

"Is there a menu anywhere in this place?" Drew asked. "Mongolian Beef would hit the spot now. Though, on the other hand, sausage and mushroom pizza wouldn't be bad, either."

While sending out sweet, fragrant waves of Flying Dutchman tobacco from his pipe, Philly chuckled to himself.

"Andrew, Woody doesn't serve either of those things," Dad said, as if that should been obvious.

"But the sign outside reads, 'Pizza and Chinese food.' What's that if not…?"

"I don't care, son. All Woody serves is waffles."

"Why?" Drew stammered.

A voice behind me said in a whining tone, "Like, for the fun of it, man."

I turned and saw Woody slouched there. He'd aged since the last time I saw him, but he hadn't changed much. When I was a little kid and he a teenager, I always thought of Woody as the undead. That was before vampires became the dashing heroes of popular fiction. He was the whitest white guy I'd ever seen, without being an outright albino. The only breaks to his otherwise ghostly paleness were dark circles under his eyes, and a pair of black eyebrows that looked like caterpillars on steroids.

It wasn't only the fairness of his skin I found creepy, but his whole appearance. It was like he'd been put together with spare monster parts. His unusually prominent cheekbones were like iron balls that stretched his skin extra tight, while cheeks so gaunt they screamed of starvation lay below them. Crowning them both was a pronounced forehead and a square head, like Frankenstein without the studs. Despite the skeletal cheeks, now that he was approaching forty-five, Woody had put on quite the middle-aged gut, which sagged over his belt, though his face still hadn't filled out.

"Yo, Trace," he said with no apparent enthusiasm.

While placing him shy of Hinky on the weirdness scale, I still limited my greeting to a wordless wave.

Dad grabbed Woody's large bony hand for a strong clasp. "Woody, my boy, meet Drew, my son-in-law. Why don't you rustle up a couple of plates of your best waffles for him and Tracy?"

A sharp look from Dad stalled any objection Drew might have voiced right in his throat. "Sure, waffles would be great," Drew said, his tone belying the words.

Whatever enthusiasm Drew lacked, Dad more than made up for it. When Woody shuffled off toward the kitchen, the way Dad beamed at him, you'd have thought the guy made from odd monster parts spent his time saving orphans and bringing about world peace, instead of desecrating Route 66 diners.

As always, Dad's apparent fondness for Woody gave me a sinking feeling in my gut. I couldn't imagine what about him engendered Dad's relentless affection. Nor why he continued to foot Woody's bills. Despite his grumbling over the cost of the building's ongoing paintjob, he always forked it over. I suspected it was Woody, not Route 66, that brought Dad here year after year. And why? Maybe because Woody and I shared the same DNA.

There, I said it. Don't make me repeat it. Was it possible? Not to brag, but I am my parents' offspring. I don't exactly break mirrors. Could the man who produced me, along with the breathtaking Lucy Crier, actually have sired Woody?

Don't get me wrong, I wasn't some petulant only child who refused to share. I'd always longed for siblings. Truly. If you think

I wanted to shoulder the lone responsibility for the loonies who brought me into this world, you're outta your mind. It was just that while I'd always wished for a brother, I didn't want him to be a creepy dweeb like Woody.

Dad continued sharing stories about Lucy, fond anecdotes that I'd heard countless times already.

Woody pushed through the door from the kitchen. "If you're talking about Ma, she shouldn't have done what she did. Shouldn't have taken what was mine."

Even if waffles weren't what Drew wanted, he looked longingly at the plates that hovered above our heads.

"You mean your father?" I asked. "She shouldn't have killed your father?" The general belief was Lucy's victim, Billy Rob Royce, her on-and-off married lover, must have sired Woody, though Lucy had never publicly confirmed it. I wished I were as certain.

"Well, yeah. What else could I mean?" Woody demanded, as he noisily tossed plates down before us, before returning to the kitchen in a huff.

"These waffles are charred." Drew picked at a blackened area with a fork.

Woody's outrage at his mother, after all this time, seemed excessive. Once I was old enough to understand, like Dad, I questioned Lucy's guilt. I never understood why she rushed to plead guilty, when a trial might have cleared her. Her lawyer only needed to establish reasonable doubt, and loads of people could have wanted Billy Rob Royce dead, starting with his wife. I wondered whether Lucy might have been protecting someone else. But who would she be willing to take a life sentence for?

While I stared across the table, an unformed thought caused my gaze to fall on someone Lucy might have cared enough to protect.

Despite my best efforts, I couldn't stop staring at my dad.

CHAPTER NINE

MEMORIES OF ROUTE 66
PHILLY

Thirty-three years ago, and it was like yesterday. Every day he awoke to the memory of what happened, and it still felt raw. When that guy died, even if it wasn't actually Philly's fault, some of the light he carried within him dimmed. Maybe nobody else could see it, but he knew. And if they couldn't see it, that was because he felt he owed it to that guy to live his own life with as much gusto as he could. Like maybe it wasn't right to take a minute of it for granted, since someone else got snuffed.

It had happened in Chicago, the start of Route 66. Philly hadn't spent a whole lotta time in the States in those years, preferring instead to bum around Europe. He'd been born in New York, but he had good reasons to avoid that place. It got to be tough sometimes seeing his sister Charlotte and her kids. Especially her kids. Especially...well, it was better for everyone if he stayed away.

But now and then he'd get homesick for the U.S. One day when somebody mentioned Chicago, it felt right. He hopped on a plane without giving it another thought. How could he have known it would change his life?

Philly had never been a big time crook—he had no illusions about that. Hell, his cons didn't rise to the level of Internet spammers today. It wasn't even that he got off on cheating people. He just wasn't cut out for honest work, and a guy had to eat.

But he had to admit back then he'd admired the bad boys at the top of the crime world. He loved their style, their swagger. Philly always knew them all. The criminal world was as small as any other. But he was never part of the inner circle of anyone important.

Until he met one of Chicago's rising crime figures, The Actor, as people called Tag Kowalski. They called him that because the boy was so smooth he could put anything over on anyone. He wasn't a big guy, but he'd cast a big shadow. Philly knew he wasn't in Tag's league, but he lost any objectivity when The Actor began to pal around with him.

Philly was so flattered by The Actor's attention, he never admitted to himself that he was getting conned, too. He never acknowledged that his friend liked to hurt people. He savored the uncharacteristic chance of being associated with a guy even the big crime bosses talked about.

When Tag asked Philly to borrow a car and pick him up, Philly never thought to ask why The Actor didn't simply use his own car. Philly borrowed a car from a neighbor at his rooming house.

Him and Tag—they were cruising down Michigan Avenue, for all to see. Philly felt like a million bucks.

Then The Actor smoothly instructed him to take a few turns, until they were driving in some immigrant neighborhood.

"Pull up in front of that grocery store over there, will you, Philly, my Main Buckaroo," The Actor said, pointing to a corner store. Tag called everyone "Buckaroo," but it made Philly feel special when tacked on the addition of "Main" to the name for him. "Gotta get me some smokes."

When Philly started to cut the engine, The Actor added, "Don't bother to turn it off. You can wait here."

What the hell, Philly thought. If Tag wanted him to sit there with the engine idling, who was he to argue?

"As sure as the sun's gonna set out California-way, I'll be back in a flash," The Actor promised.

Tag and his expressions. Philly knew if anyone else said the things that he did, Philly would regard them as corny. But The Actor made everything sound cool.

Tag stepped from the car, ambling across the sidewalk with that cocky strut of his. He paused outside the grocery store door, and yanked a cap from his pocket and stuffed it on his head, pulling it low over his eyes. Tag punched the door open with his fist and sauntered through. Philly didn't pay much attention after that. He was too *busy puffing on his ever-present pipe and wondering whether all the poor slobs passing by knew what an important fella he was.*

Suddenly, he heard shots. The sounds so shocked him, it took Philly a moment to realize they were coming from inside the grocery store.

The Actor ran out the door and leaped into the car. "Drive," he ordered gruffly, without a shred of his usual style.

Philly stared at him, as The Actor stuffed some greenbacks into his shirt pocket, with a hand smeared in blood.

"Drive, dammit!" Tag shouted.

Philly slammed the accelerator as ordered. It was only the next day, when he read the newspaper that he learned what happened. After robbing the till, The Actor pistol-whipped the clerk. And when that wasn't enough to satisfy him, he shot the guy, killing him instantly.

They dumped the neighbor's car a couple of blocks later, and stole another parked nearby. Tag told Philly he was setting out to see the country, along Route 66. Philly left Chicago that day, taking a cab straight to the airport. He returned to Europe on the first flight out. He never went back to Chicago. Never been on Route 66 again until this trip with Alec.

He never saw The Actor again. Sometime later Philly heard that Tag had gotten into counterfeiting, and thereafter, that he'd had a bad accident during another trek somewhere along Route 66, and got really banged up. Then, nothing ever again. Never heard of him high up in the crime world, like you'd expect him to be. Maybe he died from his injuries, or was still too beat up to work. Or maybe he was still quietly printing out the funny money, though it wasn't like The Actor to do anything quietly. Tag had always been such a showman.

But Philly had lived all these years knowing what he'd been a part of. He didn't long to be a bad boy anymore after that—he saw those guys for what they were.

And every day of his life, he'd mourned the shopkeeper who got killed. Wasn't that being punished enough? Maybe the law wouldn't see it that way, but anyone else would. So why was the past rising

up now? Why had it come back to haunt him?
　And what in hell was he going to do about it?

CHAPTER TEN

Only moments after Woody stomped back to the kitchen, he informed us he was closing in his own sweet, passive-aggressive way. With no warning, he cut the lights, leaving us there in the dark. After the lights went out, I heard a door slam at the back of the restaurant. Since neither Drew nor I had eaten much of our blackened waffles, I didn't think any of us would care. Still, I considered it shoddy treatment of his benefactor, even if Dad didn't seem to notice. Dad and Philly just rose to leave. Maybe that was how Woody closed every night.

"What about all your papers on the table?" I asked.

"We leave them here," Philly said.

Obviously, The Kontiki Room wasn't any more burdened by customers than I suspected. When we filed out, Dad told Drew to turn the lock in the doorknob and yank it shut.

"No alarm?" Drew asked.

"Andrew, it's Route 66," Dad said. "No crime waves here."

Especially in restaurants that didn't attract customers to add to the till.

During the short walk to the motel, Dad explained that instead of getting us a room of our own, we'd be staying in their suite. "The Presidential Suite," he added.

Drew seemed impressed by that. See what I mean? A total mark. Did he really think a place with Zs in its sign attracted many presidents? The lone governor in the area wasn't even staying here. I couldn't say whether there was really a sucker born every minute, but I knew one who was *re*-born that often.

The Rest Ur Head typified Route 66 lodging. Two rows of rooms opened directly into parking areas, while their windows looked out on a central courtyard with an office, a small kidney-shaped pool, and a cracked patio with some sun-bleached lounges.

As we approached our suite on the end of one wing of rooms,

in the glow of an overhead light, I saw Woody enter a room at the other end.

"Woody lives in the motor court now?" I asked. "Not in the rooms over the restaurant, like he and Lucy used to? Even though he has to pay rent here?" Or *someone* did.

While fishing the room key from his pocket, Dad shrugged. "Woody says he's not comfortable in Lucy's old place after what happened."

Who knew he was such a sensitive guy? If it bothered him that much, how was he able to operate the restaurant? That was where Billy Rob had been killed, not in the apartment.

"Besides, he says he's kept the rooms upstairs exactly as Lucy left them. As a tribute to her."

Didn't sound like the Woody I remembered. "Are they really exactly like she left them?"

"How would I know?" Dad asked, in a frosty tone.

Philly coughed pointedly into his hand, reminding me of the kids who say, "Asshole," to their parents, under the cover of a fake cough. What was going on here?

As I figured, the suite wasn't exactly presidential caliber. Ancient knotty pine paneling covered the sitting room walls. Most of it had been adequately nailed to the studs below, though here and there unfastened portions curved to form gaping holes, some the size of my fist. Everything else in the room, including the worn carpet, the furniture, the draperies, was in various tones of pink, except for a tufted sofa in faded crimson, whose trim took on the shape of a heart, confirming my suspicion that this had once been dubbed "the bridal suite," until it occurred to the motel's owners that it's only the kinkier newlyweds who need three bedrooms.

After a grunt, Philly disappeared through one of the doors off the sitting room. Dad grabbed a walnut coffee table that had been shoved along the far wall, and dragged it to the seating area, angling it vaguely before the sofa, although it stuck out into the traffic lane from the entryway. He fell onto the heart-shaped sofa and propped his Italian loafers onto the end of the scratched coffee table. He motioned us to join him in the worn pink chairs. The Rest Ur Head's owners had obviously made a wise choice in not going all out on the furnishings. The guests who stayed here didn't appreciate them.

"So, Drew, found a job yet?" Dad asked. Neither of my parents ever received high marks for subtlety.

"I told you, Alec, I'm not looking. The universe—" Finally, he seemed to rethink the value of continuing to trot out the universe's plans for him. "Tracy is going to write a travel article."

There it was again, his equating me with the whole freakin' cosmos.

"*Be the river, not the rock*—that's my motto now," Drew said.

Hey, I was the one who spouted moronic mottos, not him. Come to think of it, I was the river, too. But a river needs a rock. Didn't he know that?

As if he'd been reading my thoughts, which weirded me out, Dad gave a kindly tilt to his head and said, "Consistency is overrated, honey."

And people wonder why I turned out like I did.

Showing how thoroughly he embraced inconsistency, Dad said to Drew, "Kind of an iffy way to live, son."

And demonstrating how well I appreciated changeability myself, I turned it around on him. "Gee, Dad, it hasn't hurt Woody."

Dad momentarily busied himself picking at one of the buttons on the faded couch, before announcing that it was past his bedtime. He disappeared behind another one of those closed doors.

"What do you suppose is behind door number three?" Drew asked.

"My guess would be the worst bedroom."

After a quick trip back to the Volvo for some of our luggage, we confirmed my suspicions, finding ourselves in another paneled room with a double bed that sagged in the center. We fell into the awful bed and were asleep within minutes.

But the sound of voices elsewhere in the suite woke me sometime later.

I stretched out on my back, studying the shapes on the water-stained ceiling. After a moment, it occurred to me to wonder why the room seemed so much brighter now than earlier. I went to the window and saw that the clouds that had hovered low when we arrived had all drifted away, leaving a brilliantly clear night under a full moon.

Our room faced the western side of Woody's restaurant, the way we'd approached it earlier. I saw some movement along the side of Woody's building. Someone seemed to be hovering there. Maybe I was still asleep and dreaming. I blinked hard and stared again. In the clear bright moonlight, there was no mistaking what I saw. A figure did hover alongside the building's outer wall, but not in midair. Someone stood on the ladder that rested against the building.

Going up or going down? I watched for a while and determined the direction to be down, although it seemed a slow descent. After a moment, another person, a shorter, lumpier form, shuffled along the ground, from the front of the restaurant, and took hold of the bottom of the ladder to steady it. After that the climber made faster progress.

I rushed back to the bed. Just before I shook him awake, I noticed Drew's broad naked shoulders peeking out from the top of the blanket. Then I still wanted to wake him, but for a different reason. Decisions, decisions—nosiness or sex? Who was I kidding? Nosiness, then sex. No, nosiness, then food, then sex. Jeez, what a thing to admit.

I reached over and gave Drew a hard shake. "Drew!" I murmured. "Wake up."

When his sleep-puffy eyes fluttered open, he said, "Is it morning already? We're going to have to find someplace else for breakfast. No way will I endure another one of those waffles."

"Shush!" I said, though there was really no need to whisper. "It's still nighttime."

"You better have a good reason for this."

"The best. I saw Dad and Philly sneaking out of Lucy Crier's apartment."

CHAPTER ELEVEN

S trictly speaking, I didn't know whether Philly had ever joined his partner in crime in sneaking *into* the apartment. It looked like he'd been off somewhere around the front of the restaurant and only returned to hold the ladder for Dad. But he might have climbed down earlier and gone off briefly. All I could say for certain was that those two old coots were hiding more than they wanted me to know.

Drew and I yanked the blanket free from the bed, and we curled up on the floor, with our ears pressed to our room's door.

It didn't take long for our lost sheep to find their way back. They probably would have made it back to their rooms without revealing anything, only Dad had left that coffee table angled into the path to his room. He plowed right into it.

"Ow!" he cried aloud. "Who left that table there?"

See what I mean about consistency in my family?

"Quiet, Alec! You'll wake the kids."

"Oh, they must be sleeping like the dead," Dad said, but softer now.

Behind our door, we snickered to ourselves, like real little kids fooling the adults.

"Your choice, Alec," Philly said with a sniff. "Do you really want to run the risk of Tracy learning what you've been doing?"

Ooh! The good stuff. Neither of them knew it, but they had waved a red flag before a bull. Had Dad forgotten my childhood? Didn't he remember the ridiculous lengths he and Mother had to go to keep anything from me?

We listened in silence for a while longer, but the codgers didn't spill anything more before returning to their rooms. We gave them enough time to fall back to sleep. Then, after hastily dressing, we crept from the suite.

While traversing the stretch of land between the motel and the restaurant, Drew lamented, "It's a shame I locked the restaurant door when I closed it. It's not as if Woody seems to care who comes and goes."

I cared. Sneaking in through a second story window was way more fun than simply walking through an open door. I rushed to the ladder, still propped against the side of the building, before Drew could suggest trying the door. But despite the brightness of the moon, I discovered it's not that easy to climb a ladder at night. I had to place each of my sneakers carefully on the rungs. Dad must have been pretty determined to do this in leather-soled shoes.

At the three-quarter point I glanced down and saw Drew well below me. Why was he taking so long?

When I reached the top, I noticed Dad had lowered the window to within a couple of inches of closing. I hoped years of warping hadn't rendered it tough to open. But when I pushed, I found it slid effortlessly along vinyl runners. New windows. Dad had sure invested plenty in the upkeep of Lucy's building.

Many people would insist that if I truly needed money, I could tap the same source as Woody. As much as I enjoy spending other people's money, I'd rather lick dog drool. Generosity from my parents always came with strings. Sure, I'd accepted Mother's old country home, but that was because she couldn't afford for that house to pass to strangers because of something hidden within it. I was able to make that seem like I was doing her a favor. To accept help from the people who already tried too hard to control my life was not an option. I'd rather write the stupid travel article, which, despite my claims, I actually had no intention of doing.

I slipped over the windowsill, hoping Dad hadn't positioned any furniture strangely in this room. But I stepped comfortably on worn, but serviceable, wall-to-wall shag carpeting where I waited for Drew to join me.

He sure took his time about it, though. Jeez, I almost went back to sleep standing there. Eventually, he approached the liftoff point— and stalled there, on the top rung of the ladder. It was getting hard to follow his flip-flopping.

"Trace, do you really want to do this? Maybe we should think about it," he said, speaking to me through the open window.

"Think?" I said, like it was an alien concept. "Drew, we thought about it back in the room. Now is not the time for thinking."

"But this is breaking-and-entering."

"And going through the door would have been...what? Just entering? It must be wonderful to be a lawyer. You always know how they're going to nail you." I waited. "In or out, Drew. Are you the river or the rock?" I bit the insides of my cheeks to keep from grinning. This was the rock I knew and loved.

Still, he hesitated.

"Drew, the universe left the ladder here. What's that, if not a sign?"

With a sigh, Semi-Rock-Guy motioned for me to move aside so he could climb through. "I'm going to regret this, I know it."

"Big hairy deal. I can say that about most of my choices."

When we paused to orient ourselves in the shadowy room, a little light suddenly appeared and began drifting about the room. I was almost about to buy into that universe-providing crap, until I discovered it came from a penlight flashlight Drew held.

"Where'd you get that?" I asked in a whisper.

"I keep it on my key-ring. I realized we'd need it."

See what I mean? A guy that wonderfully anal wasn't meant to be a free spirit.

With the aid of his little light we scoped out the room we'd entered, which appeared to be Lucy's old bedroom. Woody wasn't kidding when he said he hadn't altered a thing. But if you're thinking of something on the order of a shrine, forget it. Clothes were strewn everywhere, as if her last act had been changing for a date, instead of heading off to the pokey. Her son hadn't even cleaned up after her, and Lucy had apparently been as big a slob as me. Bigger even, since a couple of old-fashioned stockings were still tossed on one of the old blue vinyl chairs from the café that she'd placed next to the full-sized bed. I don't wait decades to wash my undies.

Despite Lucy's mess, I could see that someone else had hastily searched the place. Dresser drawers were left angled out, and through an open closet door, I could see the contents had been shoved aside.

Maybe so the floor and rear wall could be checked for hiding places?

"What do you think Dad was looking for?" I asked.

"T.K. Mann's missing loot?" Drew said with a chuckle. "The TV show that gave you a crazy dream said they're offering a reward to anyone who finds it."

Right. Like the sleek, stacked Lucy had transformed herself into either a small, wiry guy or a tall, bony one—depending on which description of the hijacker you believed. And like my dad, a guy known in Hollywood for still clutching the first dollar he ever made, needed a reward.

Mother is a wealthy woman, thanks more to the efforts of her financial advisors than the huge sums she's made, since that woman spends like she expects all the world's stores to close tomorrow. Dad was another story. Despite his generosity with people like Woody and Hinky, and even Philly, Dad had always been careful with a buck. But things hadn't always been as easy for him.

Mother had been so sure she would make it in Hollywood, she left her family's California farm as a teenager and promptly snagged herself a studio contract. Her first role set her on the path to stardom. Dad was different—he hadn't planned it. He was a local boy, Hollywood born and bred, who happened to be a good enough craftsman to score a job as a set carpenter. That he'd been singled out for fame and fortune seemed an incredible long shot. He couldn't have known a director would spontaneously cast him when an actor was injured in a set accident, nor that the critics and the public would take to him as they had. He'd never expected it to last. Even after all these years of fame and wealth, old habits seemed hard to break.

So what could he have been searching for? Could Lucy have had something on him? Had she blackmailed him from jail? That might explain his payouts to Woody, but not the devotion he'd always shown to both of them.

I made my way to Woody's boyhood bedroom, which also looked like it had been preserved in time. In contrast to the baby blue walls and the puffy clouds painted on the ceiling were fading gangster movie posters tacked onto the walls. I remembered how

Woody used to have a real fascination going with godfather-types. Legos structures and toy guns still filled the shelves mounted on the walls—some Legos pieces and model car parts were also scattered across the bed and the rug. Apart from the gangster-art, it seemed more like a little boy's room, than that of a kid in his teens.

We continued searching, but we were following a well-worn path. The apartment wasn't large—just those two bedrooms and a sitting area—and Dad had pulled it all apart. Without knowing what he was looking for, we didn't have a chance of doing better.

Still, I'm temperamentally incapable of admitting defeat. So, after shaking down both bedrooms, we turned to the sitting room. It was a rectangular space that ran the length of the front of the building. That room had been roughly divided into two halves. On one side, a rickety cart held a tiny TV set across from a worn gray tweed couch, and covering every surface in that part of the room, from the top of the TV, to the arms of the sofa, were stacks of old fashion magazines.

The other end of the room had been set up as a sewing area. I hadn't realized that Lucy used to make her own clothes. Considering how young I was the last time I saw her, I probably didn't know people *could* make them. I probably believed they appeared spontaneously in their natural habitat—the boutiques along Rodeo Drive in Beverly Hills. But as I studied a nearly completed dress hanging from a hook on the wall beside the machine, I saw that Lucy had been a real artist. Forget about having had the stuff to be a model—she could have been a successful designer, if she'd only known how to pull her life together. With its blousy bodice, trim waist and dirndl skirt, there was a stylish Gypsy quality about the challis dress. If someone only completed the missing sleeve, that garment could have commanded big bucks in some trendy shop.

I wondered why Lucy hadn't finished it. With the café closed during the weeks leading up to her imprisonment, she couldn't have had much to do. I pawed through the plastic laundry baskets that she used to hold fabric remnants, and it looked as if she'd busied herself making workout wear and burlap toys for a while. That was Lucy, all right—no follow-through.

In a metal cabinet, whose lock yielded after I jiggled it, I found albums filled with Lucy's designs, as well as lots of loose pages piled up on the shelves. Drew had gone off somewhere with his penlight, leaving me with nothing but moonlight to examine the contents of those albums. Even in that scant light, I could see how good Lucy really had been. Sure, I knew she'd brought strong artistic skills to her lunch pail paintings, especially since she probably never took an art class, but I hadn't imagined her design instincts would be this good.

As I continued skimming the album pages, I wondered if I could get Mother to interest one of her designer friends to take a look at these. Fat chance. In all the years Dad had been visiting Tecos, I'd never heard her even acknowledge Lucy's existence. I clearly wasn't the only one who had suspicions about Dad's relationship with Lucy and her son.

Still, I gathered up Lucy's albums and all the loose pages, and went in search of Drew. "We're not finding anything here," I said. "Let's go back to bed."

I started toward the window with the ladder, but before I stepped out, I realized Drew hadn't followed me. I found him poised beside the stairway to the restaurant downstairs.

"Uh, Tracy...in for a penny." He shrugged sheepishly.

That had always been one of my mottos, although I didn't know what it meant in this context.

"I'm starved, babe. What do you say we go downstairs and make something to eat? Even if there's nothing in that kitchen but waffle batter, we can't wreck it as badly as Woody."

With a nod, I agreed. Hell, if we got caught, the cops would probably go easier on us if they thought we were just stealing waffle fixings.

With Drew's little flashlight leading the way, we pounded down the stairs. The staircase deposited us outside the restrooms, down a little hall from the restaurant. Drew pushed at a swinging door that should have led to the kitchen, but it stuck.

"We'll have to break into the kitchen from the restaurant side. Come on," I said. I plopped all the albums into Drew's arms and snatched his little flashlight, and used it to lead the way down that short corridor.

We pushed through the restaurant's door, which swung open easily. I paused inside of it and wiggled the flashlight around to scope out the joint.

The beam of light fell on the reason why we hadn't been able to open the door from the hall. Something blocked it. Someone.

Woody sat propped against the door, slumped over, as still as a doorstop.

CHAPTER TWELVE

We stood there stupidly, staring down at Woody, while he remained slumped in the flashlight's beam.

"Is he...a goner?" Drew asked.

Gallows humor now. He *was* becoming more like me.

Making that determination seemed to have fallen to me *again*. Just as when Philly went splat on the road, the answer was obvious, even if the outcome proved to be the exact opposite. Unlike Philly, Woody's chest didn't rise and fall anymore. Even more telling, someone had brought a rock shaped like a wedge of pie, and used its narrowed side like a hatchet, parting Woody's skull along a ruby red line. The rock had been left beside Woody's still form. I didn't touch it, in case the killer had left fingerprints, though given its craggy surface, it was unlikely to take any good prints.

I'd always avoided contact with the icky guy in life, and I felt no more desire to cozy up to him now. But I'm nothing if not thorough. Most of the time. With a sigh, I reached through the wrinkled collar of his dingy shirt and felt for a pulse. Woody wasn't the *un*dead anymore.

"He's with his dad now," I said, clinging to the idea that Billy Rob had sired him, not a certain well-known actor. But they hadn't been together long. Jeez, Woody was warmer than I was, especially since finding him had given me a distinct chill. "Funny, huh? I always figured he'd end up where they sent his mom."

"What was he doing here at this hour?" Drew asked. "Why did he close, only to come back? Surely he wasn't desperate enough to eat his own cooking."

I remembered how Woody had hustled us out earlier. "Maybe he planned to meet someone here, and he didn't want us to know."

In that shadowy room, my preoccupied gaze met Drew's. The scary thing about a long relationship is that, eventually, you can read each other's thoughts. Really scary for me, considering how much I kept from him. In the instant our eyes connected, I sensed we shared the same idea of Woody's meeting partner. I turned away fast to break the connection.

As if I could run away from the thought, I pushed through the door into the darkened restaurant. After a moment, Drew followed me. We groped our way back to the old boys' table.

"We gotta call the cops, you know," I said to the shadowy form sitting across from me.

The form jerked. "Are you out of your mind?"

The universe was cockeyed, all right. There I was all for taking the conventional route, while Drew opposed it. That was just wrong.

"How are you going to explain the little matter of our breaking in?" he asked.

The thought of Woody's theoretical companion, the one who must have left him dead, consumed my brain cells. Fortunately, I can easily speak without my mind being in gear. "We'll tell them we had to break in upstairs because we found the front door locked."

From within the gloomy shadows, I heard Drew sigh. "You're getting more like your mother every day."

Now he was just being insulting. I remembered that I'd had Drew's key-ring flashlight. What had I done with it? I tapped the pockets of my jeans until I found a lump. Once I illuminated the light, I stretched my other hand across the table. "Give me your wallet."

Drew hesitated, but he finally handed it over. I shined the light into the money compartment. He had *scads* of bills in there. Man, had he built up a stash. Now I had proof that he should continue in the money-gatherer role, while I belonged on the disperser side. I pulled the loot from the wallet and stuffed it into my pocket, and then I tossed the wallet onto the floor under the table. Even if I hadn't managed to confiscate this before we left home, it was mine now.

"There. Now, here's how we'll play it: When you found your wallet was gone, we pounded on Woody's motel room door to let us in, only he didn't answer. Nobody waits until morning when his wallet is missing. Since we're old friends of the family, we were sure Woody wouldn't mind if we snuck in to see if you dropped it here. Hell, us four are the only ones who know we actually locked the door. We can say we found it open."

Drew nodded his approval. "You're getting as devious as your mother, too."

Now that was a compliment. Reality is so flexible, the way I use it anyway.

Despite having worked out our story, we didn't act on it. We continued to sit there in silence, breathing in the smell of burned waffles and congealed maple syrup from the plates we'd pushed aside earlier, which Woody hadn't bothered to remove before closing up. A guy we knew was rapidly turning into lumber in the other room, and we didn't move a muscle. Such is the power of denial.

Finally, Drew asked, "Why would you assume Woody was meeting someone here? He could have forgotten something and came back for it and surprised a thief."

"Good idea," I said. As long as the person Woody surprised wasn't the same one I avoided mentioning. "I guess the coincidence of his dad also being killed here just struck me strongly."

"His father met someone here? When he was killed, you mean?"

I shrugged. "That was what the police surmised. But the rest of it doesn't apply to Woody. They think Billy Rob met another woman here, which so incensed Lucy, she killed him."

"I thought Lucy *was* the other woman. Wasn't the guy married?"

"They figured there was *another* other woman."

"And with all the motels along this stretch of road, he met her in his girlfriend's restaurant after hours, below her bedroom? Was he an idiot?"

"Pretty much."

"*That* much of one?" Drew demanded. "Did they ever identify the woman?"

Lawyers—do they always see those loopholes? "I was just a little kid, so nobody shared too much with me. That was what Lucy confessed to, Drew. Why should the cops doubt it? Apparently, she built a pretty good case for her guilt." But now that I thought about it, I couldn't remember a woman ever having been named. Why would Lucy have killed him if another woman wasn't involved?

Drew seemed to mull that one over for a while. "What was he like—the man she killed?"

"Billy Rob Royce?" I snorted. "I always thought his name sounded like one of the drinks my parents favored back then. But my dad never liked Billy Rob. He always put on this friendly act, but I could feel Dad's tension around him. Because of Lucy, I guess. He'd always insisted she could do better." I never asked if he had anyone else in mind.

"Good looking?"

"Really not. He had these prominent facial bones. You know, thick features, heavy, protruding brow."

"Like Woody."

"More like Bigfoot, or Cro-Magnon Man. I think one of his legs must have been shorter than the other because he walked funny. Not with a limp, but kind of leaning to the short side." Another memory drifted back to me. "There was also a cruel streak in Billy Rob. That's why people believed he was nasty enough to taunt Lucy with his bimbo. He used to tickle me unmercifully. Some people think little kids like it, but it's actually mean. Dad told him to stop it, but Billy Rob kept doing it, every time he saw me. So, Dad and I rehearsed precisely when I should haul off and give a kick."

"You nailed him in the nuts?" Drew chuckled.

"Sure did. It's not every father who'd teach you how to do that." It also wasn't every father who broke into old friends' homes, either. I shouldn't cheer his originality too much.

I couldn't bear the weight of the unspoken any longer. I leaped to my feet, so fast, my chair crashed to the floor. I reached across table and groped in the dark for Drew's wrist.

"Come on, Drew. Let's get out of here."

We switched sides again. "Trace, we have to call this in."

"No, let's just leave. Someone else will find him."

He sighed. "At least let me get my wallet."

I yanked harder, though he didn't budge. "Leave it."

"Tracy, do the words *identity theft* mean anything to you?"

"Do the words *my father's in the clink* mean anything to you?" Had I totally lost my touch with denial?

Drew snorted. "You think Alec...? That *he* was the person Woody was meeting?"

Hadn't we both thought it? Had I misread his expression in the dark? "Given the timing—who else could it have been? Woody must have caught him searching for something."

"And whatever it was, you believe Alec would *kill* over it? Kill someone he's show incredible devotion to all these years? Someone he could talk to at any time, without a clandestine arrangement?"

I should have talked to Drew earlier. "When you put it that way..." But then I bit my lip. "Only...I'm starting to remember something else..."

CHAPTER THIRTEEN

MEMORIES OF ROUTE 66
TRACY

"Get down those stairs, twerp."* Punctuating the hard words had been a bony knee thrust into my back, which sent me tumbling to the floor. My keeper just laughed.*

After all the fun of my first trip along Route 66, I figured these getaways would always be great. But Lucy killed Billy Rob, and now that she'd been hauled off to serve her sentence, we were back again to clean out the Lunch Pail Café. As if Dad's mood wasn't enough to sour the trip, he'd hired Terry, a drifter we'd met there last time, to fill some time capsule we were supposed to put together before we went home.

Dad also left it to Terry to take care of me whenever he was busy, and since he made frequent trips to see Lucy at the prison, that ended up being most of the time. I'd never encountered an adult as lousy to me as Terry was, and that included lots of movie directors who threatened to bar me from their sets and one or two teachers who thought my parents deserved a commendation for putting up with me. I could never get Dad to believe how Terry changed whenever he wasn't there. My father might not have been the sharpest knife in the drawer, I knew now, but after a lifetime of acting, he understood people. Yet he never saw through his miserable assistant.

Nobody did except for me. Even as young as I was, I'd already noticed grownups get taken in when people tell them what they want to hear.

Terry was always quick with a grin and a match to light someone's smoke, and people seemed to believe he smiled just because it gave him joy to serve them. As young as I was, I sensed the source of his amusement was the knowledge that the last time he used that book of matches was to burn down someone's house, and the memory gave him a warm glow.

Though I'd never forget him, I also couldn't describe him. His face had the soft, rubbery quality of Silly Putty. Apart from his flat, murky hazel eyes, anyway. They looked like raisins I'd once left in the yard that'd gotten rained on—mushy things, lacking all color and character.

But Terry wasn't totally responsible for ruining that trip. I remember waking up one night to the sound of my dad sobbing in the sitting room of our suite, at the motel next door to Lucy's café. Unless he was making a movie, I'd never seen my dad cry. Nothing, including some breakups with Mother, had ever saddened him that much.

After Lucy went away, Dad assumed the task of closing up her restaurant for the last time, even though it meant bailing from some film he was supposed to make, and that caused some legal brouhaha for him. At first he hadn't seemed in any hurry to pack things up. We had a little time before we needed to be back in California to dedicate that time capsule. Even then, I sensed he was stalling, and that was his way of holding onto Lucy.

But all at once, everything changed. That was the first time when Terry hit me with his knee, throwing me to the floor and laughing about it. Still, the sense of urgency didn't come from Terry, but Dad. That day, when I went downstairs to the restaurant, I saw that the lunch pails he hadn't had the heart to remove before had been stripped away. He'd stuffed them all into a large rental trailer that he had hooked to the bumper of his Lincoln.

Dad hadn't looked his usual carefree handsome self that morning, either. From trying to stuff the lunch pails into the trailer really fast, his face had become red, and sweat slicked back his hair.

"Get in the car now, Tracy," he'd said breathlessly. "We need to leave."

Since I didn't see all of my things in the car, I'd balked.

"With Terry along, we don't have enough room for all our luggage. We'll pick up some new things for you later, honey."

I'd left my doll in the motel room, and I refused to leave without it. *"Not my dolly, daddy. I need my dolly."*

Dad never treated me harshly, but he came close that morning. "Get in the car, Tracy. We'll find you a new dolly."

"I don't want a new one." I felt my chin begin to quiver.

After a heavy sigh, Dad had knelt down before me. But impatience strained the already-tight muscles of his face. "Honey, we have to leave now."

"No," I wailed.

"Yes, Tracy—now," he had snapped for the first and last time in my life. He took a moment to soften his voice when he repeated, "Now." But the sound of urgency never wavered.

CHAPTER FOURTEEN

Despite my impassioned relating of Dad's hasty retreat from the restaurant of death, Drew prevailed and we alerted the police. The cop shop dispatcher instructed us to wait in the café, well away from the body in the kitchen, and not to touch anything. I might have agreed to call them, but I had no intention of leaving Lucy's design albums behind, as they'd doubtless expect, since the police invariably view everything as evidence. To my surprise, Drew agreed. We rushed to our car and hid them in the trunk. It was still dark outside, but the sky was beginning to brighten.

On the way back to the restaurant, Drew asked. "So you have no idea what caused Alec to bug out of here in a hurry back then. What is it you think?"

I gave a reluctant shrug. "Maybe some evidence surfaced that implicated him in Billy Rob's murder."

"No evidence was surfacing, Trace. Lucy had already started serving her sentence. The police stop investigating a crime by that point." He gripped my shoulders and turned me to face him. "And the Alec Grainger I know wouldn't let an innocent woman go to prison for a crime he committed. You of all people should know that."

I gave Drew a confident nod, while inside, the doubts I kept trying to smother refused to die.

I didn't have time to dwell on them, though. The cops in small towns must sit around waiting for calls like ours. In no more than mere moments after we took our places back in the restaurant, I heard the sound of approaching sirens.

A minute later, the door to The Kontiki Room flew open. At the sight of the man suddenly filling the doorway, I went into a laughing spasm that I tried to cover with a cough. Too bad that cough didn't come fast enough.

In the doorway stood the world's most glittery Rhinestone Cowboy, an African-American man, whose embroidered Western shirt and decorated leather spats sported so much fringe, he had drastically reduced the world's supply of it. There must have been clackers hidden within that fringe, too, because when he strode into the place, he jangled.

He tipped a gigantic white hat, which matched the accents in his black shirt and spats, and said, "Ma'am. Hear tell someone blew out poor Woody's light."

Huh? Was his getup and lingo a joke? If we'd been back in L.A., I'd have assumed this guy to be an actor in some Western movie parody. Here, I figured he'd been yanked from his other job, rodeo clown. Were we on reality TV? Was Woody going to jump up and surprise us? Nope, that wasn't going to happen. I remembered checking for his missing pulse.

The rodeo clown introduced himself as Chief Roy Fricker. A more jovial expression should have gone along with that costume, but with his high cheekbones and prominent jaw, Chief Fricker's face was as flat, hard, and as lacking in affect as a board. Hooded lids made for sharply narrowed eyes within that flat surface. Though for an instant, I saw excitement burning hot and bright within them. Well, why not? How many murders could they get around here?

He paused beside Drew and asked, "Where's Woody at?"

It was impossible to gauge the chief's age. While the slight sag below the prominent jaw might have meant he was creeping up on Medicare, the washboard abs beneath his fitted shirt rivaled any surfer boy's.

Drew pointed toward the kitchen.

Fricker removed his hat and ran a large hand over his closely shorn hair. "Can't say I'm all that surprised someone flipped Woody's hash browns. He's always been like someone riding 'round with a wasp up his nose. Always looking for a porker to kick."

Was that English?

Those hooded eyes narrowed in on Drew. "You're mighty calm about all this, son. As cool as a skunk on a dark night." He indicated me with a nod of his head. "While the little lady's as nervous a bit-up old mule in fly season."

I was not! Jeez, who did he think he was? I was just trying to act like I was in shock, so he didn't think I tripped over stiffs all the time. *Show 'em what they expect, if you want the edge*—that's my motto.

"I'm a lawyer," Drew explained. "That is—"

"Aren't we lucky."

Some things are universal.

Through the open doorway, in the light of The Kontiki Room flashing sign, I saw another patrol car pull to a stop outside, which produced two uniformed officers. When they entered the café, I watched their young faces to see if they found anything odd about their chief's garments. Not a flicker of surprise or amusement. Was this the way he always dressed?

"Juan, you come with me," Fricker said to the shorter of the two. "Paulie, keep an eye on these folks here. And don't let them sit together." With that the chief and his deputy strode into the kitchen.

Officer Paulie looked about as slow as a pig in molasses. Hey, I was getting into this cowboy gibberish. Drew took a seat in the booth where Paulie directed.

"You sit somewhere else," he said to me.

I sat in the booth right behind Drew's, with my back to his. Paulie frowned at that, but he didn't object. We all sat there in silence, for so long, I felt sure they must be selling snow cones in hell by now. The deputy Juan came and went occasionally with evidence bags. A woman, carrying a medical bag, also arrived and disappeared into the kitchen, as did a man who parked a hearse outside. And even though the sun hadn't yet risen, most of the town's folks must have gathered there as well, judging by the chatter I heard through the door they'd left ajar.

The curious thing was that neither Dad nor Philly came to the restaurant. Maybe there was another cop outside who had turned them away. Or maybe, when they saw the commotion, they cleared out. My stomach began to ache so badly, you'd think I'd eaten one of Woody's waffles.

In one of the rare moments when Deputy Paulie left us alone,

Drew asked. "Why do you think Fricker didn't ask us anything about finding Woody?"

"He had more important fish to fry, Drew." Jeez, I did have my own slang. "He's not through with us yet."

Showed what I knew. Apparently, after keeping us there for most of a lifetime, he *was* through with us. When Chief Fricker strode from the kitchen, he asked, "Y'all staying at the Rest Ur Head?" Then, before waiting for an answer, he told Paulie to let us go.

As annoyed as I felt that he'd kept us there for nothing, I wasn't about to give him a chance to change his mind. I wiggled out of the booth and rushed toward the door. To my surprise, Drew wasn't right behind me. I turned and saw that he stood beside Fricker.

Drew's lips thinned to a grim line, the way they did when he seemed to be psyching himself up for something. "Uh...Chief. You're probably wondering how we came to find Woody."

What was he doing? Now *that's* the reason why honest people should never go into the law. With his strict ethical code, Drew was wise to get out of that cutthroat game.

Fricker's eyes narrowed in on him, but not before I caught a flash of something within them. "Son, I spotted your wallet on the floor when I came in. Let's just say that was what you were looking for. We both know it wasn't to rustle up any of Woody's grub. Everything here tasted like lemonade made from dirty shorts."

The Rhinestone Cowboy had seen Drew's wallet? I wondered if I underestimated him.

"Now why don't you fetch your billfold and be on your way?"

Drew moved toward the table where we'd tossed the wallet. But instead of merely leaning in, he crawled all the way under it. And then he didn't emerge right away. Had he decided to set up camp down there? Fricker watched for an instant, before marching out of the restaurant. Only then did Drew reappear.

We walked from the restaurant without exchanging a word. People in the crowd gathered outside the place immediately assaulted us with questions, but Fricker shouted a caution for us not to talk with anyone, and the disappointed crowd lost interest in us.

Only once we were far enough away to talk, did I say with a

sniff, "What were you thinking, Drew? Have you learned nothing from me? Honesty will kill you every time."

"I'm not as honest as you think, babe."

I snorted.

"I mean it. I found something under that table, Trace."

"Yeah, your wallet. Remember? We threw it there."

"Something else, and I withheld it."

Maybe my guidance was paying off, after all. Drew glanced over his shoulder, before producing a folded slip of scrap paper on which someone had printed in block letters, "How much is it worth to you to keep your past hidden?"

I gasped. "I knew it! Someone *is* blackmailing Dad."

"Think again."

He flipped the sheet over so I could see how the note had been addressed. In those same blocky letters, someone had written, "Philly Chase, sidekick of The Actor."

CHAPTER FIFTEEN

While we walked away from the crime scene, the sight of *Philly's* name on that blackmail note so stunned me, I tripped and landed facedown in a little Mother Road dust. Drew pulled me to my feet, but not before I swallowed some of the stuff. The grit between my teeth felt the same as any other dirt.

"Philly!" I blew out across my tongue, in the hopes of clearing the dirt, but it only caused me to choke. "I can see Dad getting blackmailed, but not your uncle."

Drew gave his head a toss. "Think about it: Which of them has the colorful past in the world of crime?"

Talk about exaggerations. Drew's con man uncle wasn't exactly a mob boss, and he never denied his nefarious past.

"Which one is the public figure, who'd have the strongest need to hide it?"

Drew gave a rueful laugh. "I don't know, Trace. Your dad's celebrity has really hit the skids when he's referred to merely as, *The Actor.*" He stewed in silence. "Should we confront them?"

I shook my head, which just tossed dust into my eyes. "Not until we've thought this through." I rolled my eyes in big circles, to move the dust out.

Some man in a plaid flannel shirt headed toward where the crowd still gathered outside the Kontiki Room. But the sight of my reeling eyeballs must have stopped him in his tracks.

"Is she having some kinda fit?" he asked Drew.

"Sure is. She'll probably fall your way if you don't tell me quick where we can find the best breakfast in town."

No! We really had changed roles. I stifled a sob.

But Drew's gambit worked. The man hastily spouted directions, while inching around me. I continued to roll my eyes, as Drew helped me into the Volvo.

A short time later, we found ourselves seated on opposite sides of a booth in the red, white, and blue All-American Route 66 Coffee Shoppe. Though this shoppe, with its over-the-top flag theme, didn't look the least like Lucy's lunch pail place had, it offered the same homey feel. Why had Woody discarded that in favor of his bizarre nightclub-waffle mutation, with those strange holes he'd punched in the walls?

While plates of eggs and hash browns, stacked up on the arms of servers, called out to me as they moved past, when our waitress arrived, I ordered waffles. So did Drew.

"We want to remember what they're supposed to taste like," Drew said with a sheepish shrug.

The sardonic gray-haired woman responded with a knowing snort. "Woody's place, huh? You won't do that again."

No kidding. Neither would anyone else.

Once the waitress left, Drew leaned his forearms across the table. "So...Philly? When you saw Alec climbing down the ladder, you said Philly had returned from the front of the building. He couldn't have been inside—I know I locked that door when I closed it."

I snorted. "That pitiful little lock wouldn't have stopped Philly if he wanted in." Hell, it wouldn't have stopped *me*. It was sheer luck that I didn't have to suspect myself.

"He couldn't have...you know...?"

"Snuffed Woody, you mean?" I asked.

I guessed, from his pained grimace, that he found that statement a little too direct. So much for our shared gallows humor. I clung to this difference between us like a lifeline.

"He never met the guy till a week ago," Drew went on hastily. "And Philly doesn't even get mad enough to curse out anyone, not to mention..."

True. I'd never met anyone more comfortable in his own worn-out sack of a suit than Philly Chase. Though he had seemed uncharacteristically sad when we encountered him dressed as Lucy out on Route 66.

"Besides, Philly's lived most of his life out of the country. I doubt he'd been west of the Hudson until he moved in with us."

Who was Drew trying to convince? "You *doubt* it? Could you *swear* to it? Or anything else about Philly's past?" Despite Philly's openness about the dubious way he'd made his way in the world, he did have his secrets. I stumbled onto one a couple of years ago, when Drew's sister Marisa was kidnapped before her wedding. I'd promised Philly I'd never share it with Drew, and I hadn't. A guy with one big mystery in his past could have many more.

"Besides, what are the odds that he and your dad *both* have connections here?"

The waitress paused at our table and slopped more coffee into our thick, white mugs.

"Pretty good, actually. Route 66 is a vortex of coincidence. An amazing number of paths cross here."

"But a major motion picture star and a down-on-his-luck con man?"

They were here together now, weren't they? I sensed Drew didn't want to hear that. What I said about Route 66 was true, though. In adulthood, I'd discovered that friends of mine had actually been here at the same time as me when they were kids. It was just chance that we hadn't met then.

Drew grabbed a glass saltshaker with a dented chrome top and absently slid it back and forth across the table. "Whatever Philly's hiding—one thing is certain: Alec must know what it is. They are friends, after all."

I wasn't as sure. Though Philly was Drew's uncle, and I'd only known him a couple of years, I understood him much better. I knew why he might keep secrets that others would regard as pointless, since I did the same. You never know when some innocuous little fact will come back to bite you on the ass. If you don't spill it, even to your nearest and dearest, you don't have to worry. Besides, secrets are fun to keep.

Drew's hands, spread about a foot apart, began to slide that saltshaker across the table with increasing speed. The sound of the glass scraping against Formica rolled on relentlessly, threatening my brain with meltdown. As it flew past one time, I grabbed the little jar, to silence that noise. At that moment, an illusive connection that had been eluding me since the night before, finally clicked in my mind.

I slammed the shaker down against the tabletop. "That's it. That's why we're here! I see it all now."

"All I see is that you stole the saltshaker."

"Look…Dad tried to light a fire under us with that silly phone call about Lucy running around on Route 66. But here's the thing, Drew: I think he did it for Philly, at Philly's suggestion."

Drew answered that with a skeptical lift of one eyebrow. They must have classes in law school where they perfect that gesture. Such intense scrutiny might have caused me to back down, were I not so certain I was right.

"We keep saying it: Dad taught me to do Route 66 in a certain way. It was part of our ritual to visit the plaque, and to stop at every gaudy bit of Americana along the way. And he insisted we visit Hinky's storage yard. Despite his dangling that little mystery before my nose, he knew we wouldn't make it here quickly."

Drew nodded slowly.

"It was *Philly* who griped about how long he had to maintain that Lucy charade while dodging traffic. *He* thought we'd rush straight here."

Just as understanding floated into Drew's sherry colored eyes, the waitress placed our waffle dishes before us. But neither of us dove in immediately. I knew I needed to work through the logic of whatever game the old boys were playing, and I guessed Drew did, too.

"I don't know what inducement he used, but Philly must have convinced Dad to find a way to get us here faster. Dad's obviously got a few secrets of his own, so there are bound to be buttons that Philly would know how to push. But it was *Philly* who felt desperate enough to perform that ridiculous Lucy stunt."

"Why?"

"There's only one reason: Because your uncle is in big trouble, and he needs our help. The blackmail note proves it."

"You think he'd just ask," Drew said in a sour tone before finally starting to eat.

He really didn't get Philly at all. "Ah, but that wouldn't be playing the game, and you know he's all about games." As was I. "He's going to make us figure it out."

"How? It won't be easy, will it?"

"More like damn near impossible." We weren't on our home turf. There wasn't a fixed circle of suspects. "People reinvent themselves along Route 66. Who can say which of the locals recognized Philly from some prior life and smelled opportunity?"

"What if we don't put it together in time?"

I shrugged. "Then he loses. That's a big part of gamesmanship, too." My heart ached over the mere idea of it. How many guilty old coots could I worry about?

The old anal Drew surfaced, as he absently sketched a pair of neat little boxes on the table with his hands, with a distinct separation between them. "This isn't another chance for you to play detective, Tracy. We'll limit ourselves to Philly's blackmail. Woody's murder is a job for the police."

Mr. Daredevil's flip-flops were giving me a headache. "Hey, I'm a full service amateur sleuth, capable of multi-tasking."

His eyes bulged.

"Oh, un-bunch your shorts, Drew. I was just having some fun with you. Fricker is welcome to Woody's murder. I didn't like the guy in life, and I'm not enough of a hypocrite to pretend to care now." Okay, so all murders lured me. I resisted its appeal.

Drew actually exhaled in relief. He really wasn't playing in my league. "Then we're agreed, right?" He thrust his hand across the table. "Blackmail only, no murder?"

"You bet," I said, giving him a firm shake.

Unless…Woody's murder really was tied into Philly's troubles, as it could be. Or whatever Dad was trying to keep under wraps, which I also intended to get to the bottom of. Then all bets were off.

CHAPTER SIXTEEN

W e headed back to the Rest Ur Head, determined to cut through the pile of buffalo chips the old boys had scattered so heavily on the ground that we needed hip boots to wade through them. We would have made it back there sooner, only we couldn't agree on our approach. Me, I usually relied on the inspiration of the moment, but Drew liked to be prepared. That was the lawyer in him—apparently, they don't win many cases when they just wing it in court. To my mind, the trouble with preparedness is that you simply can't plan for every eventuality. But that didn't stop Drew from trying.

Despite his having sketched out various approaches, none included the likelihood that we'd catch the old farts trying to kill each other. Yet the sound of angry voices coming from the suite greeted us on our arrival. I had sensed some tension between the Odd Couple, but I didn't expect it to break out in full-fledged warfare. Maybe we wouldn't have to ask any questions to get the answers. We stood outside the suite, and once again, we pressed our ears to the door.

"You're full of it, Alec," Philly shouted. "You don't have the slightest idea of the stuff regular people have to deal with."

"That's not fair. I've found myself in some tough spots."

"And with your celebrity and money, you slip right through them."

They were both right. Despite Dad's insistence on his regular guy status, he was clueless about how the other half lived. He did try to understand, though.

"I can't help it if—"

"Can't or won't?" Philly cried bitterly. "Don't matter no how."

Drew must have sensed that Philly's stampede was about to begin, and he jumped out of the way. I wasn't as quick. When the door flew open, it knocked me down.

"Outta my way, kids," Philly said as he stormed out, leaving a whiff of pipe smoke in his wake. "You don't want to stand in front of this runaway train." He stomped off through the parking lot.

I noticed Philly wore his old brown tweed suit again, something I hadn't seen since he started wearing castoff clothing from some of Dad's pudgier friends.

Drew turned to go after him, but I held him back. "Let him cool down. Besides, there's gold to be mined in there." I gave my head a toss toward the room.

If I expected to find Dad broken up, I was in for a surprise. He was too distracted for that. We found him rushing back and forth between his room and the sitting area, too busy packing to notice Philly had gone. His suitcases covered every surface, while Dad moved between them, tossing his possessions into whichever seemed to have a bit of space. The messiness of this hasty packing didn't fit a guy with knife-sharp jeans creases.

Drew expressed his surprise by pursing of his lips. I was too stunned to react. My dad was fleeing this place *again*. And I could only think of one reason why, even if I couldn't bring myself to put it into words.

Somehow, by halting my thoughts, I also short-circuited my speech. Whoa! I would never have guessed that thoughts and speech could be connected. For the first time in my life, I was rendered mute.

Fortunately, Drew's voice hadn't abandoned him. "Going somewhere, Alec?"

Okay, so he wasn't very original, but I wasn't in a position to complain. Hell, if I had the voice to complain, I wouldn't need Drew's crappy lead-in.

The only thing that cheered me was that, despite his determination to bug out, Dad didn't act guilty. Commanding his full attention at that moment were the pair of cashmere sweaters he held, as he seemed to weigh the question of which suitcase pile he should toss them onto.

"No reason to stay now that Woody's gone," he said.

So he did know that Woody had been killed. He must have been part of the crowd gathered outside the café after all, at least for a while.

Drew gave his head a sorry shake. "Really a shame about Woody."

Dad's eyes finally focused on Drew. Still holding the pair of sweaters, he sagged against the sofa's arm. "Poor Lucy. Now she has nothing left to live for."

"Are you still going to try to get her freed?" Drew asked.

Dad hurled both sweaters to a bare spot on the coffee table. "That was never gonna happen, son. You know how hard it is to win someone a new trial?"

Drew nodded.

"I should never have listened to Philly. He was so sure you two could turn up something."

After my former muteness, now I had to clamp a hand over my mouth to keep from shouting, "Told you so!" I *knew* it had been *Philly,* not Dad, who maneuvered to get us there. But it wasn't so we could help Lucy. Philly was the one who really needed the help.

Once my voice finally became unleashed, I let it fly. "Dad, there's a lot of *déjà vu* in this room."

His white head swiveled from corner to corner, as if in search of something physical.

"I'm thinking of another time when we left here in this much of a rush. Remember, after Lucy went away—you stuffed those lunch pails in the trailer you rented, and we flew away from here. Why was that, Dad?"

He offered me one of his signature screen smiles, the ones that make the lines about his eyes crinkle so attractively. "Baby, don't you remember. That wasn't me—you were the one who was eager to get away."

Whoa! He sold that so well, I almost believed it. And I knew better. Where had I gotten the idea that he didn't know how to lie?

"Are your pants on fire?" I blurted.

He actually looked. Drew was right—Dad wasn't the brightest bulb in the marquee. Or maybe I was just feeling spiteful because he could lie that easily to me.

Dad produced a strained chuckle, despite a jawline that had grown rigid trying to hold that expression. "Oh, I get it. You think I'm fibbing. It's true, honey. You did want to leave. The young guy I had working for me then told me so."

The whopper wasn't delivered quite so well that time. He held my gaze a bit too long. A director would have insisted on another take. But it was a good move, blaming it on the dweeb who worked for him. Too bad I'd never said anything about leaving to either of them.

Philly walked back in at that point, leaving the door open behind him. He didn't acknowledge any of us. He simply strode over to a table below the window, on which someone had placed a gallon-sized bottle of water, along with a stack of cheap plastic glasses. From where I stood, I could see that his hands shook as he tried to remove one glass from the stack. I wondered whether Philly returned to give an apology or to collect one, or simply because our cars were the best way he had to get back to California.

Charm suddenly glazed Dad's voice. "He was sure something, wasn't he, sweetheart? That Terry, I mean, that young guy I hired to help us. He was such a character." A warm chuckle rolled out from Dad's belly. "Remember how he always called everyone Something Buckaroo?"

Philly's shaky hands dropped the gallon of water onto the table.

"Dad, you found that funny because he always called you King Buckaroo. You wouldn't have liked it as much if you ever listened to what he called me." I tried to recall his voice, but only remember the guy's smarmy smirk and some of his other colorful expressions, not the actual timbre of the voice. "'Sure as the sun rises in the East,'" I said, mimicking him, " 'you're a Little Shit Buckaroo.'"

In the silence that followed, I heard the gluck-gluck, gluck-gluck of water pouring from the bottle. Yet Philly made no move to pick it up. Had something else happened, something worse than that blackmail note? What could have left him this shattered?

Dad squinted skeptically at me. "Are you sure you're remembering that right, Tracy? It doesn't sound like—"

Philly had turned back toward us, his ruddy face having now

taken on the peculiar blue-white color of the dead. And having seen one member of the dead lately, I was able to give expert testimony on that. Dad broke off at the sight of his pal's pasty face.

Never in my life had I ever met anyone who rolled with things as well as Philly. Now this threat had rendered him helpless. Maybe Dad was right—we should leave this place. But what if the blackmailer followed us? What if Philly couldn't outrun him?

"Alec, I—" Philly started to say.

Dad's eyes clouded over. He might not know what life was like for poor schmucks like Philly, but he cared about his friend's suffering. He looked pained by Philly's attempt to crawl back. Obviously, I'd learned my own one-upmanship from Mother, because Dad didn't practice it.

He gave his hands a hard clap. "Philly, my friend, this place is getting us down. We need to hit the open road and find somewhere with a better holiday spirit." With a glance, he included us in the plan. "All right, everyone. Anything you can't pack in the next five minutes, you don't need. Let's just leave here now."

As if someone had thrown a switch, we all went into motion— Dad, Drew and me, and even Philly—as we started toward our respective rooms.

And just as fast as we had begun to move, we came to a dead stop—when we heard the sound of jangling from the open doorway. I turned and saw Chief Fricker, in all his cowboy finery, standing there.

A nasty smile reshaped his oddly flat face. "Ain't y'all as quick as the first rattler outta the sack? Why your feet must be so itchy, you're like a pack of spiders with athlete's foot."

I didn't understand a word of that, but I knew what it meant before he uttered his next line: "Nobody's going anywhere."

CHAPTER SEVENTEEN

Even though Dad's suitcases claimed most of the space in our suite's sitting room, Fricker ordered us to sit. Dad perched on the edge of a chair and Drew claimed a tiny place on the end of the sofa and pulled me onto his lap. That relegated poor Philly to a spot on the floor right beside the water he'd spilled.

Fricker jingled through the short pacing strip left in the center of the room, while swinging his enormous cowboy hat at his side. "The way I see it, there's not a one of you who mightn't have had a motive for killing Woody."

Cutting through his labyrinth of conflicting negatives, I was pretty sure he said we *could* all have a motive for killing Woody. Hell, loads of people *could* have motives. I thought I'd shown great restraint by not offing him decades earlier.

Drew slowly raised a crooked finger, in the manner of the kid in class who doesn't want to get called on, but who still wants credit for volunteering. "In my own defense, my only issue with the man was that he served me a dreadful waffle."

When had he gotten this chatty? I was supposed to be the one who never knew when to shut her trap.

Fricker's stoic features gave nothing away, though a light momentarily surfaced in his eyes. "That'd do it for me. I've tasted Woody's waffles." The Chief suddenly spun around on the heels of his cowboy boots, first to me, and then to Dad. "The pair of you were here for not one, but two murders. That's a mighty big coincidence to swallow."

"Whoa!" I said. "I was little more than a toddler during the first murder. It was days before anyone even told me what had happened."

Fricker acknowledged that point with a nod.

"If you swallow that, you don't know my Tracy," Dad said with a jovial laugh. "Even as a little one, if she wanted someone dead, she could have done it."

Man, was I lucky. To think, some people never get that kind of approval from their fathers.

"How about her daddy?" Fricker asked. "Could he have?"

No question, a total disregard of consequence must come through the genes. What possessed Dad to give Fricker an opening like that?

Fricker spread a speculative glance over all of us. "Why don't the rest of y'all make yourselves scarce, so Mr. Grainger and me can have a little chat?" He formed it as a question, but it was an order.

I felt pulled in conflicting directions, like the rope in a game of tug of war. I hated to see Dad in the hot seat, especially since I didn't know what he was hiding, and how much trouble it could cause. But Philly didn't even seem to be in Fricker's radar. One relief.

Philly and I scrambled to our feet, while Drew didn't budge. "You two go. I'll stay with Alec."

"What say, Mr. Grainger? Need your lawyer here?" Fricker asked in a tone that equated wanting a lawyer with a signed confession.

"Drew's not my lawyer, he's my son-in-law." Dad flashed his best movie star grin. "Don't worry, Andrew. I don't mind answering a few questions for Chief Fricker. I have nothing to hide."

If only that were true. People with nothing to hide don't search their friends' apartments.

Drew shrugged. "Doesn't matter, Alec. The Chief knows, under our system of justice, everyone is entitled to have a son-in-law protecting his interests." When he brought his gaze around to Fricker, his steely look made it clear he wasn't budging.

I stopped before Drew and sent him a look of appreciation. Not a mere *thank you*-expression, either, but a *buddy, you're in for some cyclone sex*-look. I paused for a brief respite, during which I imagined us playing "Tracy and the UPS driver" in my mind. Until reality, that snotty enforcer, pushed back in me.

When I saw Philly heading toward the suite's exit door, I hooked my arm through his and guided him instead to our room. I checked to see whether Fricker would object, but he'd already directed all his attention to Dad.

After I shut the door, Philly started to say something, but I shushed him. Once more, I cozied up to that door.

"Looks like you've done this before," Philly whispered behind me.

The Philly I knew would have huddled next to me. He alone in this family rivaled me for childish nosiness. Instead, with a sigh, he sank onto the end of our bed. Seeing him so defeated tugged at my heart. *Save one old coot at a time*, I reminded myself.

Fricker must have been facing away from the door, because I couldn't make out his words clearly. "Something something suspect," I sorta heard him say. Fortunately, he must have turned my way at that point because then he came through clearer. "Thing is, while nobody 'round here particularly liked Woody, nobody disliked him much, either. Most of the time, ol' Woody was as quiet as the bark of a cement dog."

Was that actually true? It was hard to imagine that other people hadn't found him as objectionable as I did. Maybe Fricker hadn't been in Tecos long enough to pick up on the subtle dislikes. Or maybe he was lying. Hadn't he told us the opposite when he first came to inspect the body?

"Tracy, you don't have to eavesdrop," Philly said. "You can ask me whatever you want to know. Alec and me don't got many secrets from each other."

Just a few really critical ones.

"I'll get back to you on that." I said, keeping my ear right where it was.

Fricker asked Dad where he was when Woody went on to meet Billy Rob in hell.

"Took my friend Philly out for a spin, so I could show him some of the sights," Dad said.

Tecos had sights? He delivered that lie much better. Dad was getting more fluid with the fibs.

"In the dark?" Fricker asked.

"Aw, Chief, I'm surprised you haven't noticed how picturesque your town is in the moonlight."

He might have been delivering his lies better now, but they were still stupid. Like he'd been taking lying lessons from Lucy. If he needed help, he should have come to me.

"It seems you're his alibi," I said to Philly.

"Yup, that's how it works with Alec and me. I alibi him, and he does the same for me."

How nice that neither one actually felt a need to share where they really were when Woody bought country real estate. But Philly's blathering on about how alibis functioned in his life and Dad's caused me to miss some of the conversation beyond the door. Fricker had moved on to questioning the state of Woody's finances. Did that mean he accepted Dad's alibi, or just that he didn't think he'd break it? What Fricker seemed to want to establish was that, while Woody had lived with his grandmother after Lucy went up the river, Dad had been his trustee.

"But Woody's been as big enough to hunt boars with a stick for some time now," the Chief went on in his hokey drawl. "Yet you still tell him what to do with his property?"

"Guess I got stuck in my role as Woody's advisor. No actor ever gives up a part he likes." Dad ended with a too-hearty chuckle. He was about to add a worst-actor award to his collection now. How desperate did he have to feel to fib this badly?

"His advisor or his benefactor?" Fricker asked. "Thanks to you, Woody got as lazy as a hound dog in a sunbeam."

Dad allowed that he had been generous with Woody, but then, he was a good friend's son, without anyone left in the world to care for him. Imagine that—a forty-five year-old man without anyone to change his diaper. How had he survived so long?

"Trace, I'm telling ya—" Philly began again.

"Who does the property pass to now?" Fricker asked in the other room.

I shushed my companion. "Pipe down, willya, Philly? They're talking about who inherits from Woody."

Philly chortled softly. "Didn't you know your pop just got a little richer?"

So Dad inherited it. Drew, who hadn't even earned weeknight, *I don't care, what do you want to do*-sex, finally jumped in. "Chief, Mr. Grainger is a wealthy man. You really can't believe he would kill his friend's son, someone he's supported all of his life, to take possession of some rundown building in Nowhere, New Mexico."

Nice going, Counselor. Why don't you insult Nowhere's Chief of Police?

"Mr. Grainger wouldn't be the first rich fella interested in Woody's property. There's a pair that rolls into town in a Ferrari, rich enough to kick mud in new boots, always to up their offer on Woody's place."

A pair of what?

"And there's some lawyer in California, who never reveals his client, who makes occasional offers on the property. Has for years. Woody used to brag all over town about his prospects."

"No way," Drew said, sounding hopelessly flatfooted. This period of unemployment had obviously robbed him of some of his legal cool.

"Way, son."

"You can't have it both ways, Chief," Drew said, finally taking back a bit of that savvy. "You can't blame Alec for spoiling Woody with too much generosity, while simultaneously claiming he killed Woody to get a building he's probably paid for many times over."

"People make offers on Woody's restaurant?" Dad asked, finally catching up. Talk about flatfooted. "That's not possible."

"Alec," Drew said. "Don't say—"

"Woody told me everything," Dad said, ignoring Drew's order.

I had a bad feeling that Dad had given himself another motive. I knew Woody's having shown some independence wouldn't have threatened him. Hell, he and Mother made me their equal before I was out of the cradle. We were all pretty fuzzy on the roles we were expected to play in this family. But Fricker couldn't know that.

Proving my point, when Fricker's chuckle rolled through the door, it sounded pretty satisfied. "Sir, ol' Woody might have seemed as useless as a four-card flush, but he surely had a few secrets."

Who in Nowhere, New Mexico didn't?

CHAPTER EIGHTEEN

Fricker warned us not to leave Tecos. He said he'd jail us as material witnesses if we tried, and if we managed to make it back to California, he'd extradite us. Well, he didn't say it like that. He said something unintelligible about tying a bobcat with a string, but that was what he meant.

"Can he do that?" I asked Drew.

"Extradite us? Nah, he has nothing on us. But I wouldn't put it past him to shoot us at the state line."

Kidding, right?

The old boys wanted to run. They were so jittery, you'd think their chairs had become popcorn poppers. Jeez, Fricker's colorful imagery really was rubbing off on me.

I made a vow—I would stay and try to get to the bottom of their troubles, despite their efforts to impede Drew and me. But if the threats against them got any more serious, Fricker could eat our dust.

* * *

The next morning, Philly snuck out while Dad and Drew were at breakfast, back at the All American Coffee Shoppe. I stayed behind because I figured he might try to ditch us. I tailed him to a rundown bar in the shadiest part of town, well away from Route 66. Wherever he traveled, Philly always made the slummiest dive his home away from home. I had hoped he might be meeting someone there. No dice. Though I kept peeking through the dusty front window, all he did was hole up in the corner, nursing coffee, and making trips to the back alley for an occasional smoke.

I had intended to cozy up to the some of the shopkeepers in town, after Drew took over the tailing-Philly duties, only Dad dropped a bombshell on me.

He waited until we were alone to say, "Tracy, Lucy wants to see you again."

"Uh, you mean back in the clink?" I should have figured that he'd have gone to see her. He wouldn't let her hear about Woody's murder from a stranger.

"That's where they keep her, honey."

Nothing good ever comes from a jail visit. The last time I did it on impulse, and still, the memories of Drew behind bars nearly overwhelmed me. I didn't want to risk that again. Besides, Lucy was going to ask me to find Woody's killer, and for what must have been the first time in my life, I didn't care about solving a particular crime. I guessed I was stuck going to see her, though. Under the circumstances, I couldn't refuse to see her, and it wasn't as if I could ask her to come to me.

When I agreed, Dad placed a roll of quarters in my hand. I must have stared back at him stupidly.

"For vending machines. I always bring change with me. You'll be allowed to bring that in and give it to her."

Ooh! Way too real.

I borrowed the Bentley and reluctantly set out for Grants. I realized for the first time that the prison was also located on Route 66. Though Lucy left town to serve her sentence, she never left the Mother Road. I couldn't decide whether that was outright sad, or just fitting.

In the dark, I hadn't gotten a good look at the place. Now, in daylight, the squat one-story facility looked like some generic junior college campus, where they weren't big on windows. I didn't mind their patdown and metal detectors, since they were like airport security. It was the sounds in those places that always got to me, and today was no exception. All that heavy concrete, to guarantee the inmates didn't dig through it, made for ominous echoes. Especially the sound of metal doors clanging shut. As soon as you passed through one, it slid closed behind you, trapping you in the tomb the cement hallway made between that door and the next. I always had to fight the impulse to claw my way out.

Without Drew along, I wasn't eligible for the attorney interview room we'd used before. Why would he want to give up that perk? Instead, I followed a group of husbands and a few kids to the visitor center, a big open room, filled with individual wooden tables and benches.

The change in Lucy when she appeared tugged at my heart. No runway beat this time. She shuffled in, an old woman with reddened eyes.

"Lucy, I'm so sorry about Woody," I said, inadequately, once we were seated.

She reached into the top of her jumpsuit and pulled out a wadded-up tissue she must have tucked into her bra, which she used to dab at her eyes.

I took the plunge. "Dad said you wanted to talk to me about something."

She leaned on the table and directed a peculiar zeal my way. "Tracy what is it you do. You write detective fiction, don't you?" When I didn't answer, she urgently clutched my hand and said, "Honey, I think you should stick to what you know, writing books about detectives, not trying to be one."

Wait! That wasn't how this was supposed to go.

A stout female guard tapped the table. "No touching, Crier," she said, though not unkindly.

Lucy jerked away, but the intensity of her expression never lessened. "Alec said you like to play at solving your little mysteries, but it's nonsense to think ordinary people can solve crimes. That's the stuff of books, sweetheart, not real life. Believe me, I know. I am a library director, after all."

The old Lucy Liar had surfaced there. Library director? She was an inmate shelving books in a prison library. An accomplishment within these walls, but she sure didn't run the joint. Next she'd swear she was the warden.

Tension made her voice sound brusque. "I want you to forget all of that and just let my poor Woody rest in peace."

I didn't know what to make of her demand that I leave Woody's murder alone. The relatives of the victim always want justice. They *need* it to move on. Yet here was Lucy insisting on the exact opposite. No question, this twist surprised me. But it was my own reaction that left me absolutely stunned. While all murders tweaked my antennae, I *really* hadn't cared enough about Woody to want to secure justice for him. Besides, I had Dad and Philly to worry about. Yet now I found myself oddly reluctant to agree to a request that supposedly coincided with what I thought I wanted.

"It's not up to me. The police—"

She snorted. "The Tecos police have never been good at anything but catching tourists in speed traps."

She'd clearly only seen them pre-Fricker. Still, I couldn't bring myself to agree. When you consider that I'd broken more promises in my life than horsetails swat flies, to use a Fricker-expression, that shouldn't have bothered me. But I couldn't lie to her, not with all that life had dumped on her. What was wrong with me?

Stalling, I changed the subject. "Lucy, I saw your design albums. You did some amazing work in them."

She frowned. "How did you happen to see them?"

Oops! I could hardly tell her I climbed through her bedroom window and swiped the whole lot of them. "Woody showed them to me."

Her expression brightened. "He did? My boy never expressed any interest in my work before." She dabbed at her eyes with the used tissue.

I told her about my plan to try to interest some clothing manufacturer in them.

"Gee, hon, you'd do that for me? That would be swell."

Despite her apparent interest, I sensed she didn't care about her designs anymore. That had been part of another life. Had she glommed onto it to distract me from looking into Woody's murder? Her next remark proved it. "You work on that and forget about Woody. You and Alec should both stop trying to raise the dead."

This time, I knew, she wasn't talking about her son.

In the moments we had left, Lucy's peaceful aura returned. She seemed secure in the idea that we had settled things about Woody, when we hadn't decided anything at all.

When it was time for her to leave, Lucy paused at the door and sent a little wave over her shoulder. She looked so much like she used to in the old days, when she'd send off a jaunty little salute to Dad and me as we drove off, that my throat tightened.

But as I sat there after the other visitors left, I realized that despite her transformation, I didn't believe her. I couldn't explain her angle, yet I felt certain it had nothing to do with letting the dead rest in peace.

Lucy was hiding something, I decided when I finally made my way out of that place. Perhaps she knew something bad about Woody, and she didn't want it coming out. She might have been protecting her son's reputation even now, the last thing she could do for him. Or was it her own past that needed shielding? Hard to imagine. She'd been convicted of murder—how much worse could things be?

CHAPTER NINETEEN

B y the time I returned to the suite, someone had pushed an invitation to a memorial service for Woody under the door. I thought scheduling a service for this evening was rushing things, considering the body had scarcely cooled off. Either the people of Tecos genuinely loved Woody, or they needed to sell the lie that they did. Either way, I hoped to learn something there.

With Philly hiding out in his room, he didn't get a vote on whether we should all go. Drew and I planned to attend, since it provided a perfect opportunity to meet the locals, one of which might have been Philly's blackmailer. But Dad refused to.

"Don't you realize, one of those people must have *killed* Woody?" he said, aghast.

"No!" I'd said, confident he wouldn't pick up on my sarcasm. Why else would he think I'd go to Woody's memorial? It sure wasn't to honor the lazy oaf.

I secretly cheered that Dad didn't want to join us. I didn't need him continuing to try to convince Fricker what a good little hit-child I could have been if I'd set my precocious mind to it.

Drew donned the black sports coat he brought along "just in case" on this, the most casual of trips. The guy takes a jacket for funereal emergencies, and he thinks he's not anal. Since after a particularly nasty teasing, I'd once screamed at Woody that I'd wear red to his funeral—a threat I'll admit I copied verbatim from Mother—I kept that promise now, with a scarlet T-shirt and tattered jeans. Maybe my lack of restraint would loosen the tongues of some of the hypocrites I hoped to find there.

Drew groused when I wanted to leave the suite early, but I had stops to make. Our first destination was a hardware store, where we bought a couple of strong flashlights, as opposed to Drew's little penlight. Then we went to a craft shop, where I picked up four skeins of mismatched wool from a sale table, spending some of the stash I'd swiped from Drew's wallet. He looked askance at the wool, since I don't knit, but he didn't say anything. How weird this was for both of us. I'd have predicted that I'd like having him as a sidekick right about the time that pigs began to fly out my butt, but I had to admit including him in my caper made it easier than sneaking around behind his back, even if it wasn't as much fun.

We finally arrived at the destination all the other stops had led up to, the Tecos Caves. Though the approach to the caves was about a half-mile and several turns off Route 66, on a dirt road, ultimately the sprawling underground structure curved around behind Woody's restaurant. Old-Drew put in an appearance at the entrance, when he mulishly came to a halt before the aging sign that declared the attraction to be "Closed," on which someone had stuck a banner that promised to be "Reopening Soon."

"We can't go in there. The sign says it's closed," he insisted.

"Do you believe everything you read, Drew?" I'd expect a more challenging attitude from even a recovering lawyer. "It's lettering on a sign. Nobody has shut the holes in the earth."

Before I could move, a red Ferrari sped past, cloaking us in the cloud of dust it left behind. You see everything in Route 66 towns.

I began picking my way over the large rocks piled up before the entrance. After folding his jacket neatly in the car, Drew did the same.

The first sizeable cavern we entered showed signs that it had once been a popular attraction. A paved path wove through the cave, wide enough to carry good-sized clusters of tourists, and electric light fixtures hung from the ceiling. But it was also clear that the crowds hadn't come through lately. The place was caked in dirt and the cracked pavement was crumbling along the edges. No evidence that anyone had started repairing it, either.

The cavern was shadowy, but not as dark as I expected, even after we moved away from the entrance. Stray lighting seemed to be spilling from somewhere deeper in the system of caves, although the ceiling electrical lights weren't lit. Even so, I pointed the flashlight at the roof of the cave, and as if by magic, a spray of cobalt-colored glitter appeared.

"This is one of my favorite spots. When I was little, I asked Dad whether someone had flung Mother's jewelry box at the ceiling," I said with a happy sigh. "And hey, listen to the sound of my voice." There was a peculiar reverb in those caves that gave voices the richest, most velvety sound. I started singing, since I'd always thought this was the only place my voice sounded good.

While ignoring my impromptu concert, Drew pulled his cell phone from the little case that hung from his belt. "Look at that. I've got a signal in here."

Why did he care? I started the song over. "Do you believe my voice sounds this good?"

"How is that possible?" he asked. I sensed we were still on the subject of cell signals, not my voice, which was what mattered to me.

"Who knows? There are openings all over the place." I shrugged. "What I find crazier is when you're so close to three cell towers that your brain turns to green mush, yet your phone doesn't show a single bar. Who can explain cell phones? Now voices..."

"Can you beat that?" While still trying his phone in various directions, he continued to marvel at it.

"Yeah, it's a freakin' miracle. Come on, Phone Guy, you gotta see more." Last time I'd waste a concert on him.

I put Drew on flashlight duty, while I began unwinding the yarn and draping it along the path. I'd explored all those caverns as a kid, but I doubted I could find my way around today. Hence, the trail of woolen breadcrumbs

"So there is a method in madness," Drew said.

"Who knew?" I said, cheerfully unoffended. I liked to keep him guessing. If he thought I was nuts, it was that much easier.

A few caverns in, we came upon the source of the light, a battery-operated standing torch at the mouth of the next cave. Why use a battery-operated lamp, instead of running the electric lights? It couldn't cost that much to turn on the power, could it? I also heard movement in there, but from where I stood behind Drew, I couldn't see in.

"Who's there?" a gruff voice called from within that cavern.

Drew directed a flashlight beam through the opening. "A couple of your constituents, Governor."

I came alongside Drew and saw the caves' owner himself standing there, California Governor Kyle Tandy, shielding his eyes from the flashlight beam with his hand.

"Governor-for-the-moment, you mean," Tandy said with a droll chuckle. So the recall effort hadn't taken him by surprise.

Close up and covered in dirt, Tandy's chiseled face looked as flawlessly featured as it did in photo ops. And that blues-belting voice sounded every bit as craggy and engaging. He wasn't a tall man, or all that young, but the abs beneath his sweat-stained T-shirt remained in taut form. Beside him stood a wheelbarrow filled high with rocks and soil, and on the ground, a cooler. I figured that meant he really was cleaning up a cave-in as the news reported. Or digging for something. But why would he dig?

"You two are going to have to leave. I can't risk anything happening to you. If you were hurt, after I pay my fine, I won't have a penny left for your medical bills, not to mention your pain and suffering," he said with a wry crinkling of his green hooded eyes.

"We'll take responsibility," Drew said.

Tandy snorted. "You say that now. So did a certain staffer of mine, who never did step up, unless that's how you'd describe his suicide."

So the rumors were true, or at least what he wanted us to believe. Tandy's few remaining supporters insisted his dead assistant had been the one guilty of corruption, not their fearless leader. Philly said as much, too—after all, the dead guy had been living in the free house that some state contractor had put in Tandy's name. Some still said Tandy had nothing to do with taking that bribe. But he was the one convicted of it.

"If that's true, sir, your case should be reopened," Drew said, ever the lawyer.

Tandy shrugged. "No proof. Besides, you know what they said about where the buck stops. Now you really have to—" He broke off in a sigh. "What the hell. Pull up a rock. Someone was over in

Y-273 or 274 a while ago—I heard him shouting, but I was too tired to go there and kick him out."

I didn't know what that designation meant, but I had news for him—no matter what he said, I didn't intend to leave.

Tandy sat on a squat boulder. Drew and I plopped ourselves down on similar rock stools. Tandy yanked the top off the cooler and offered us either beer or soda. Drew took a beer, and Tandy opened a can of Coke for himself, but I declined, and awfully stiffly for me. What was it about this guy that irked me? He was good-looking, had charm by the bushel, not to mention that catchy voice, and he didn't take himself too seriously—what was not to like?

Drew, on the other hand, seemed ready to start a fan club.

Tandy pulled a crushed pack of cigarettes from his pants' pocket and lit one up. He squinted at me through the smoke. "You're the Grainger girl, aren't you? I remember seeing pictures of you with your parents in *People*, back in my studio days. Your old man blew off a meeting with me once, but I still like his work. Both his and Martha's."

Funny how my father told an entirely different story about that missed meeting. But it was just as likely that Dad had tweaked his story, to make Tandy the one who cancelled it, instead of him. In his prime Alec Grainger would never have been asked to read for a part. While he groused about the demands of celebrity, he also resisted the downgrading of his status.

"Maybe you shouldn't have left the studio," I said. "Hollywood's more forgiving about shenanigans than politics."

Drew flashed me a nasty look, while Tandy shook his head. "Not my way. You should know that."

Me? I only met the guy five seconds ago.

"I told the voters I'd come into office, fix a few things, and then I'd be on my way again. I'm a rolling stone-kinda guy."

Ah, he meant us voters, not me personally. Someone should have told him how fickle we were. I couldn't remember whether he had actually fixed anything in state government.

Tandy rose and stretched. "Well, I've had enough community service for one day. Will I see you two at Woody Crier's memorial?"

I told him he would. "How did you know Woody?"

"Met him when I came to town. Foolishly stopped there for dinner. Sure as the sun sets over the Pacific, I never made that mistake again." He choked out a short laugh. "But he was an engaging guy to chat with."

Really? I'd always found Woody about as engaging as a sinkhole.

To make up for my earlier rudeness, I asked if Tandy wanted us to dump that wheelbarrow full of rocks for him. It still surprised me that any part of this sturdy cavern system had come down. They were natural caves, after all, untouched for centuries. It wasn't like someone dug those tunnels and didn't support them.

"It'll keep till tomorrow," Tandy said. With a nod toward his empty can and Drew's bottle, he added. "But you could deposit our empties in the recycling bin you'll find out front." With a nod that sent his graying hair forward into an appealing forelock, he picked up the cooler and walked out, promising to see us later.

After a few moments, I heard the faint sound of an engine starting up from way in the distance, and then the faded opening bars of the theme of *Jaws.* I waited until the sounds drifted away before saying, "He recycles even. And we're kicking him out of office."

"Nice guy," Drew said. "Now I wish I voted for him."

"Not me. I still don't like his eyes."

"An informed voter, I see."

"Well, it is a citizen's responsibility to make the serious choices."

With time to kill before the start of the service, we gathered up the recyclables and took our yarn and flashlights and started exploring again. When I reached the end of one skein of yarn, I tied it to the start of another, continuing to trace our path. At one point, I noticed small metal plates over the entrances and exits of the individual caves, designating them with letters and numbers.

We came across a couple of burlap bags draped along one side of a narrow passageway. They were dirt-stained, but given how loosely they lay along the ground, I suspected someone had shaken them out recently. As they weren't too grungy, I took one to hold the recyclables and the excess yarn.

I never did see Y-273, but we did come upon Y-274. I knew

instantly that another trespasser had been in this cave. Unlike the dank, earthy odor filling the rest of the place, both sweet and acrid smells hung in the air here. My nostrils twitched.

Drew caught it, too, better identifying one of those smells than I did. "Philly's not the only person who smokes Flying Dutchman tobacco."

But he sure was one of them, and that was the sweeter smoky smell now fading in the air. A few cigarette butts also littered the ground. Though it was impossible to say when the butts were left, I wrapped my hand around the plug of tobacco that had been tapped out onto a rock, and it still held a wisp of warmth.

While checking on that tobacco, I spotted a scrap of paper caught between a pair of boulders. The same kind of paper, filled with the same squared lettering that we'd seen on the blackmail note we found in Woody's restaurant. On one side, our unknown printer had repeated, "Philly Chase, sidekick of The Actor," while the other said, "You'd better pay attention to me!" Along with a date and time when Philly was ordered to come to this cave.

I felt the lurch of regret in my gut. If I'd skipped the shopping spree, we might have started out earlier. Would we have run into them? Could we have ended it here and now? Then again, maybe Philly's blackmailer had only toyed with him. Tandy spoke of hearing only one voice. Had his tormenter stood him up? Had Philly been shouting in frustration?

"He might not be the only Flying Dutchman user," I said, holding out the note to Drew. "But in a town this small, I bet he's the only pipe smoker being blackmailed."

CHAPTER TWENTY

MEMORIES OF ROUTE 66
PHILLY

P*hilly had come to hate Route 66 with a vengeance. The worst parts of his life had happened on that lousy road. How he'd love to leave Tecos, stick out his thumb, and hightail it outta that hellhole of Americana. He couldn't do it, though. It wasn't Fricker's threat that held him there—the cops had nothing on him. Not yet, anyway. But the blackmailer had not only sworn to deliver evidence on Philly's past to them, he also vowed to kill Alec if Philly left. Philly had always been a cut-and-run-kinda guy. Even if this trip had put the kibosh on his friendship with Alec, Philly still couldn't duck out on him.*

The vacation started out so great. Him and Alec on the open road, combining the best of both of their worlds. Cruising along in the Bentley like a pair o' swells, but eating in roadside diners and bedding down in regular joints, like Philly would have chosen if he'd been alone. And never once did Alec act like those dumps were beneath him. Though they'd started out as rivals for Martha's affection, Philly had soon realized that was just a pipe dream. Despite that start, he and Tracy's pop had gotten close in the months of working together to fix her old house. Out in the world, where people could recognize him, Philly hadn't known whether Alec would seem the same. But him and Philly, if anything, they got closer.

Philly felt sure that him and Alec would be BFFs, as the kids said. It would have happened, anyway—if Woody Crier hadn't entered the picture. Philly hadn't really taken to Woody, but the guy had had a tough break with his mom being sent away. And if Woody was important to Alec, Philly vowed to warm to the boy.

But that first blackmail note changed everything. They'd finished one of the horrendous breakfasts Woody served in The Kontiki Room, and Alec left to visit Lucy in prison, while Philly stayed behind to read the newspaper over a second cup of sour coffee. But when he returned from a trip to the men's room, Philly's whole life took a tumble. Propped up beside his cup was the first of the blackmail notes, demanding ten million dollars or the cops would know all they'd need to come after Philly with a felony murder charge. The threat rattled him, but the part that shook him all the way to the core was that the note had been addressed to: "Philly Chase, sidekick of The Actor." That alone demonstrated how much his blackmailer knew about the past.

Everything within Philly shattered in that moment. After a while, he got his wits about him. There was nobody in the café, except for him and Woody. Philly rushed to the kitchen and confronted Woody, but the kid claimed to know nothing about it.

"Man, you gotta lay off the weed, you know?" Woody had said. As if a con man would dull his wits with dope. "Somebody else musta slipped into the dining room while I was in the kitchen."

Philly might have believed him, except for a coupla things. A door chime sounded, in the dining room and the kitchen, whenever anyone entered the place, alerting Woody to the presence of a patron. Not that he had ever rushed to attend to them. More important was the sly smirk that stole across Woody's thin lips, and the knowing look that came into his murky eyes. He had placed that note there beside Philly's cup, all right. Somehow Woody had known about Philly's past.

How was that possible? He would only have been a little kid during Philly's old Chicago days, and Alec swore Woody had never left Tecos.

Philly wanted to turn to Alec, his friend and benefactor. Lay the whole seamy story at his feet and beg for help. But how could he share the tale without implicating Woody? How could he hope to win if he came between Alec and the person Alec cherished most, apart from Martha, Tracy, and Lucy? Woody was like a son to him.

When it came to rejection, Philly always acted like it beaded off him like raindrops on a well-waxed car. Just a cheerful vagabond who took nothing personally. That was the story he sold about his sister Charlotte and her obvious contempt for him. But he couldn't quite pull off that good cheer when it came to Alec, not as devastated as he felt right now. So he rejected Alec before his pal could reject him. Called him a dilettante, dabbling at being a regular guy. Anything to avoid the rebuff that was sure to surface in Alec's once-warm eyes when he learned the truth.

He couldn't even turn to Tracy, who was more like him than anyone in either clan. She'd saved his sorry hide plenty of times. But she was her pop's little girl. Philly couldn't tell what she'd thought about Woody, but there was no way she would take anyone's side before her beloved father. Philly's trouble was that he never mattered enough to anyone.

After Woody died, and the letters kept coming, it was clear that Woody hadn't been the blackmailer, after all. Now notes were pushed under Philly's motel room door. He eventually traced them to the Rest Ur Head desk clerk Duncan, who said they were pushed under his door, with instructions and forty bucks.

Maybe that was all it had been with Woody, something someone paid him to do. But Philly couldn't shake the conviction that Woody had been in league with his tormentor, not to mention enjoying his role in the operation. Who would Woody have been in cahoots with?

Maybe that was why Woody had been killed. A falling out between bad guys? Would Alec hate Philly more for keeping that theory to himself?

What choice did he have? Philly had always made it his highest priority to protect his own skin. He'd been a coward all his life. This time, for once, he was trying to protect Alec, too. And Alec, his friend—his best friend—would never know it. That made Philly sadder than anything else.

CHAPTER TWENTY-ONE

Our caving fun evaporated once we realized how close we might have come to ending Philly's nightmare. I wanted to kick myself. My mood reached outright funk-level by the time we stumbled out to the sunlight, clutching our flashlights and the bag of unraveled yarn.

Drew obviously shared my gloom. "We're not making much progress helping Philly out of this mess, are we?"

No flies on him. "What would you have us do, Drew?" I flailed my arms at the passing cars. "Shout to all the drivers flying by, 'Which of you bastards is putting the screws to my uncle?' We're not getting anywhere because we haven't turned up a single clue. That's why we're going to the memorial service, so we can take a closer look at these folks."

He gave a rock a nasty kick. "And the fact that you probably find it sexier to investigate a murder has nothing to do with our clueless state, I suppose."

Not fair. I'd really had left Woody's murder alone, precisely as I'd promised him. But given my reaction to Lucy's request, I didn't feel I could make that defense. And that meant I probably shouldn't confess that I'd gone to see her again.

"Hey, this is how investigations work," I said instead. "You find a thread, you follow it, without questioning where it might lead."

I chose a rock of my own and gave it a kick. Unfortunately, I exercised less control than Drew. For a second there, I thought it might come crashing down on the Volvo's windshield. I tried not to sigh too loudly when it landed safely on the far side.

Fortunately, Drew seemed too intent on staring at the road to pay attention to flying rocks. "Okay, Tracy, you follow your threads—I'm going to follow the Governor." With a nod, he indicated Tandy's Jeep sailing past. With a shrug, he added, "I forgot to bring the directions to the church hall."

We threw our gear into the Volvo and took off. But Tandy led us, not to the church where Woody's memorial was to be held, but the Tecos Town Hall. The rustic adobe building contained entrances to both the police department and the section for the town government. While Drew parked, Tandy entered the PD side. We leaned against our car's dirty fenders, waiting for him to come out and show us the way.

Before he did, another man bounded from the door to the town hall side. With his penny loafers and white socks, and blue jeans rolled up around his ankles, the wiry dandy looked like he'd dressed for a role in *Grease*. The theatrical theme extended to his bouncy strut to such a degree, I expected him to tap dance his way across the road and to take a swing on the lamppost on the far side. Instead, he stopped before us.

"Hey there, folks. You look lost. I'm Mark Baker, mayor of Tecos. Any way I can help?"

When Drew told him about our need for directions, Mark rattled them out.

He squinted at me. "You're Tracy Grainger, aren't you? I remember you from when you visited here when you were little."

"You mean I haven't changed?" Good to know age wasn't catching up with me. Or even adulthood, considering how I felt about it.

Mark flashed me a cocky, *you got me*-grin. "Well, I might have caught that piece on you in *People* when you and your mom signed a contract for the book you wrote together. But I do remember you from when you were a kid. I was a boyhood friend of Woody's."

I doubted that. He wasn't a big man now, so he must have been a scrawny little kid. Woody always believed the smaller boys existed to provide action for his fists. Besides, he looked closer to my age, younger than the Wood-Man. After introducing Drew, I led the conversation back to Woody.

With a hairy enough hand to make a monkey proud, Mark smoothed his fifties' pompadour. "Woody...what can I say?"

That was what I wanted to know. But as silence stretched

between us, I got the idea the unspoken answer to that question was, "Not much."

Finally, he said, "Woody sure made a mean waffle, didn't he?"

Hey, Dude, no points for the literal truth. You'd think a boyhood friend with loads of wedgie memories could have done better. Mark excused himself, claiming a need to arrive early at the service. Then he actually leaped toward his truck, like he was off to rumble with the Jets.

Tandy finally sailed out the PD door. A moment later, a man in a coat and tie, a rarity in these parts, emerged as well and called to him. "Governor? You forgot your community service record." He held out what looked like an oversized index card.

Tandy took the card. "I appreciate your meeting me here today, Mr. West."

The stranger offered a smile that seemed eager to please. "Glad to do it. We'll have that ankle bracelet turned off tonight, but remember, at midnight you turn back into a pumpkin."

"His parole officer, would you say?" I asked Drew. "Awfully accommodating, isn't he?"

Drew shrugged. "Maybe he's never had a politician among his clients."

It surprised me that politicians didn't fill every parole officer's case files.

Fricker stepped out the PD door and paused to watch the jovial pair, but Tandy and his parole officer parted ways before they actually hugged. With a nod, Fricker ambled over to us.

Today Fricker's Western shirt was teal and black, and he wore it over charcoal leather spats. Was everyone on Route 66 playing a role? My actor father was starting to seem like the most normal person there. It wasn't often I could say that.

Before Fricker could spit out one of his folksy zingers, I attacked him with, "What did you do? Buy out the contents of some cowboy shop?"

His lips parted in a rare grin. "You mean, why am I always wearing my flashiarity?"

Was that a word?

"I didn't always display enough splendor to outdo a peacock. I used to be a homicide cop back in Detroit, and I dressed as ordinary as everyone else." He lost a bit of the Western drawl. "But I've always loved tales of the old West. My wife Jenny and me, we planned to retire somewhere out here. But cancer took Jenny faster'n a cat with his tail afire. After she passed on, I asked myself how long I planned to wait to live the life I wanted. Took the first police chief job I found, and I brought my own style to it. And I don't take no sass about it, even from ladies as smart as bunkhouse bed bugs."

I might take issue with his description of me, if I understood it. But his remarks about his life hit a sore spot. It was that freedom to make his own choices, however aimless they seemed to me, that I wanted to deny Drew. Maybe I'd have to write that lame travel article after all, along with loads of other dreaded articles, and quit frittering away my book advances. Even worse, I might have to give up this adolescence that I'd clung to for so long.

A red Ferrari pulled out from the driveway beyond the far side of the town hall and waited to pull into traffic. I know I said you see everything on Route 66, but you don't *keep* seeing it.

With a nod of his black hat, Fricker said, "That's the pair I told you about. The folks who hanker for Woody's place. They'll likely hit up your daddy at the service."

I trotted out Dad's excuse of being too devastated to attend, rather than his accusation against the town's people, and asked Fricker to explain this "pair" business.

"They're Sean and Kitty Clement. Fraternal twins. As to the 'pair,' you'll have to meet them to understand that." He flashed another brief smile. "Their grandpappy Angus used to own the caves Governor Tandy is fixin' to donate to his two favorite states. Used to live 'round these parts, till the family moved away."

"Wasn't he the town drunk?"

"Before my time, but I hear he stayed drunker than an apple orchard sow after he lost the caves in that poker game. He's passed on now, but I've been told the family was so hard up after he lost the caves that they were always trying to keep the wolf from having pups at their door."

Their family fortunes had risen considerably if they now included a Ferrari. The showy red sports car cut into traffic with a screech of tires.

After leaving Fricker, Drew and I followed Mark Baker's directions to the church hall where the memorial service would be held. When we pulled into the parking lot, I saw the red Ferrari parked along the side of the meeting room.

I gestured to Drew. "Pull up behind the Ferrari, blocking it from view." This was too good a chance to pass up. Those two had grabbed my interest.

"Why?" he said, though he did as I asked.

Rather than answer, I leaped out and ran to the side of the convertible sports car. Drew hastily cut the Volvo's engine and came to my side. By then, I'd leaned over the passenger side door, to keep a low profile, and had started pawing through the Ferrari's glove box.

"Tracy, what are you doing?" Drew demanded, aghast.

"Oh, please. If they didn't want people snooping, they'd have a roof."

I pulled a sheet of paper out and held it up to read. It was a car rental agreement for the Ferrari.

A rental? So Fricker wasn't the only one with "flashiarity." Truly, everyone on Route 66 was putting on a show. The question was, who was the intended audience?

CHAPTER TWENTY-TWO

The church hall was already crowded by the time we went in. Most of the mourners stood around in little clusters, though some gathered at the small round tables and chairs scattered about. Either those people really did love Woody, or they'd go anywhere for a potluck dinner. Then again, maybe they gathered together to reassure themselves that he was really dead.

Apparently, the mayor had already come and gone—so much for his lifelong friendship with the dearly departed. I hope he'd found something better to say than to remark on the meanness of Woody's waffles, before leaping out in a move from modern dance. Governor Tandy was there, as was Chief Fricker, and even "The Pair," who rented the Ferrari.

Drew went off to check out the potluck tables, spread along one wall. Since I'd asked Dad to bring me some take-out from the restaurant where he went for dinner, I skipped the potluck fare. I did take a glass of what I thought would be a fruity punch, which proved to be a better than average sangria. While I sipped my drink, a woman put out jugs of wine.

I moved to the back of a cluster surrounding the Clement twins and watched them for a while, finally understanding why Fricker called them "The Pair." The fraternal twins in their late twenties looked so androgynously alike, I couldn't tell which was the boy, Sean, and which the girl, Kitty, though I noticed that one of them had a stubby little pinky, considerably shorter than the other's. Their hats, with their pinwheel designs in peach and mint green, covered the bright red, and equally short, hair they shared. Their satin clothes, also in peach and mint, looked like old-fashioned golfing outfits, with baggy knickers that ended below their knees, where high socks took over. Rather than being identical, the satin suits alternated each other, with one wearing the peach top and green bottom, while the other reversed those colors. Together, they looked like a small, insane checkerboard.

Even stranger than their getup was the way they finished each other's sentences. "Even though Woody would never sell us his restaurant…" Green Top said.

"…we drove from Corrales…" Peach Top took up.

"…to honor him," Green Top ended.

Corrales? Near Santa Fe? For such a short trip they needed to rent a crazy-expensive and totally impractical car? Perhaps they were simply trying to sell the idea that they could afford to keep upping their offers for Woody's property, confident in the knowledge that he would never sell. Why bother? When their little cluster broke up, I moved toward them, but a guy blocked my path.

"Hey, Presidential Suite. How's it going?" the path blocker asked in an oddly high-pitched voice.

Was he talking to me in that girly voice? I guess there was something vaguely familiar about him, though with his shaggy, mouse-brown hair and small, mushy features, he was too forgettable for me to make a connection.

"It's me—Duncan."

Finally, the "Presidential Suite" reference hit me. Duncan was the desk clerk at the Rest Ur Head Motel. His voice was so shrill, I'd seen dogs gather around the office whenever he spoke.

"You're Tracy, right? Yeah, I seen your picture on the back of your last book."

He might have that ear-shattering voice, but it cheered me to know he read my books.

"Alec sent a case to Woody, and he gave it to me. The front door at the motel won't stay open."

My career was sure on the rise when my father had to buy whole cases, and they ended up with a guy who needed a doorstop.

Duncan leaned into my face and said, "Damn shame about Woody, huh? He was the greatest guy. You know he used spell me at the desk so I could get some extra time off. Actually closed the restaurant to do it, too."

I muttered something noncommittal. While Woody hadn't

exactly been burdened with customer rushes, it still seemed an oddly generous act for such a lazy guy. When Duncan suggested that while I was here, I might want to fill in for him occasionally, I made my escape. Didn't he get days off?

I ran into Drew, holding a paper plate overflowing the assortment of foods you see at potlucks, salads and tamales rubbing against brownies. Had he forgotten we were there to mingle?

"Trace, there's a detailed map of the area on the wall over there," he said, gesturing with a plastic fork. "Did you realize the caves extend back almost all the way to Woody's property line?"

I nodded. "When I was a kid, that was usually where I slipped into them. But the cave openings there are so small, today I'd probably have to crawl in."

With a shred of irritation, I reminded Drew that we had gone there to learn something useful to help his uncle. Wasn't he the one who bitched about how little progress we were making?

I also shared that I wanted to get a closer look at "The Pair," for no reason other than pure nosiness. I had to know why they rented that flashy car and dressed the way they did. Drew suggested we corner them from two sides. Yet each time we came at them, they managed to give us the slip. At one point, Green Top pushed one of those small tables, which proved to be on castors, between us. It was starting to seem like they really didn't want to talk to me. If they were so freakin' eager to get Woody's restaurant, shouldn't they have wanted me to pass along an offer to Dad?

The minister whose church we were meeting in, Reverend Don Cannon, a boyish-looking guy with rosy cheeks and a wide grin, stepped up to the podium at one end of the room, and spoke into the microphone. "We're gathered here today because we've lost one of our own. I know Woody wasn't the easiest man to love, but he was one of God's children, too. We can't always judge people by the image they present to the world. Look at my dear wife Genevieve." He gestured to an unusually pretty woman in a baggy gray jacket and shapeless blue dress. "People around here warned me I'd be crazy to marry an ex-beauty queen—she was Miss Florida, you know. A runner-up for Miss America." I heard a few groans at that line, making me wonder if he'd said it once, or maybe a thousand times, before. "But she's become a fine pastor's wife."

Behind me someone snickered. Why was that funny?

"I happen to know that Woody was on a stronger spiritual path than most people would think. Genevieve had been ministering to Woody, and she's assured me..."

Someone bumped into me hard enough to dislocate my arm, and just kept going.

"Excuse me for not getting out of your way," I muttered after him. But I quickly got the idea, from the way he staggered toward the wine table, that his blood alcohol level might be higher than the Sangria's.

Reverend Don Cannon, who must have concluded his remarks while I was having my shoulder removed, appeared at my side. "I knew it was a mistake to allow liquor here. Neither my wife nor I imbibe, you know. But this isn't a church function, it's a town affair."

That made more sense. I would have expected Woody to be a parishioner of the Church of Satan's Shoes.

The drunk was an old man, whose fan of facial wrinkles rivaled the folds in the shirt he had clearly slept in. The minister hastily excused himself and rushed toward Blotto Man before he could upend another bottle.

Genevieve, the beauty queen who'd turned into such a good pastor's wife, introduced herself. Even without makeup or a flattering hairstyle, the photogenic facial lines that had once dazzled the Miss America judges were quite evident, but her dowdy, loose-fitting duds hid the swimsuit body that had paraded down that runway. Her only vanity seemed to be her nails, which were nicely manicured with pale pink polish. Green eyes that might have once sparkled for nationally televised cameras looked haunted today.

"So you...what?" I asked. "Prayed with Woody?"

Her husband joined us again. "She was also charitable enough to help him clean his place, since he couldn't afford to pay someone to do it." Reverend Cannon's wholesome looks lent him a Jimmy Olson-quality. First Mayor Mark Baker and now Don Cannon—

there must have been something in the water here that made guys look especially boyish. Too bad they hadn't shared it with Woody.

I didn't let on that I had good reason to know that Woody could easily have paid for a cleaning service, thanks to Dad. "At the restaurant?" I asked, confused about what kind of work she might have done.

"No, his home," Don said.

I no longer questioned why Jimmy Olson never wondered why his pal Clark Kent kept ducking into phone booths. Woody lived in a motel, with maid service. It took all I had not to make eye contact with the good pastor's wife, though now I understood those snickers I'd heard. I tried to muster a benign smile for her naïve husband, but I need not have bothered. He was focused on the podium microphone, where Blotto Man stood.

"No! It's Tom again," Don said. "I'd better..." He dashed off.

He didn't reach the podium before a sloshed silly Tom screamed into the microphone, "I'm glad he's dead, ya hear me? *Glad.* Laughing my ass off over it." With the turn-on-a-dime emotions common to drunks, the old man's red eyes welled up. "Woody was a real sombitch. He was mean to my old friend Angus Clement, powerful mean."

Angus Clement? The Clement twins' grandfather? Was Tom Angus's old drinking buddy? I looked to the last place I'd seen the twins, for some sign of recognition, but they were gone.

Drew whispered into my ear, "Who is that?"

I glanced around to see if people seemed shocked or angry. What I mostly saw were heads lowered to hide laughter. I was right. Nobody had loved Woody, apart from Dad and Lucy.

I leaned close to Drew and said, "That's the most honest man in town."

CHAPTER TWENTY-THREE

I was back on the plane with T.K. Mann. We stood together once more before that open cabin door. No disco this time; in the background, I heard the strangled sounds of some awful atonal jazz, played by someone who must not have ever heard music before. Though the plane was still in the air, the passengers were all gone, as if they'd all somehow deplaned, while T.K. and I waited to jump.

Right before my eyes, the T.K. Mann I vaguely remembered from the first dream turned into a different guy. Smaller now, and wiry, with less of a photogenic smile and more of a smartass grin. The new T.K. wore a thin pair of dark glasses, blades that barely covered his eyes. But while that exposed more of his face, I couldn't seem to grasp what he looked like. Dreams are crazy, huh?

Talk about understatements. All at once, he changed again—this time, into a toad. Not a euphemism for a bad looking guy, but an actual frog-thing. Only it was my size. A giant toad wearing T.K. Mann's backpack.

"T.K., make it stop!" I shouted. "You keep morphing into different things."

The toad flashed me a set of decidedly human teeth and said in the T.K. voice from the first dream, "*Morphing?* That sounds more like something from your time than mine. Remember, Tracy, a guy's gotta have some mystery."

I popped right out of this dream. For a moment I felt disoriented. But then, in the moonlight streaming through the window, I saw that I was lying in our bed in the Rest Ur Head, with Drew at my side.

"T.K.," I muttered softly into the darkness. "We gotta stop meeting over burrito fumes."

Last night when we returned from the memorial service, Dad had a pair of take-out burritos waiting for us. Since Drew had filled up on the potluck grub at the service, I scarfed down both of them.

Now surfer-sized waves of acid filled my stomach. I slipped from the bed, and remembering to snag my robe from the hook on the door, I made my way to the sitting room.

I threw the light on. The brightness blinded me initially. Then the sight of the mess I'd deposited earlier in that room continued to irritate my eyes. Neatness was always a challenge for me, but never more than in hotel rooms. Tonight, I'd left my purse and cell phone there, along with all the T-shirts I'd discarded the prior evening, before settling on the red one. Well, Drew had also neatly folded his jacket across the sofa arm, so I wasn't completely to blame for the mess.

I slumped into a side chair just as my cell phone rang. Who calls in the middle of the night? I grabbed the phone before it woke the others.

Hinky's voice came through. "Alec's kid? Is that you?"

Alec's kid? Did he think that was my name?

"I wanted to let you know, I'm heading out for a little casino crawl, so I probably won't be here if you need me to show you the way to Alec's unit again, when you come back this way."

I told him I thought I could find it next time. I hesitated, before adding, "You know, Hinky, your slot machine really doesn't get you into shape for winning. What do you hope to gain with this casino trip?" Man, I really was turning into an adult. I had to short-circuit this slide into maturity.

Hinky, while older than me, managed to hold it at bay. "Alec's kid, you still ask too many questions." He abruptly ended the call.

"Yeah? Eat dirt, Hinky," I muttered into the dead phone. Having recently consumed dirt myself, I knew it was no fun. I hurled the cell phone into my purse.

I remembered that I had stowed Lucy's design albums in the Volvo's trunk, along with all the loose papers I'd scooped up in the dark when we searched her apartment, and I hadn't looked through any of that yet. I reached into Drew's jacket pocket for his keys and went out to the parking lot.

The moon was full and the stars twinkled gloriously against the midnight sky. I threw my head back and drew in the night show.

The sound of screeching tires interrupted my moonlit reverie. A red Ferrari came from behind Woody's building and burned rubber peeling away. Oh, yeah, "The Pair" and I were gonna rumble soon, preferably where they couldn't push a table into my path.

I spotted Woody's RV in the restaurant parking lot, unused, according to Dad, and now, never to be. While staring at the camper, The Kontiki Room's neon sign, dark since Woody's death, also caught my eye. With only the moon's scant illumination striking the neon tubes, rather than brightly colored lights glowing from within, something about the sign struck me as strange. I stared at it for a moment. But when nothing came, I rescued the overstuffed albums from the trunk and went back to the suite.

Studying them in the bright light of the sitting room, I was even more awed by Lucy's designs, than I had been that night in her darkened apartment. The body conscious quality she brought to clothing put her way ahead of her time. Mother had dragged me to too many fashion shows not to know that. I could easily see these garments being sold today.

With a turn of a page, I came across a manila envelope stuffed between two album pages, on which a sloppy hand had written, "Genevieve." If that referred to the woman I'd met earlier this evening, the minister's wife and Woody's cleaning lady, this envelope couldn't have been Lucy's. When Lucy went away, Don Cannon's Genevieve wouldn't have been more than two or three years old. But it wasn't a common name.

It's not often that anything shocks me. When you consider that, as a youngster, my father brought me to meet the woman who might have been his mistress—that wasn't a surprise. So it was nice to know that some things could put me into jaw-dropping mode.

I gaped at the photos that envelope had held in disbelief. It was Genevieve Cannon, all right. But she wasn't two years old in those pictures. The first eight photos caught her having sex with some heavily tattooed muscle-bound guy, but in the later ones—riding her was Woody. Ewww!

Despite my revulsion, I studied them. Both tête-à-têtes had been captured from the identical angle; whoever operated the camera stood in the same spot both times. No matter what else I tried to look at, my gaze kept being drawn back to Genevieve's face. I've heard it suggested that there's only the slimmest of lines between agony and ecstasy. Whoever believed that clearly hadn't studied enough agony. I'd never seen such utter disgust reflected on a human face as in her sessions with Woody. With the tattooed stranger, she looked confused, and maybe regretful, but she still seemed to be enjoying herself.

I shifted my attention to Woody. In one photo, while grinning triumphantly like a silly idiot, he stared right at the camera. Had he known it was there? His arm stretched toward it, while he held a small black object between his fingers. A remote control! Woody snapped those pictures himself, while Genevieve serviced him.

I gasped aloud as possibilities tumbled through my mind. If Woody had been the secret chronicler of Genevieve's first encounter, he may have forced her into the second one. Nobody doing something by choice looked as pained she did.

Was this what Lucy had been trying to hide? It was hard to imagine that there could be something even slimier in Woody's past. How would Lucy have even known about it? Would a guy share with his mother that he extorted sex?

The idea that Woody might have blackmailed Genevieve continued to leave me stunned, especially in light of Philly's current squeeze. How many extortionists could there be in a town this small? I couldn't imagine how Woody might have learned about Philly's hidden past, especially since we didn't know a thing about it, but I didn't doubt that he might have put the screws to Philly. And we had found that first note in the café.

Yet Philly's attempted extortion continued past Woody's death. Did Woody have a partner who carried on without him? Was his murder the result of a falling out between them? Then again, perhaps Woody had left blackmail notes with someone else—someone like the desk clerk, Duncan, who had reason to be grateful to him—and the threats he'd engineered were now delivered from the grave.

My head began to hurt as badly as my tummy. But excitement finally made my heart sing.

Good dirt should be shared—that's my motto. I woke Drew up and dragged him out to the sitting room. The sight of his sleep-tousled hair and naked chest above his sagging pajama bottoms, got my own motor humming. I almost jumped him. Only then I remembered something else about those photos—that they appeared to have been shot in this motel—and it shut that impulse down damn quick.

Drew whistled when I showed him the pictures. "Those beauty pageant judges have all the luck."

With a testy snort, I pulled away the ones with Genevieve's mystery lover, Tattoo Man, and made him focus on the shots with Woody. "Don't you see what this means?"

"Yeah. The minister's wife needs to rethink how she makes parishioner visits."

I clicked my tongue. "To think I actually chose you as a sidekick." I shared my coercion theory as the basis for her encounter with Woody.

Drew scratched his head. "I don't know, Trace. She might have been genuinely attracted to him. There's no accounting for taste. I can't tell you how many people at my old law firm told me that."

"Surely, you misunderstood them," I said coldly. But I directed Drew to really study her face, and I told him about everything I'd noticed the night before. The laughter when Don Cannon talked about what a good wife she was, the haunted look in her eyes. "She realizes that other people know, that it's only a matter of time until someone tells her husband."

As Drew shuffled through the photos, he identified the thing I'd also noticed, which had shut down my own amorous juices. "These were all shot somewhere in this motel. There can't be many dumps that look exactly like this."

He hadn't spent enough nights along Route 66. But it did look like the Rest Ur Head. "You know what that means."

"That we're not having sex again until we get home?"

I really expected better from my gossip partners. "Well, that, too." I gave those warped paneled walls an uncomfortable glance. "No. It explains Woody's unexpected generosity." I'd already told

Drew what Duncan said at the service, about Woody working the front desk for him. "Woody must have taken those shots from another room. That's why he offered to spell Duncan—to have access to it. With Duncan away, Woody had run of the whole place. "

I trotted out the rest of my half-formed theories: Woody as the town blackmailer. That he'd had a willing partner who killed him, or an inadvertent one like Duncan carrying on without him.

To my surprise, Drew listened in silence, not objecting to my dragging the murder in, as I thought he would. "So...Woody's murder really might be related to Philly's troubles," he said slowly.

Okay, I'd get to keep my secrets for a while longer, and he'd get to keep participating in my fun and games for another day. Only I figured that day would be tomorrow, not tonight.

Drew popped to his feet, pacing frantically. "We need to scope out that peephole spot, as well as Woody's room when Fricker takes the police seal off it."

Finally, my investigative zeal was catching fire in him. But now that my stomach had cooled down, I began yawning. "Yup. Those rooms, and we need to look through the rest of the albums for whatever else I may have grabbed from Lucy's sewing cabinet. First, though, we should to visit the prim little pastor's wife, and confront her with what we know." I yawned again. "But tomorrow. Now I think I can get back to sleep."

I couldn't wait to plop my head back on the pillow. But I took another look at those badly paneled walls, so similar to the ones in Genevieve's photos. No way would I trust the security in that dump with anything important. I told Drew we had to put the albums back in his trunk.

When we walked outside together, I glanced at Woody's sign again. "Drew, do you see anything wrong with the Kontiki sign?"

He choked. "You mean you see something *right* with it? It's only slightly less offensive now that it's no longer lit."

Sure, that was it. It just looked different to me. Why was I harping on this?

The sound of something scurrying passed behind Drew, and he jerked away. Probably a lizard or some desert critter, because there was nobody outside the motel now but us.

"You know, Trace, Route 66 feels lots more sinister than you let on to me."

More than I let on to me, too. I felt like a chump for getting taken in by this Americana crap for so long. And I couldn't help but look over my shoulder, before rushing back to the safety of the room.

CHAPTER TWENTY-FOUR

The next morning, we returned to the church. Set back from the hall where the service was held was a blue and white cottage with a wide front porch. It wasn't a bad looking house with its white porch rails and dormer windows. But someone had really hit the place with a cutesy stick. The boxes attached to every window overflowed with pink flowers, as did the many clusters of pots. Every window showed evidence of frilly curtains. And the rattan furniture on the porch overflowed with flowered chintz cushions. That cavity-forming house was so freakin' adorable now, it made my teeth ache.

Genevieve, the probable designer of the cloying décor, struck the only odd note. We found her seated on the porch. In a departure from the baggy duds of the night before, she now wore tight knit pants and midriff revealing top. The top showed lines of dust along the shoulders, as if it had hung unused in a closet for some time. She'd replaced last night's anxious look with one of complete devastation. The dark circles under her eyes almost hung to her knees.

"I'm not receiving visitors today," Genevieve spat, in a way that was simultaneously formal and rude.

Drew hesitated, but it took more than a bit of impoliteness to send me packing. "Good thing then that I consider myself an intruder." I marched onto the porch, tugging Drew along with me. I held the manila envelope at my side.

She shrugged indifferently and reached for the pack of cigarettes resting on the white rattan table at her side. "I've taken these up again," she said, lighting up. She had also bitten down her pretty pink nails virtually to the quick.

I opened Woody's envelope and passed the stack of photos to her, plopping them on her lap. Her eyes widened at the sight of them, and her hands jerked away.

Her gaze switched to me, narrowing in contempt. "You're too

late to pull what Woody did," she said. "I already told Don…what I
did." She grasped the stack and threw them back to me. "Besides, I
don't have anything to give you to keep this quiet. No money." With
a toss of her head at Drew, who stood beside my chair, she added,
"Unless you thought you'd get me to do your old man."

"About that…yeah…nobody does my love monkey but me."

Drew sputtered. He was a keeper in so many ways, but the jury
was still out on how good a sidekick he'd make. I brought the heel
of my shoe down on his toes to silence him.

"Why did you do it? I'm not asking about Woody. I can see he
coerced you. I mean Tattoo Man."

"I wasn't always as discriminate as I should have been. When
I met Don…well, he believed in me. I really wanted to change for
him." She took a drag and blew out a thick stream of smoke. "But
the parishioners never took to me. And you can't imagine how they
treat a pastor and his wife. They come into my house—well, the
church's house—and they snoop through everything, the clothes in
my closet, the food in the pantry. And none of it was ever good
enough for them. People who pride themselves on their Christian
charity never showed any to me."

I thought I understood her sugar-sweet approach to home décor
now. She wanted to be above reproach. "And Tattoo Man?"

"You know what Route 66 is like. Everyone's path seems to cross
with yours. He was an old boyfriend, passing through. The night
before, I'd overheard a conversation about me at the church hall.
A group of women were imitating Don's 'beauty queen' remarks.
Something snapped in me, and I made the worst mistake of my life."

"Until Woody made you repeat it."

"The really horrible part was that even after I…did that with
him, Woody told people anyway, when he promised he wouldn't."
Disgust seemed to roil through her body, rising up from her stomach.

"Doesn't that give you a pretty good motive for getting rid of
him?" I asked.

Genevieve happened to be sucking on her butt again, and the
smoke caused her to choke. "Is that why you're here?" She laughed
hysterically. "You can't know how many times I fantasized about

driving a knife straight into his miserable excuse for a heart. But I didn't do it."

"Can you prove it?" Drew asked, jumping in at last.

She nodded. "You can check with Pete Rivera, the bartender at the Sagebrush Cantina." When I frowned, she said, "You must know it. From what I hear you've been here loads of times. You've probably logged more accumulated time in Tecos than I have in my two years."

Maybe so, but I didn't know all the bars. Mother and Dad might be the ringmasters of the circus of sex, though they'd never pulled me out of preschool for a pub crawl. But we'd find it. And we'd determine whether or not the beauty queen-pastor's wife gave that slug in waffle batter what he deserved.

* * *

With its red tile roof and walled patio, the Sagebrush Cantina looked like an old Mexican roadhouse. While much of Route 66 is strictly vintage Heartland, another aspect I'd always loved were the little pockets of local color that you find. The Mexican theme carried through the interior, from the hand-painted tiles that lined the bar, to the chili ristras—strands of red chilies strung together—that hung from the ceiling. Sure, it still had the pool table and small band stage required of all neighborhood bars, but the local touches lent it unexpected flavor.

With his gray silk shirt and flashing black eyes, Pete Rivera looked like a Southwestern impresario. He was the bartender at present, but he was in the process of buying the bar.

He described the changes he planned to make to the charming cantina. "Slick, that's the look I'm going for." With arms waving in all directions, he went on to describe Lucite surfaces and flashing colored lights. "Like a nightclub in L.A. or New York."

Didn't anyone like the character of wherever they lived? It sounded to me like he wanted to turn this charming little cantina into the reincarnation of Studio 54.

To my surprise, since we were there to verify Genevieve's alibi, Drew diverted the investigation by offering to review Pete's

purchase contract and give him a second legal opinion. Clearly, Mr.
I don't want to be a lawyer anymore just didn't want paying work.

Before they could get too lost in legalese, I broke in with,
"Genevieve Cannon says she was here the night Woody Crier was
killed. She's the—"

"I know who she is. She and my girlfriend are in the same book
club. Yeah, she was here. First time, too, I'll tell you that."

When he and Drew went back to legal matters, I broke in again
with, "You're sure she was here the whole evening? She couldn't
have left for a while and come back?"

"Yeah, absolutely sure. Our cocktail waitress didn't show up for
her shift, and I had to ferry drinks to Genevieve steadily throughout
the night."

"She was drinking? Liquor?" I remembered Don telling me that
neither one of them drank.

"Like they were starting Prohibition again the next day. When I
cut her off and called a cab for her, she tried to get someone else to
buy her another drink."

Drew brought his attention back to the contract. "Pete, you might
want to look at this clause."

"How do you know it was *that* night?" I asked, interrupting
again. "The night Woody was killed. I can't remember one day from
another."

Pete sighed with obvious annoyance. "My sister-in-law is a
dispatcher at the PD. She told me right after the call came in." He
looked from Drew to me. "After you two called it in, I guess. She's
probably supposed to keep stuff like that confidential. You won't
rat her out, will you? She knows I've had issues with Woody and
figured I'd want to know."

Drew finally remembered which side he was supposed to be on.
"What kind of issues?"

Pete ran a hand through his dark hair. "He tried to stop me
from buying this place. He said this town wasn't big enough for
two nightclubs. But my place will run rings around Woody's dump.
Good food, great bands—I'll have it all. What did Woody ever do
with his café, other than ruining waffles? He didn't even have a

liquor license. What kind of club is that?"

"Sounds like you had a pretty good motive yourself," I said. "How do we know *you* didn't sneak out during the night?"

"Didn't you hear me? I told you, my cocktail waitress bailed. Fifty people in here saw me all night. And like I said, I ran back and forth between the bar and Genevieve's table throughout the evening."

"Where was she sitting?"

He gestured toward an arched doorway on the far side of the room. "In the back room. Funny thing, exactly where her old man is getting shit-faced right now."

Drew and I shared startled looks. "Don Cannon is here now? Drinking?" I demanded.

"He was waiting outside when I opened today."

I left Drew to deal with Pete's contract and went through the arched doorway. Don Cannon, slumped alone in a corner booth, was in his cups, all right. Watery eyes, slack lip—the whole drunken works. Strangely, there were only two beer bottles before him, and one looked only half empty.

"I don't want company," he said, when I slid into the other side of the booth, interrupting his pity party. I repeated my intruder line. I wasn't making up new material for these Cannons—they were too distracted to appreciate it.

After a pause, I said, "She made a mistake."

"A bad one. And then she made it again. With Woody Crier, of all people. Scum o' the earth."

So much for his being one of God's children. Don loved Genevieve, I felt sure. He wouldn't hurt this much if he didn't. Still, I bet he never acknowledged how badly his parishioners had treated her. He was too busy selling his beauty queen wife to notice they weren't buying.

Though his eyes were bleary, I hoped he wasn't too wasted to take in what he ought to hear. I told him everything she'd shared with me. Every snide comment, every time she overheard trash talk about herself.

"Always happens. She shoulda known that." He took a tiny sip of beer.

Maybe she would have known what to expect if he'd prepared her.

He wiped his mouth with his sleeve. "Doesn't matter. It's over."

"Over? Are you nuts? Think about all you have in common." Drew came to stand beside the booth, along with Pete.

"Like what?" Don asked.

How did I know? I only met them yesterday. "Well…for newbies, you're both great drinkers."

With no warning, he pitched forward. He would have smashed his head against the table if Drew hadn't caught him.

"Jeez, Pete, how much did you let him drink?" I asked.

Pete picked up the bottles and held them up to the light. "Two… no, one and a half beers."

Some people just *want* to get drunk. The guys dragged him from the booth and stuffed him into our backseat for the ride back home to sleep it off. Pete thanked Drew for the legal advice and invited us back for a few on the house. There must have been other legal matters Drew could review for Pete, when he was supposed to be helping me. Drew wasn't shaping up to be a consistently good sidekick, but I grudgingly admitted I wouldn't have been able to lug Don Cannon home on my own.

But Drew's sidekick status unexpectedly rose a notch while we were driving away from the bar. "You know, Trace, it occurs to me that there's no question that Genevieve didn't kill Woody. She was clearly here that night."

Talk about stating the obvious. "So?"

"So what about Don? We only know when Genevieve *told* him about her infidelity—we don't know when he actually *learned* it."

CHAPTER TWENTY-FIVE

When we delivered Don Cannon home, I'd hoped to question Genevieve about her husband's whereabouts on the night Woody was killed, while she was out getting waffled. But Chief Fricker was there, right on the front porch, staring out as if he expected us. Was he considering the same suspects, or following us?

"To think I worried that y'all would try to leave Tecos," he said, after helping Drew tuck Don into bed. "I didn't know you'd be as busy as a one-armed chimp in a flea circus."

If I was interpreting his gibberish correctly, he knew we were poking into the crime he was charged with solving. I limited my response to, *"Watch what you wish for*—that's my motto."

Bottom line, though: We had to skedaddle, with our questions left unasked.

Back at the suite, we found the old boys in residence. After their little patch-up before Fricker ordered us to stay in Tecos, I thought they were on solid terms again. No dice. Apparently, they'd returned to feuding now. I wasn't even sure why. Was this still about Dad being a dilettante?

It occurred to me if I sent them off to question the Cannons, not only might we get some answers, they'd have to work together. Two crows down with only one slingshot. Three crows, actually, since we'd also get rid of them. We needed to follow up on some stuff at the Rest Ur Head, and we didn't need them around, getting in our way.

I called them both to the sitting area. They emerged from their rooms like a pair of sulky schoolboys, alternately avoiding each other and sending hopeless glances the other's way.

I caught them up on what we were doing. Though Dad hadn't understood why we went to the memorial service, neither one seemed surprised that we'd begun sleuthing. Despite Dad's lifelong devotion to Woody, he didn't seem particularly interested, either. I shared Drew's theory that Don might have learned about his wife's infidelity earlier than he claimed, and explained that we needed them to verify his alibi.

"I don't know, Trace. I'm not good with Thumpers." Philly began backing up toward the door to his room, scratching his bristly hair until it stuck out like a porcupine's quills.

"They're not thumping that strenuously right now," I shouted as he made his escape, slamming the door behind him.

Dad looked longingly at the closed door, but he also raised objections, though more diplomatically. "Tracy, I can't ask him if he's a murderer. He's a man of the cloth."

"Less of one than you think, Dad. Just do it, huh?" With a look at Philly's door, I made a choice. "But wait until I roust your partner in crime."

I burst into Philly's room without knocking, shutting the door behind me. He glanced up indifferently from where he sat on the bed.

"Gloves off, old man. I want to know what the hell you're involved in." I waited, but he didn't utter a peep. With a sigh, I sat beside him. "Philly, haven't I always been there for you? Have I ever let you down?"

He cupped his rough hand around my chin in a rare show of affection. "Kid, I love you like you're my own, but I got nothing to say."

This was starting to look like way more than the gamesmanship I'd predicted to Drew that Philly would play. It was also completely uncharacteristic of him. Philly was no towering oak, he was a willow, bending with every breeze. What could possibly matter so much to him as to make him hang tough?

"Look, Philly, I know it was *you*, not Dad, who plotted to get us here faster. That whole dressing-like-Lucy scheme—that was your idea. You wanted us here, and not so we could help get Lucy released. You knew *you* were in deep doo-doo, and you needed our help. Don't bother to deny it."

His eyes widened in shock, and he opened his mouth, as if to speak, only to shut it again. When he finally spoke, he surprised me.

"I made a mistake, okay? I should never have involved you." He ran his hand through his spiky hair. "Trace, there's nothing here for any of you now. Woody's gone, and Lucy's in there for the rest of her life. We all know that. Why don't you and Drew take Alec and go home? Get as far as you can away from this wretched place."

And leave him behind? Was that what he really wanted?

"I warn you, Tracy—you go sticking your nose in where it don't belong, like you always do, and you and me are through." With that, he stormed out of the room, slamming the door behind him.

"Philly, how deep a mess did you get yourself into?" I whispered to the walls around me. "And why do you think you have to handle it alone?"

The only bright note was that after exploding at me, Philly must have felt so contrite, he agreed to go along with Dad to wheedle some answers from Genevieve and Don. By the time old farts departed, I was too preoccupied by this unexpected turn of events to draw any satisfaction from turning them into our band of Route 66 Irregulars.

Drew had also left. We'd already decided that he would tackle Duncan, the Rest Ur Head desk clerk, on his own. Since I'd blown off the idea of filling in for Duncan on his job the way he wanted, we weren't sure he would accept a change of heart from me. But now that we knew we needed to get rid of him, spelling him at the front desk would provide the perfect opportunity.

Alone in our suite, I reviewed my conversation with Philly.

It made no sense on so many levels. Why would he plot to get us there, only to threaten me if I tried to give him the help he once thought he needed? Something else must have happened between the time when Dad made that call and now. Philly's extortionist had clearly continued communicating with him—we'd found another one of his notes in the caves. The only conclusion I could draw was that his blackmailer had threatened one of us, or even all of us, with danger, and poor Philly was trying to protect us the only way he could. By keeping us out of his troubles.

I pounded on one of the sitting room's awful knotty pine walls in frustration. With nothing more to go on, somehow I had to find a way to save Philly—while keeping all of us safe—even if it meant losing him from my life.

* * *

Still bummed by frustration long after they'd all gone, I grabbed the TV remote from the table at my side and tuned it to the midday news. The news back in California wasn't good for Tandy. They'd organized rallies all over the state yesterday, with thousands calling for him to step down before they tossed him out.

As if I weren't already sufficiently bummed by politicians and bureaucrats, another one popped onto the screen for the next story. He was a blond man, with a ponytail down his back, and a tan that probably came from a tanning bed, but which looked like he'd baked on the back of a horse under a Western sky. The news anchor identified him as Cary Chandler, some Undersecretary in the Department of the Interior, in charge of National Forest land trades for New Mexico, Arizona, and California.

Cary offered us out here in TV land an engaging grin, while absently fingering the bolo tie he wore under the collar of his cowboy shirt. "Open space is a legacy we owe to our children and grandchildren," he said with an appealing Southwest drawl.

He went on to discuss the land the Forest Service would be selling off, but promised the proceeds would go to new land purchases that would increase the public acreage.

Right. Same-old, same-old. It was purely coincidental that the land the government sold off was invariably what developers wanted most, while instead, it bought acres nobody valued at all. Politicians and bureaucrats should have to wear uniforms like racecar drivers so we can see their corporate sponsors. I snapped the TV off before my cynicism hit bottom.

Fortunately, that was when the sitting room door opened and Drew popped his head in. From the twinkle in his brown eyes, I knew he'd succeeded in his mission.

"You talked Duncan into leaving?" I asked.

"Already gone. Get your snooping hat on, girl, and let's get moving."

As if I ever took off my snooping hat. Finally, this sucky day was looking up.

While we made our way across the cracked surface of the motel patio on the way to the office, I questioned Drew about his encounter with Duncan. "Did he suspect you wanted him out of the way?"

Drew snorted. "If he did, it sure didn't come up. And it would have. Unless he's a better actor than Alec, Duncan doesn't have a bit of guile."

Nor a drop of testosterone, given that voice. "Did he confess to being in league with Woody?"

"Not in league exactly, but he did admit to being Woody's errand boy."

"You mean...?"

Drew grinned. "Yup, he dropped off notes from Woody to various people. He told me he continued to pass them out even after his benefactor died, because Woody had already paid him."

"Pretty honest for someone who might have been handing out a blackmailer's communications. Was Philly one of the recipients?"

Drew frowned. "That was the one strange part. He claimed not to remember where they went."

Sounded suspicious. Yet judging by our brief encounter at the memorial service, I'd bet some things did flow straight through Duncan's brain.

We paused outside the office's glass door. Taped to the door was a sheet of paper on which Drew's distinctive handwriting read, "Back in five minutes."

"Could it be that easy?" I asked with a sigh. "Could Philly's ordeal be over already, because Woody was his blackmailer and Woody's dead?"

Drew began to gnaw at the inside of his cheek again. "I know I haven't been investigating as long as you have, Trace, but I don't think Woody was the one blackmailing Philly."

I choked. "Drew, how many extortionists could there be in a town this small?"

"Two, ten—how should I know? Maybe it's a cottage industry here." When I started to object, he gave his head a decisive shake.

"Hear me out, honey. Yeah, Woody extorted sex from a desperate woman, and I'm sure he squeezed more sleazy payoffs from other people. But think about the nature of the communication Philly has been receiving. How did the first note read, the one we found in the café? 'How much is it worth to you to keep your past hidden?' Don't you hear confidence there? Arrogance, even? And look at the one Philly left in the cave, which said, 'You'd better pay attention to me!' Anger filled that one, though the arrogance was still evident. Did they really sound like something a goofy guy like Woody would write?"

He was right—I felt it instantly. I should have known, too. I was a writer, after all—Philly's notes simply weren't in Woody's voice.

I didn't admit that to Drew, though. Instead, I glared at him and said, "First rule of being a sidekick—never upstage the detective."

With a laugh, he threw the glass door open. I trudged along behind him.

I hadn't seen the front office since we had taken up residence in Dad's suite without checking in. They'd spruced it up a bit since the last time I was there. There was now a faux granite counter, instead of the old wooden one. One of those front desk key-holders, with pigeonholes for extra room keys, filled the wall behind the counter. That made more sense here than most hotels, since the Rest Ur Head still used old-fashioned keys, instead of the electronic cards most places had switched to. A computer now sat on the desk, too. But otherwise, it was a pretty Spartan affair.

Drew popped behind the counter and pocketed the extra key to Woody's room. Then he led me through the door to the desk clerk's unit. Despite all the times I'd stayed there, I'd never seen that suite.

I stopped inside, surprised somehow. I didn't know what I'd expected—maybe something skuzzier. What we found instead was a tidy room, mostly lacking in distinction. A taupe loveseat covered one wall, while a large TV and some electronic doodads filled a wall unit on another. The only decorations were a pair of forgettable motel-type paintings.

"What does Duncan do with the extra time off he wangles?" I asked.

Drew gestured toward the wall unit. "You may not have noticed, but Duncan likes video games."

I had noticed. The only things he'd added to the generic motel décor were Xbox and Wii units, as well as a couple of hand-held games, all of which filled spaces in the wall unit. And while large, the TV was the one the motel provided, one of the older models with rounded corners, not a big plasma. Duncan didn't seem to be throwing around fistfuls of loot.

"What he really likes, he told me, are arcade games," Drew said. "But there aren't any in Tecos. He sneaks off to Albuquerque to play in the arcade in some bowling alley there."

"Did he hit you up for money to play?"

"Nope, he just threw off a giddy 'thanks' and ran out before I could change my mind. I heard the exhaust of that old Camaro he drives a moment later."

We walked into the next room, which was a small, and equally neat, bedroom, and after that, a clean little bathroom. Duncan sure wasn't shaping up to be the bad boy I'd hoped he was.

"Let's find that peephole," I said sourly. "Before guests arrive and we actually have to check someone into this joint."

The walls in that unit were drywall, not paneling, like ours. Any holes there should have stood out. Too bad nothing did. Just to be sure, Drew ran his hands over the walls of the sitting room, while I checked the bedroom and the bath. But if anyone was peeping through those walls, they had Superman's x-ray vision.

I yanked open the door to the unit's lone closet. A few garments and extra hangers were spread across the short rod. I pushed them to the side. And there it was—the peephole we'd sought. Smack dab in the center of the closet's back wall, someone had drilled a good-sized hole.

I started toward it, to test it with my eye, but I caught myself before I stepped into the closet. Instead, I studied the floor. Three black marks, spaced as they might be for a tripod, had streaked the ceramic tile floor. Only after I pointed out the marks to Drew did I try the peephole. The bed in the next room was empty now, but that looked like the room in the photos. I shivered, thinking about the price Genevieve paid for the mistakes she made in that room.

I sighed and turned to Drew. "What do you do when someone you never had any respect for suddenly deserves even less than you thought?"

Drew tossed the key he'd taken from the front office. "You search the bastard's room."

CHAPTER TWENTY-SIX

The police department hadn't sealed Woody's room, they simply crisscrossed crime scene tape over the door. But they'd taped it at eye-level, making it a simple matter to unlock the door and crawl under the tape barrier.

The squalor I'd expected to find in Duncan's room waited for us here. It was superficially clean, apart from the unmade bed, which the housekeeper hadn't been able to get in to make the morning after he died, and the black fingerprint powder the PD had left behind. But the stomach-churning scent of overly ripe clothing hung heavy in the air. Woody might have washed his clothes at some time, but probably not in the last several months of his life.

On the wall beside the door, above the light switch, a small, handwritten sign said, "Tiki-Man's Keys." Wood-man, Kontiki-man, Tiki-man—he wasn't too fond of his nicknames for himself. This had been his room—who else's keys would they be? Four cup hooks lined up under the little sign, two of which were empty. He must have had his room key and the one for the restaurant on him when he went out to meet his killer. Those had to be in police custody now.

Two other keys dangled from those hooks; both for cars, judging by the remotes that hung from them. Drew took them and leaned out the door, clicking them in different directions. I heard a car beep from somewhere outside.

"The second one doesn't register with anything parked out here," he said, pocketing both sets. "But the first one's for that cool red Mustang convertible in the corner of the parking lot."

Nothing but the best for the Wood-Man. "The other key is probably for the RV, which is parked over by the restaurant, beyond the remote's range."

This place reminded me of his teenage bedroom over the

restaurant. Once again, it looked like the personal space of a boy, not a middle-aged man. He had given up on the godfather movies, trading them for martial arts flicks. Curling posters for Kung Fu movies, with the fierce faces and fit bare torsos of Asian actors, lined these paneled walls. In addition to the motel's standard furniture, Woody had added three tall bookcases to the space. But rather than housing books, they held model cars, antique toys, and some other gadgets. They also held labeled display racks for guns—real guns according to the labels, not toys—but if guns had ever graced those display pieces, the cops had removed them.

The shelves didn't contain a single one of Lucy's painted lunch pails. Dad and I brought more sentiment to those things than he did.

Many of the antique toys weren't from Woody's own youth, but decades earlier. All of collectible quality, if I was any judge. Some of the toys I was familiar with. Things like marbles and jacks and vintage sets of Tinkertoys. But some were gizmos I'd never seen before. A mechanized marble shooter caught my eye. Attached to it was a little tube that held six marbles, and at the front of the device, a firing lever. Without giving it a thought, I clicked the lever. The coiled action was so tight, the marble shot across the room.

"Whoa!" I dashed across the room to pick up the marble that had fallen to the floor. But not before I saw that it had dented the paneling.

Drew, who'd been standing too close for comfort, snapped, "Tracy, quit fooling around! You could take someone's eye out with that."

Despite that danger, I felt such a visceral longing for the marble shooter, I decided to keep the damn thing.

My hypocrisy hit me at once. I'd only just been critical of Woody for the fact that his room looked like a kid's, yet there I was stealing a toy. Okay, so maybe I embraced my inner adolescent, too. Whatever. Consistency is overrated in my opinion.

"Come on, let's finish searching this place," Drew said. "The smell is starting to make my eyes tear."

We found a tripod outside the bathroom, with rubber tips on the end of the legs that could have made the black marks on Duncan's closet floor. We got excited when we saw the digital camera still screwed into the tripod. Too bad someone had removed the memory card.

"Fricker wouldn't have missed that," I said.

I felt a moment of dread for whatever poor slob might have been caught in the photos on that card. The dread mushroomed into full-blown fear, when I remembered the secretive behavior both Philly and Dad had shown on this trip. But what was I thinking? Neither one of them would have been engaging in some extracurricular canoodling in the room next to Duncan's. Their secrets, I felt certain, were all rooted in the past.

We tore the whole place apart, checking every drawer, the pocket and hem of every garment. We'd really hoped to find more photos of his victims. But if there were any good leads in that room, the police had clearly carted them away. All we found were some skin mags hidden below the mattress. Like a kid hiding them from his mom. Or a creepy older guy hoping to gross out the maid.

Drew crawled out the door under the crime scene tape. I turned back, and stared at the angry faces of the fighters in those Kung Fu posters. I willed them to give up the room's secrets. When they refused to utter a peep, I banged the wall above the Tiki-Man's keys.

Remembering to grab the marble shooter and a handful of extra marbles, I followed Drew out.

* * *

After searching Woody's room, we returned to the suite. I shared with Drew my conversation with Philly, and my conclusion about why he was keeping us out of things.

"A threat against one of us. Makes sense," Drew said. "Which of us do you think it is?"

I shrugged. "Dad maybe. They were together here before we arrived. The blackmailer must have been watching them. But it could also be you—you are his nephew."

"Why not you?"

"Oh, anyone who's been watching us should know I'm a wild card, that there's nothing I won't do."

Drew pursed his lips, clearly considering that. "Not a bad thing to have on your side."

So he finally got it. Good to know.

We decided to split the work once more. Drew agreed to look through the rest of Lucy's design albums for anything else I might have stuffed into them in the dark when we tossed her apartment. Since he insisted he needed caffeine, he went in search of a place where he could review the albums over a cup of java.

My task was to give Lucy's place another look in daylight for anything we might have missed. I rose from the suite's faded crimson couch determined to tackle the apartment once more. But how? The police had removed the ladder from the side of the building where it had been propped up.

I opened the door to Dad's room. There, on the dresser, rested a manila envelope. When I drew closer, I could see that it was stamped with the words, "Tecos Police Department." And under that, the name, "Wood-man Crier."

Wood-man? That was his real name? And I bitched about my parents.

I dumped the contents of the envelope on the dresser. Those were the things Woody must have had on him when he died, which I figured would still be in police custody. His room key was there, all right. And the restaurant key, fortunately—the label on it said, "Kontiki."

The only other items were a wallet and an iPhone. A quick check of his driver's license confirmed that Lucy really had given her son that ridiculous name. Seeing the spiffy new smart phone further bummed me. Not that I envied Woody that phone exactly. I rarely even answered my own dumb phone—I refused to accept the idea that we're all supposed to listen to any yahoo who wants to claim our time. Avoiding calls was like a hobby for me. As for texting, anyone who wanted to text me could print out the sentiment and deliver it in person, *if* they could find me. The phone was simply more evidence of how much Dad had spoiled Woody. I pocketed the restaurant key, but put everything else back where I found it.

At the restaurant, I let myself in by the front door, leaving it unlocked for Drew, and trotted up the stairs. In daylight, Lucy's apartment looked messier than it had in the dark. I saw now that she'd decorated the walls with old license plates from Route 66 states. Lucy sure had belonged there on Route 66—she had a taste for kitsch like nobody else, including me. What I didn't see was any of the black fingerprint powder that the cops had left in Woody's room. Had Fricker dismissed this space as a source of evidence? That Woody had insisted he never used the upstairs apartment made it a better hiding place for him.

I found a couple of more photos in the sewing cabinet that I'd missed in my hasty, nighttime search. One so old, it had yellowed. It was a black-and-white image of an elderly man, with the runny eyes of someone who'd had too much to drink, eyes that looked like deep pits of shame. The photo had been shot in front of the openings to the caves behind Woody's place. In his hands, the man held a length of metal pipe.

After a moment, I placed him—he was the town drunk, grandfather to "The Pair." I remembered him staggering around, publicly soused, in the years when we visited Tecos after Lucy went away. Given its yellowing, I figured Woody hadn't *just* begun his habit of catching people at their worst.

I shifted aside some of the sewing material and came across another photo, this one shot through the hole in Duncan's closet, into the room where Woody had caught Genevieve. This time, the camera captured two men, seated on folding chairs, deep in conversation. One was the town's mayor, Mark Baker. The other man had a leathery outdoors look to his tanned skin, wore Southwestern style clothing and had a long ponytail. It took a long moment before I placed him. I hadn't seen him here, but on the TV news. He was the guy from the Department of the Interior, the one responsible for National Forest Service land swaps.

Given the look of negotiation captured in the photo, I'd bet Mark was trying to sell the Feds worthless land at an inflated price. If my guess was right and he succeeded, he'd doubtless get some property on which he could build an ugly strip mall, destroying the character of his town. Not to mention making him more than a tad wealthier.

I heard the restaurant door open, and then the sound of heavy footsteps slowly climbing the stairs. I had expected Drew to join me, but wouldn't he call out, not to mention move faster? In case that was someone else coming up those stairs, I looked around for something to throw at the intruder. All I could find with weapon-potential was the sewing machine. I hoisted it up. But an instant before I let it fly, Drew peeked around from the top of the stairs.

"Drew, why are you sneaking up on me?" I vaguely noticed he wore a reticent look, but I was too excited about my own findings to care. "You're not going to believe what I found here," I said. "More of Woody's victims, maybe, and one of them makes a good suspect."

With a reluctant sigh, Drew held up a handful of sheets of paper. "I've got something that trumps another suspect, babe. I found Alec's letters to Lucy."

CHAPTER TWENTY-SEVEN

MEMORIES OF ROUTE 66
ALEC

Alec's memory of the first time he walked into the Lunch Pail Café—during the filming of his old movie, Revenge on Route 66—was still so fresh and vivid that every time he called it up, it was as if he were reliving it again.

In a career that paraded beautiful women before him all the time, he felt, rather than remembered, his first encounter with Lucy, the second most striking woman he'd ever met. The un-Martha Martha, he'd dubbed her in his own mind. So alike, yet so different. The mesmerizing hold Lucy immediately had on him spread to everything around her. Her son—well, hers and Billy Rob's—her town, even the road that brought Alec to her.

He still couldn't fathom how the place he had treasured for so long had turned on all of them now as it had during this trip.

Philly seemed to think that Alec's life had been charmed, and maybe Alec had had more than his share of good fortune. But his path hadn't been as smooth as everyone thought. The stardom that looked like such a natural fit from the outside wasn't quite as comfortable from within.

At least Philly had his pride, which was more than Alec could say. Maybe Alec was old-fashioned, but he had been raised to believe the man should be the provider of his family. There was never any question of that with Martha—she hadn't needed his support.

He hadn't had a chance to be as generous as he wanted with Lucy. Maybe that was why he went overboard with Woody. And look at what it did to the boy, sapped him of his initiative. But Alec was just trying to make up for what he couldn't do under his own roof.

He also thought a man should be strong enough to win his wife's *fidelity. No chance of that, either. Alec was Martha's old shoe, the steady guy she discarded when someone flashier came along, only to return to when she needed some help or stability, but who she'd leave again when the itch for excitement grew stronger.*

Oh, Martha loved him. Maybe more than she knew herself. Alec never doubted that. But if Martha represented love in his life, Lucy had always been hope. Even after she went to prison.

Now, with so much that he cherished slipping away from him on this jaunt down Route 66, what would he do if he lost his hope as well?

CHAPTER TWENTY-EIGHT

My gaze went to the sheets of papers clutched in Drew's hand. Dad's letters to Lucy. That Drew found them in the design albums meant that they dated back to the days before Lucy began serving her sentence.

Warring emotions paralyzed me. The nosy part of me longed to dig into whatever dirt they contained. But *suspecting* the truth about Dad and Lucy—and Woody—had been bad enough. *Knowing* it might be too hard.

"Uh...I found some good stuff here, too," I said with considerably less enthusiasm now. I rallied enough to add, "I know you just came from having coffee, Drew, but now I could sure use some." Anything to avoid plunging into those letters.

Drew laughed excitedly. "I have the best place. You're not going to believe what I found."

"Better than The Great American Coffee Shoppe?"

"Different league altogether. I found a place where they make *real* coffee. You know, with an expensive Italian machine that also steams milk."

That wasn't the Route 66 way, but, still in avoidance-mode, I didn't object. In the car, he tossed the stack of letters into my lap, where I'd already placed the photos I took from Lucy's cabinet. I eyed those letters like a scorpion set to sting.

Drew drove to a place with a sign that read, "Brewed Awakening," located on a parallel street to the Tecos PD. He grabbed the letters again, while I took the photos, and we marched through the door. At the counter, the shortest, oldest and most cheerful barista beamed up at me. Only there did my objection finally break loose.

"This isn't Route 66 coffee. You're ruining the Mother Road spirit," I said, despite the line of people that had suddenly formed behind me.

She propped small square fists on chubby hips. "I suppose you think everyone in England should live in a thatched cottage."

"Everyone but the queen, of course, but she has a castle." People behind us muttered their objections to my pontificating.

"If you don't like it here, lady, get out of line," some guy snapped.

"Wearing a suit of armor with those hats and purses?" the barista asked with a sniff. The sprinkling of freckles across her upturned nose looked like a pinch of cinnamon floating on cappuccino foam. How apt was that? "Why shouldn't the people of this town have access to the same things you do, missy? If you look around, you'll see I've honored Route 66 more than you think."

"Come on. Move it," someone else said.

Without relinquishing my spot, I glanced around, catching sight of the big mural capturing the history of Tecos on the wall opposite the counter. Maybe she'd honored it at that. Besides, hadn't I decided all that Americana had made a sucker of me? I ordered a mocha and slinked off to a distant table.

Brewed Awakening was actually a pretty interesting place. Paintings of Route 66 by local artists filled many of the walls, and there was even a small stage where, according to a hand-lettered sign, they held poetry readings. This was the kind of independence I'd always celebrated, if you could overlook the frou-frou coffeemaker.

When Drew brought our drinks, the little barista came along with him, carrying one of her own, now that a skinny guy appeared behind the counter to help the other customers. "Trace, this is Elise. Until two years ago, she was the principal of the local high school."

With a grin that demonstrated she was not the type to hold grudges, she said, "After forty years of teaching and administration, I thought I needed to be around some adults."

I hoped she wasn't including me among those adults.

"I filled Elise in on what we're doing," Drew said, as he pulled out a chair. "You know, with Woody's murder and Philly's being blackmailed."

Talk about making choices above his pay grade. He shared our private sleuthing with a stranger? Sure, I also made people I'd just met into sidekicks, whenever I sensed a kindred spirit. The difference was that *I* picked them, not Drew. Still, since he'd already blabbed to this woman, I might as well find out what she knew.

I flipped out the old photo of "The Pair's" grandfather.

"Ah, yes. Angus Clement. Such a tragedy. The man fell apart after losing the caves."

Drew took a sip from his cardboard container. "So why did he risk them in a poker game?"

She shrugged. "He used to hint occasionally that he never did, but how did that California governor eventually end up with them if he didn't?"

When I came across that photo, capturing Angus Clement clearly in his cups, I had wondered why Woody snapped it, believing he simply liked the idea of preserving the image of someone down on his luck. Now, as I blew across the surface of my mocha, another possibility occurred to me.

"Elise, was there ever a time when Angus Clement was suspected of a crime?"

"Angus really only victimized himself." After a moment, while she absently brushed aside a crumb on the table, she tilted her head in thought. "Well, there was the possibility that he had planted the bomb."

"Bomb?" Drew blurted, so loudly, people at other tables stared at him.

She made a flattening gesture with her hand, as if to tell him to hold down the panic. "Some kids who crawled into the caves out back of Woody's place found it. Scared the hell of out them, let me tell you. But it wasn't put together right, and it would never have detonated. People thought it might have been his work. Nothing came of it, though. No real evidence. Prior to Chief Fricker, the police around here weren't that swift."

Lucy had said the same thing. And those were the people who built a case against her. "Would he have had the expertise to construct a bomb?" I asked.

"Angus was an old rancher. Ranches always contain materials, if someone wants to make use of them. Fertilizer...explosives to blow up tree stumps, boulders and whatnot. It's not a stretch to think of

Angus wanting to extract revenge against the caves' new owner."

Maybe Drew hadn't done such a bad job of selecting a sidekick at that. "When was this, Elise?"

Her vague recollection put it during a time when Woody would still have been in his teens. He lived at his grandmother's house then, on the outskirts of town. I could easily imagine a boy escaping to the privacy of his old room sometimes, to get away from a fussy guardian. Had he been looking out his bedroom window when Angus staggered past? I glanced at the pipe in the photo—was that it, the bomb? I was making a leap, of course. And it didn't matter now, with Angus dead. But that old drunk, Tom, at the memorial service had said Woody was mean to Angus. I couldn't help wondering whether that man's desperate choice had provided Woody with his first taste of extortion.

After I shared that theory with my cohorts, we all sipped our drinks in silence.

I showed Elise the other photo I found, the one of Mayor Baker meeting with the man from the Department of the Interior, and explained the connection.

She nodded. "So the rumors are true. People say our mayor has hoped to make a killing off some land he was fool enough to buy. Well, what can we expect considering the little the town pays him? We were luckier with Chief Fricker."

"Yeah, he's sure a keeper." If only you could find a dictionary for hokey drivel.

"Are you planning on tackling Mr. Mayor, Tracy? Please be careful. Despite his outward bonhomie, he's a shark."

I *knew* he was acting out *West Side Story*. No matter. The Jets were going to win today.

*   *   *

I might have been a bit hasty in predicting a Jets victory. That is, me nailing Mayor Baker.

I cornered him in his office after Drew returned to the motel to check on Dad and Philly. Not all of Mark's charm had evaporated, but he'd injected it with a challenging edge now.

He pushed back across his desk the photo back I'd slapped down before him. "What is it you think you see in this picture? We were there for a poker game."

"Just the two of you?" I asked.

"The others hadn't shown up yet."

"A poker game in a motel room?"

"Gambling's illegal." He flashed a cheeky grin. "Got me there."

I pointed out the man from the Department of the Interior. "It's only a coincidence that this guy is responsible for the trades of National Forest land in the Southwest, and you have land you might like to trade?"

"Is that who he was? He never said. I didn't set up the game." Now he displayed those shark teeth. The mayor was enjoying toying with me.

I felt stymied. But a frontal assault never worked with a shark. I'd have to come at him again later with something sneakier.

"Tracy, if you think you can prove something, have at it. But Woody couldn't."

Interesting to know that Woody had tried.

Mark Baker gave his head a theatrical tilt. "And look what happened to him."

"Is that a threat?"

"Call it a warning."

Round one to the Sharks.

* * *

Back at the motel, Dad reported that Don Cannon had been running a bible study group at his church the night Woody died. I should have figured Drew got it wrong. Don wouldn't have looked so devastated when we saw him at the Cantina if he hadn't just learned of Genevieve's infidelity. At least now we knew he couldn't have done it.

But who had? The more I thought about Mark Baker, the less I considered him a suspect. Of Woody's murder, anyway. He was doubtless a crook, but a killer? Woody probably hadn't dented Baker's armor any more than I did.

For all I knew everyone in this freakin' town might have *wanted* to murder Woody, but I wasn't one bit closer to narrowing in on which one had. And forget about poor Philly's situation.

Thoroughly fed up, I decided that since I couldn't get any lower, this had to be the ideal time to read Dad's letters to Lucy. With no hope of privacy in that suite, I went to read in the car. Since it was getting dark, I used one of the flashlights I'd bought to explore the caves.

"My darling Lucy," the first letter began. With that salutation, I expected something steamy to follow. My gut clenched. I was just an impressionable thirty-five year-old, after all—what I could learn about my father might scar me for life. But that letter didn't keep up the romantic tone. It went on to relate the time I got thrown out of preschool for organizing the other kids. Dad expressed his fear that Beverly Hills wasn't an ideal place to raise a child. Hah! Like I wouldn't have been as rowdy anywhere else.

He went on to describe some shelving he built for the next preschool they'd enrolled me in, to get in good with the teacher, and what a great job he'd done with them. He signed it, "Your eternal suitor, Alec."

I snorted in disbelief at the old fraud. Dad made it sound as if he'd been there when I'd been expelled from that preschool. But he and Mother were off on some location shoot, making a movie together. My nanny and their secretary had handled everything. He'd built the shelving, all right, just as he said, but that came later.

Nosiness finally asserted itself, and I read a couple more letters. They were pretty much the same. He reported my hijinks and shared his fear about me growing up out there in the big bad world. He told Lucy about his ordinary accomplishments, yet never a word about his celebrity, and nothing about Mother. He ended them all with that "eternal suitor" crap.

A glimmer of understanding began to emerge, but I'd have to read more letters before I could say for sure. For now, I stuffed the stack into my purse and snuffed out the flashlight.

Through the Volvo's windshield, I watched Philly drag himself across the parking lot, wearing cook's whites. Dad told us he'd taken a job as the fry cook at The Great American Coffee Shoppe. Another fine eating establishment bites the dust. I'd never known Philly to have a straight job. Why was he doing it? He couldn't hope to earn enough money to pay off his blackmailer. Maybe he just needed a place to hide for much of the day.

From where I sat in the car, I could see the darkened Kontiki Room sign that had troubled me earlier. It looked as it always had. "The Kontiki Room," it read, with "the" and "room" being either higher or lower than "Kontiki." Alongside the lettering, a stick figure guy held a martini glass, from which he would have drunk if it all had been lit with neon and in motion. After lowering the window, I turned the flashlight on and began throwing the beam at the sign, quickly flicking it away. Something struck me in one of those quickie lightings.

I crawled from the car and stared at it once more. Not the whole sign now, just parts of it. Sudden understanding hit me like a runaway train.

I ran to the room, nearly crashing into some dude leaving, and dragged Drew out. "Tracy, the pizza Alec ordered just arrived. It's going to get cold."

That must have been the delivery guy I crashed into. Even if our world had collapsed, it was good that Dad was still arranging for us to eat.

"Drew, in a minute you're not going to care if the pizza fossilizes into orange stone." After positioning him across from the sign, as I had been, I said, "Now put up your hands so they hide part of Woody's sign. Block out the sections of the Kontiki sign reading, 'the' and 'Kon,' as well as 'room.' Now tell me what you see."

With a sigh, he said, "I see 'tiki' and a goofy little figure paused while drinking a cocktail. Tracy, surely this can't matter more than hot pizza."

"Stay with me," I said. "Assume the goofy little figure is male. Then say it again."

"Tiki guy."

"Try it again, Drew. More formally this time."

He shrugged with considerable annoyance. "Tiki man. That's

what Woody wrote on the sign he put over the key hooks in his room."

"Say it slower," I insisted. When Drew glared at me, I said, "Tiki man. T-K-man. T.K. Mann! With this sign, Woody Crier was telling the whole world that he had been T.K. Mann, the country's most notorious airline hijacker!"

CHAPTER TWENTY-NINE

I'd had such a good dream fantasy going about T.K. Mann. Now the revelation that the man in the plane had really been the ultimate creepy guy made me queasy. Forget about my fear that he could also have been my half-sibling—that I *really* couldn't handle.

Drew also seemed to be having trouble digesting the idea. "T.K. Mann? No. Not possible." His head whipped back and forth between the sign and me, until he finally sighed and said, "Though...Woody would have gotten off on hiding the truth in plain sight."

If my theory was right, it must have pained Woody that people didn't know about his great accomplishment. Yet he'd found a way to shout it out, without risking time in the pokey. But if he really had stolen all that money, why was his life spent on the Alec-dole? None of the marked bills paid to the hijacker had ever shown up.

"Trace, let's run this past Elise. She knows more about this place and its people than we do."

The pizza now forgotten, we raced across Tecos. Elise was just locking up Brewed Awakening when we pulled up. We waited until she reopened and placed a latte before each of us before sharing the message Woody had flashed for the world to see. Drew asked Elise if she remembered much about the hijacking.

She took a slow sip, while staring off into space. "Every adult in this country of a certain age knows where they were when T.K. Mann jumped from that plane. But since he landed in this area and was never seen again, folks around these parts *really* remember every aspect of it. For the longest time, we all suspected each other of killing him for the reward. But eventually, when nobody turned in either Mann or the money, we forgot about it."

Drew turned my way. "Were you and Alec here then?"

I said we weren't. "We came a few days later. Everyone here was talking about it, but I was too young to take it in."

"I hate to shoot down your theory, Tracy, but Woody can't have been T.K. Mann," Elise said. "The sophomores got their yearbook photos taken that day. Precisely when that plane was on the runway in Denver for refueling, when the authorities delivered the hijacking money on the cart they wheeled up to the plane. And when T.K. Mann let that one sick hostage leave."

Thanks to the news special, I was familiar with most of it, except for the business about the sick hostage. That part must have aired while I was at the door, jawboning with Loco Pepe's delivery guy.

"During the time when all that went on, Woody was in the high school gym here in Tecos waiting to have his picture taken," Elise insisted.

My BS antennae shot up. Had we made a mistake trusting her?

Drew clearly shared my skepticism. "Elise, I can see you having perfect recall of everything to do with T.K. Mann. But you really expect us to believe you remember which kids got their pictures taken for a yearbook decades ago?"

Elise shrugged sheepishly. "Call me nosy."

Hey, I was the nosy one.

"Lucy came in a week or so earlier and signed a permission slip authorizing Billy Rob to make decisions about Woody's education, or take him out of school, or allow anyone else to. Full parental authority, in effect. It was so unexpected. Everyone in town had always assumed Billy Rob was Woody's father, but Lucy had never confirmed it. Of course, who else could it have been with Woody's looks?"

Who indeed? Who had taken a lifelong interest in him?

"First thing that day, Billy Rob called the office to say he wanted Woody ready to leave school later that morning. I argued against letting him go, since I couldn't guarantee that Woody's photo would have been taken by then. But he snapped that he had every right to pull Woody from school, and I better not get in his way." Elise took another sip of her latte. "Billy Rob had never been a nice guy, unless he wanted something from you, but he sounded nastier than usual then."

"Did you ask him why he needed Woody?" Drew asked.

She nodded. "Called me a nosy bitch when I did. Rude even for him."

We asked Elise to continue her recollection of that day.

"The photographer had some trouble with his equipment, and we fell behind schedule. To keep the kids quiet, I asked one of the teachers to roll a TV into the gym. We all watched the image of that plane on the tarmac in Denver. We saw the bags of cash piled on the luggage cart that was left beside the plane, as well as the passenger sent to retrieve those bags. And eventually, we watched that same passenger deplane."

"What about Woody?" Drew asked.

"Woody was in the gym during the entire time when the plane was on the tarmac. I'm absolutely certain of that. He left school precisely when Billy Rob demanded—right after the aircraft took off again, just about the time when T.K. Mann jumped from it. Before he had his photo taken. You can check that yearbook—his picture isn't in it."

While I rolled all that around in my noggin, I asked, "Billy Rob came for him when he said he would?"

Elise flushed. "Well, no. He sent someone else he authorized to pick Woody up."

"Who?" Drew asked.

"Alice Royce, his wife." She bowed her head. "I considered challenging it. Lucy had given Billy Rob complete permission, though it was highly irregular. But Woody, who'd always been a troublemaker, was more antsy and argumentative than usual that day. Frankly, I was pretty tired of the Criers and Royces by that point, so I let him go." She shrugged again. "Later, I thought I should not have been so cavalier with a student, even if his own mother had been. I worried that I'd made a mistake. Yet Woody returned to school within a couple of days, more arrogant and aggressive with the other kids than ever, but seemingly none the worst for his outing."

We considered her story in silence. Without a word to either of us, Drew rose and went outside to the car.

"What about Lucy?" I asked. "Did you ask her why she needed

to give Billy Rob that permission?"

Elise rolled her eyes. "I did, but she just gave me one of her foolish lies. I don't remember what she said, but you know what Lucy was like."

The prison library director? Yeah, I knew.

Drew came back carrying his laptop, which we'd brought along, but had yet to take from the car. "We need to research the hijacking," he said, while setting it up on the table.

"WiFi on Route 66?" I groaned when I saw the browser load. "Drew, we should be doing this research in a library."

He ignored me, while Elise snapped, "Tracy, haven't we already discussed this Luddite quality you bring to the Mother Road?"

"Okay." I didn't really want to have to go to the library. I couldn't get a latte there.

Google turned up a few million sites on T.K. Mann and the hijacking. The urban legend had never died, but with the anniversary coming up, and the TV special that had kicked off my dreams, interest had spiked.

While Drew researched the various sites, I asked, "Elise, what did Billy Rob do for a living? I don't think I ever knew."

"He was a handyman, small-time crook, and he bought and sold motorcycles."

I chewed my lip. "T.K. Mann escaped from his landing place on a motorcycle"

"Lots of people ride bikes, Tracy. I swear to you that Woody was in the gym when T.K. Mann got his money. Woody didn't leave the gym before the plane took off again."

I downed the last of my latte. "But Billy Rob wasn't in the gym. He didn't even come for Woody," I said slowly.

"No, but then he really didn't fit the description of T.K. Mann that most of the passengers gave. They described him as a smaller, more compact man, not someone built like Billy Rob." Elise rose and gathered our cups. "It was the people on the ground who gave inconsistent descriptions."

Drew reviewed for us what he learned online. Elise was right about the times of the critical points in the hijacking. "The FBI warned the public that T.K. Mann was armed and dangerous, and that nobody should try to apprehend him. Nobody did, though sightings were called in all over New Mexico and into Arizona and Texas."

Drew went on to relate what I remembered from the news show I'd seen, and what Elise partially confirmed. On the ground where Mann was said to have landed, before he took off on the motorcycle, people reported seeing a smallish man in good shape. Others later spoke of a large, angular guy, while some described someone younger and fleshier. In all of the sightings, T.K. Mann was said to be wearing his oversized helmet, a stretchy skin-hugging garment in black, while riding a black motorcycle with no other distinguishing marks. He was seen riding in three different states, going in different directions—all at the same time.

"Eyewitnesses are notoriously unreliable," Drew said. "Ask any trial lawyer."

I walked to the front window.

"There's no way to say which of the witnesses got it right," he added.

I stared out the window, unseeing. "What if they *all* got it right?"

Drew asked, "Elise, did you spike her latte?"

I returned to the table. "What if T.K. Mann wasn't one man, but two or three? What if they all dressed the same and used identical motorcycles to create confusion?"

"They did that," Elise said. "Created confusion, I mean."

"It could work," Drew said. "One or two would have alibis, and they would all make the cops run around in circles. But who was the third man, in addition to Woody and his father?"

Elise brought her empty cardboard cup down hard on the tabletop. "The heck with the third man. Where's the money? Where has it been all these years?"

I nodded. "That is the question."

"I just remembered the lie Lucy told me when she gave Billy Rob permission to take Woody from school," Elise said with a snap of her fingers. "She told me her son was going out to make history."

Maybe that one time Lucy Liar had actually told the truth.

CHAPTER THIRTY

Drew went to dinner with Dad and Philly, leaving me alone in the suite. I begged off because I couldn't stand sitting at the same table with two guys trying so hard to ignore each other. What happened when they were alone? What if someone needed the salt? I couldn't even remember why they were fighting. Was Philly just trying to distance himself from Dad, to make sure his troubles didn't touch his friend?

I also felt too frustrated to eat. I'd let everyone down, starting with Lucy. She begged me not to look into her son's murder, but I couldn't let it go. Now I felt certain I'd stumbled onto the secret she was so desperate to hide.

I returned to what Elise had told us. How, when Lucy gave Billy Rob permission to take Woody from school, she'd said her son was going out to make history. Had she known Billy Rob and Woody were planning to hijack that plane? Would she really have let her lover risk her young son's life?

I knew for most people there wouldn't be any doubt. Lucy seemed so obviously in cahoots with Billy Rob. But the truth wasn't nearly as apparent to me. For someone who told such outrageous lies herself, Lucy never seemed to expect anyone else to fib to her. And she bought into some whoppers. Especially from Billy Rob. Even as a kid, I could see through the lies he'd fed her, but Lucy never did. She always looked so devastated when the truth finally came out.

Was that the key to Billy Rob's murder? Perhaps there never was another woman. Maybe Lucy believed Billy Rob was taking their son out to perform some noble task, only to discover he had made Woody into one of the country's most notorious criminals. She might have lost it when she discovered how he'd corrupted their son.

That could also be the key to her request that I leave the murder alone. After failing to protect Woody from Billy Rob, maybe she wanted to make up for that now by sending Woody to his grave with an unsullied reputation.

And hadn't I made a mess of it? Granted, I hadn't yet told anyone but Drew and Elise what I'd surmised about Woody and Billy Rob, but how long could I keep it quiet?

I seemed to be making a regular practice of letting people down. Look at Philly. I felt awful about not wrapping up his troubles. Maybe that was really why I didn't want to sit across a restaurant table from him—I couldn't bear to see him looking so dejected. But short of torturing him until he revealed what he was hiding, I didn't know how to get to the truth. Not here, among these strangers.

I wasn't too fed up with this rotten little town so filled with secrets.

And by not nabbing Philly's blackmailer, I'd also let Drew down. While he always bitched about my poking my nose into the crimes that fell into my lap, the one time he wanted me to solve something, I hadn't been able to.

No question, my sense of self had taken a hit on this freakin' road. If I never saw Route 66 again, it would be too soon.

When Drew returned from dinner, he found me sitting on the bed in our room, with my chin propped on my knees, still stewing in frustrated silence.

"Hey, babe, we missed you," he said. "You'd have cracked up over the lengths to which Alec and Philly went to avoid each other."

Not likely.

"Alec brought you back a burrito."

"Throw it away!" No way would I risk another dream meeting with T.K. Mann now that I'd figured out that Woody had been the one flashing me the toothy grin. As for the sexual tension we'd generated, gag me.

Drew plopped down beside me. "Not hungry, huh?"

Come to think of it, I was hungry, but not for food. I stretched my hand out, and slowly walked my fingers up Drew's thigh.

His brown eyes brightened. "Hmmm. Does that mean what I

think it does? What about the peeper who could be watching at this moment."

I sank back into the pillows behind me, drawing Drew to me. "Let him see how it's done."

This wasn't one of those gentle lovemaking sessions, in which someone could practically recite romantic poetry, it was closer to a nuclear power plant explosion. Vaguely, I remembered hearing the sound of a phone ringing somewhere in the suite. But I was too intent on the dance my tongue did on Drew's tonsils to pay attention to it, while all of his focus seemed directed to separating me from my clothes.

Somehow we shed sufficient garments and climbed beneath the covers. The only sounds I heard then were my own heartbeats pounding in my ears, along with some grunts and groans, and a whole lot of heavy breathing.

"Oh, yeah," I said with a moan, when Drew's finger brushed a critical spot. "That's what I mean."

Before he could repeat it, the door to our room flew open. I gasped and jerked away, yanking the covers over my naked breasts.

Dad stumbled into the room, with his hand plastered over his eyes. "Not seeing anything."

I know I often say I'm going to be scarred for life, but this time, I truly meant it. Talk about an instant turn-off.

"Kids, get dressed and get out here now." He turned to leave.

"Dad, what...?" I shouted after him.

"Tracy, unless you want to join Lucy in the slammer, you'll quit fooling around and get out here." He shut the door behind him.

How did he know we'd been fooling around? Wasn't there any privacy in that motel? The idea of me spending my life as Lucy's cellmate simply flew out my ears.

We stumbled out into the sitting room, dressed, though I wasn't sure we each only wore our own clothes. The first thing that struck me as bizarre was that Dad and Philly had their heads together, as if they were making plans. What brought that about?

"Kids!" Dad shouted. "Something's happened, something bad."

Everything that happened in this wretched place was bad.

What could be worse than Woody being murdered, or Philly being blackmailed? Worse than me having to assume the role of a functioning adult?

Dad said, "Tracy has to go on the lam, and, Drew, you need to go along to protect her."

Hallelujah! All I heard was "Tracy has to go on the lam." After that, it was just noise. Going on the lam had long been one of my great fantasies—it didn't matter what brought it about. To have the chance to go on the lam, I'd gladly suffer *coitus interruptus*. Who was I kidding? To have any excuse to leave Tecos, I'd take a vow of celibacy.

Drew might have sputtered something at that point, but I couldn't say. I raced back to our room, yanked our suitcases from under the bed and began tossing our belongings into them. I intentionally didn't ask Dad *why* he thought I should go on the run. What if his reason turned out to be something totally dumb-ass? Did I want reality spoiling my only excuse to take a break from Tecos and all the problems it had dumped on us? No, I did not.

"Tracy, stop packing," Drew shouted.

Not only didn't I stop, I didn't even slow down.

With a worried sigh, Dad said, "Martha called with some serious news."

That got my attention. Mother had never even acknowledged our excursions to Tecos because that would have meant acknowledging Lucy. Even after Lucy went to prison, she remained a non-person to Mother. Mother's calling now was unexpected enough to draw me back to the sitting room.

"Remember our neighbor, Myrna?" Dad asked me.

How could I forget her? She had a walk-in freezer where we'd once stowed Mother's dead boy toy until we could decide what to do with him.

"Myrna's son-in-law is in the FBI. Seems the Fed told Myrna that they were investigating Tracy for some charges that could send her to prison, and Myrna passed it onto Martha."

With a nod to Dad, Philly suddenly raced out the suite's main door. I heard his shoes shuffling away in the parking lot.

"What kind of charges?" Drew demanded.

Dad shrugged, clearly annoyed at Drew's continued interruptions. "I don't know, and we don't have time to figure it out. Now Philly and I have planned everything. You'll hit the road in Woody's RV. We'll exchange its real license plate for one of those old plates in Lucy's apartment, just to make sure the cops can't trace it. Philly's gone to get one."

Okay, that wasn't dumb-ass. Crazy, but not dumb-ass. Seeing Dad had everything in hand, I returned to the bedroom to continue packing. Running from the law required a wide range of clothing options.

"Tracy, stop packing!" Drew roared again. "Alec, we're not going anywhere. If this is true, we have to arrange for Tracy to turn herself in for questioning. I'm still an Officer of the Court—I can't be a party to her running."

While deciding where we should go, I did spare a thought to the reactions of my nearest and dearest. None of them seemed to question that I might be wanted on Federal charges. The idea that this was just a nutty mix-up didn't seem to occur to anyone.

Dad didn't even react to Drew's suggestion. "Kids, leave your cell phones here and take Woody's iPhone." A thought flashed across his face. "As soon as you can, get yourself a burn phone."

A burn phone? The last man on earth to use one knew cell phone street lingo?

Dad's face brightened with pride. "I got to say that once when I played the aging detective brought out of retirement on one of the *Law & Order* franchises."

Neither of my parents would know anything if it weren't for scripts.

Dad reined in his focus once more. "Drew, you should probably have Woody's driver's license, in case you need to show an ID anywhere."

A huffy Drew protested that nobody would believe he was Woody, while Dad insisted that no one actually looked that closely at license photos.

But then Dad turned to me and whispered, "Another reason why

I don't have a driver's license—it wouldn't do my career any good to have a bad photo of me floating around out there."

So much for nobody looking that closely at them.

Drew continued to struggle against the tide of Dad's plans. "No!" Drew shouted. "We're not going…" Nobody paid any attention to him.

My own excitement had built to outright giddiness. It was finally fun-time again!

Philly scooted in with the real license plate from the RV, which he put aside. Dad raced into his room and came back with Woody's phone and his wallet, which he stuffed into Drew's pants pockets. Drew kept shouting and sputtering, of course, but even as he did, Dad and Philly carried our luggage to the camper.

I made a brief stop at the Volvo, where I scooped up Lucy's albums and my lunch pail, since I never cruised Route 66 without it, and I checked my purse to make sure Dad's letters to Lucy were still there. Reading material for the road. I was glad to see that by the time I rejoined the rest of them, Drew was seated behind the RV wheel, reduced to muttering to himself.

Dad pressed some cash into my hand. "Don't use your credit cards. Pay with cash, or use Woody's cards. I haven't cancelled those accounts yet. And don't call us here till you buy a new phone. Until you do, we'll work out some arrangement with your mother."

Before I knew it we were on our way, living out one of my lifelong fantasies, to be on the run from the law. And also living out my more urgent new desire, to leave that blasted town. The only downside to the whole exercise was that while we escaped Tecos, we hadn't escaped the freakin' Mother Road. But finally, I thought for sure, I was outrunning my problems.

When would I learn?

CHAPTER THIRTY-ONE

While steering that land-boat down the highway, Drew said with a groan, "I can't believe I'm on the lam—again."

True, this wasn't his first time. Lucky stiff. Back when the police thought he'd killed his boss, and other prisoners kept beating the crap outta him, we busted him out of custody and hid him away in an unexpected place. I'd always envied him that experience. Now I would have one of my own, without the concern of actually being wanted by the law.

I was still buzzing inside with excitement, but Drew had been griping since we crossed the Texas state line. The penalty for harboring a semi-fugitive must be greater when you cross into other states, because he really cranked up the whining.

"We're actually on the run," he muttered for the thousandth time.

"So felon-up, dude, and quit your bitching."

"Right. It must be my fate to live a criminal life."

First meditating, then a providing universe, and now fate. Enough of the cosmic crap. "Oh, unwad your knickers, Drew. I'm not wanted by anybody." I wasn't sure whether it flattered or offended me that he bought so easily into the idea that I was. Flattered, for sure

"Then…what about the source of this little excursion?"

I shrugged. "Either Mother wanted to create some drama for reasons of her own, or Myrna decided to yank Mother's chain. But I swear to you, Drew, that while it pains me to admit it, I'm as pure as that white stuff that falls from the winter sky. You should know that—we've been together pretty continuously since you stopped working as a lawyer."

He snorted. "Trace, you can wedge nefarious deeds into the mere moments it takes me to sneeze."

"True," I said, flushing with pride. Once again it didn't seem like the right time to tell him I'd gone to see Lucy. I didn't want him to start watching me during sneezes.

"I don't get it, honey. If you knew the FBI wasn't interested in you, why are we running?"

I shuddered. "Anything to get a break from that ratty little town."

Drew laughed so hard, he almost lost control of the wheel. "So Route 66 disenchantment has finally set in, huh?"

"Happy?"

He hesitated, before shaking his head no. "Nah. I hate to see anyone's young dreams shattered. Besides, since I discovered Brewed Awakening, I didn't find Tecos half-bad."

Funny, I couldn't remember the last time I found it even half-good.

Slowly, I began to dribble out the cause of my funk the night before. How guilty I felt for what I hadn't managed to accomplish for Philly. Then, before I knew it, I blabbed about visiting Lucy, and her unexpected request.

"You went to see Lucy, huh? See what I mean about what you can accomplish even under my watchful eye?" He chuckled. "It is odd the way she warned you away from looking into Woody's death. You'd think his mother would want justice for him." He stewed in silence for a moment. "You must be right, babe. She's trying to keep something under wraps."

I shared my theory that Lucy hadn't understood the kind of history Billy Rob was taking their kid out to make, to use her words, and popped Billy Rob when she found out. "And now I've stumbled onto the truth, when she thinks I promised to leave it alone." I sighed. I'd never been a believer in suffering guilt, but I was getting way too good at it.

"We're going have to find a place to settle in for the night," Drew said. "Any idea where we might find a campground?"

How would I know? Did he think I was sneaking off to camp during those moments he devoted to sneezing? But this was Route 66—you can't move three feet in any direction without stumbling across a campground or a tacky museum. Usually, they're one in the same.

Woody's iPhone, which I'd propped between us on the console, rang. I carried it back to the motor home's living area, where I stretched out on a built-in sofa, placing a throw pillow under my head, before answering it. The unidentified caller was Mother. Dad must have given her this number.

"Anything new on those charges they're planning to file against me?" I asked, knowing I'd get more out of her if I played along, rather than calling her on the silly lie.

"Not a thing. Myrna's become a clam, damn her. But maybe now you and your father will listen to my warnings when I tell you to stay away from that ghastly place."

In what universe could never having uttered a word about somewhere be classified as a warning? But anything was possible in Martha-land. I adjusted the pillow under my head.

"For the life of me, I can't imagine why that town continues to hold any appeal for either of you." The grunt she ended with belied that sentence. She thought she understood its appeal too well.

"Mother, listen, I need you to do something for me."

"Darling, I'll do anything for my little crook."

She might be the most reality-challenged woman on the planet, but it's not everyone's mother who lends that kind of support. I told her about Lucy's designs. "You're not going to believe how talented she was. I'm flabbergasted. She understood how fabric would drape on the body, and how to flatter any figure. I want you to show them to some of your designer friends."

"Why would I do that?" she asked in a voice that could flash freeze a side of beef.

"Trust me, you're going to want one of everything for yourself."

"If you think I'd wear something that woman…" Her sigh dissolved into silence.

While Mother had never been a model of fidelity, the unspoken told me how much Dad's relationship with Lucy had irked her. Come to think of it, she hadn't tumbled for a new guy for a while. Perhaps she finally realized what a keeper she had, and now, finally, couldn't bear to lose him.

"Mother, listen…I've read Dad's letters to Lucy."

"He *wrote* to her?" she demanded with indignant outrage. "Oh, after she went to prison, you mean."

I let that go without correcting her assumption. But I noticed she knew more about Lucy than she let on.

"It was really not what you think." Not what I'd thought, either.

In shifting the pillow, I exposed something below it that scratched my neck. I yanked whatever it was out from under the pillow and threw it to the floor.

"A wise wife would do this for her husband's friend," I went on. As if anyone had ever applied the word *wise* to Mother. "And I do mean *friend*."

"If you think I care what—or who—that old goat gets into, you're sadly mistaken," she said with a sniff. "Old men can be so tedious anyway. You know I really prefer to rob the cradle."

And old crones who foist robbing on the cradle aren't tedious? Please tell me I'm adopted.

My continued assurances about the nature of Dad and Lucy's relationship must have seeped in, though, because eventually, she promised to think about what I asked her to do for Lucy. I'd find a mail center somewhere and ship the albums off to her. Once she saw them, I felt sure she'd help. If Dad was right about Lucy's cancer, with a little success, maybe the end of her life would have more meaning. Who knows? If I made Lucy the most famous designer in the hoosegow, she might forget that I broke my non-promise.

After I clicked off the phone, I looked at the scratchy thing I'd pulled from under the pillow. A burlap bag. Funny, it looked the same as the ones I'd found in the cave, only cleaner. I shook it, but nothing came out. How odd that I'd stumbled across another one. Did they sell them somewhere in Tecos? What did people use them for?

I started to rise, but a realization caused me to sink back onto the couch. The money paid to T.K. Mann had been packed in plain burlap bags, which he'd transferred to his gigantic backpack before jumping out of the plane. And now we had stumbled across a few burlap bags of the same design.

If I was right that Woody, Billy Rob, and some unknown person were the combined T.K. Mann, the caves would have been a good place to hunker down after that little performance of appearing simultaneously in multiple states. An ideal spot to hide the loot, too. I could see the bags being left behind there, but why here? Was it just a souvenir of the high point in Woody's life that he kept around to relive his moment of glory, like the café's neon sign? If he had the bag, what had he done with the money?

When the RV went into a turn, I fell to the side. After I pulled myself back into a sitting position, I glanced out the picture window along the side of the camper and saw that Drew was pulling into a campground. A sign we drove past directed us to the office, and also indicated that, "IDs will be checked."

How unusual. From what my friends told me, campgrounds weren't like European hotels, where you had to turn in your passport. They said they never had to show anything. Some told me they paid with a credit card online, or tucked the cash in an envelope stuck to a pole next to their assigned spot. Mostly they never saw anyone in charge. I knew Drew would grumble, but I secretly cheered that we'd turned up at the one campground that would force him to use Woody's ID. My fun quotient just shot up another notch.

I slipped into the passenger seat as Drew brought the RV to a stop before a small building with a red tile roof. He turned to me. "Since you're not really wanted by the law, I can check-in with my own ID, can't I?"

"Aw, Drew, that isn't playing the game. Besides, Dad kept your wallet."

In a panic, he patted his pockets, and pulled out the only wallet in them, Woody's.

With a sigh, he climbed from the cab, clutching Woody's ID, as he headed for the office door. I skipped along behind him, not hiding my not-actually-sought face at all. I wanted Drew to play the game, not me.

After confirming that they had a vacancy and telling him how much it would be, a scrawny little woman at the check-in desk, as tanned as an Egyptian mummy, asked Drew for his license. "Since 9/11, we take security seriously."

Drew squared his shoulders for the ordeal, but he opened Woody's wallet and passed over the license. Would she buy it? Drew was a hot guy in his thirties, while Woody had been ten years older and had looked like a toad.

The woman glanced from the photo, to Drew, and back again. "You sure clean up good, Wood-man, but you should sue the motor vehicle folks over this photo."

So much for security.

I'd confiscated Drew's cash when we tossed his wallet under the table at the café, after finding Woody's body. Since he was so insistent that I become more responsible, I intentionally kept it all. I'm nothing if not hopelessly adolescent. So, as with everything we'd bought lately, it fell to me to pass some moolah over to the burnished campground gatekeeper.

Back outside, while Drew maneuvered the RV into our assigned space, I glanced out the windows. As a first-time camper, it surprised me to see how close we were to our neighbors. There was an even larger RV blocking the view to one side of us, while two small tents filled the opposite space. Finding that view better, I watched our tenting neighbors for a moment. There were two of them, a man and a woman, seated on the ground around a small barbeque grill. Parked beside their colorful tents was an old rusted pickup truck.

I spotted their red hair first. Flaming red that they shared, which flared brightly in the sunshine. How odd that I'd see two redheaded pairs of people in only a few days, first the Clement twins back in Tecos, and now these strangers. After a moment, I realized there weren't four such people, after all, only one "Pair."

Hallelujah! The mystery gods were once again working in my favor.

I flew out the RV the instant it came to a stop and rushed to their campsite. They were the Clement twins, all right. Roughing it on a west Texas campground, not showing off in a small New Mexican town, with a wildly impractical Italian sports car. Kitty, the girl, looked up first. Recognition dawned on her face, and then apprehension. The boy, Sean, sputtered something incomprehensible.

I cut him off. "Can it, pal. It's time we talked."

CHAPTER THIRTY-TWO

MEMORIES OF ROUTE 66
LUCY

*A*ll those years she'd spent running the café, the ones when she played around with Billy Rob...they felt so distant now, they might have been part of someone else's life.

Lucy had always been a foolish girl, never studying, always boy-crazy. She thought success would just find her somehow, despite the bad choices she made. She had a major motion picture star offering her the world, but all she hankered for was a married, out-of-work bike mechanic. Not that Alec meant what he always hinted at—he was devoted to Martha, even if he didn't always realize it himself. If Lucy had set her mind to it, though, she might have made him forget his glamorous wife. But then, she might have done a lot of things.

Maybe it was just the regrets that made that time feel so far away. If Lucy let them, the regrets would choke her. She still felt bad about how she and Billy Rob had treated his wife Alice. If she could, Lucy would try to make up for that.

Mostly, though, she regretted that she hadn't been a better mother to Woody. He'd deserved someone who really cared how he turned out. She'd always intended to take him in hand, to make him do his homework, treat other boys better. But she'd been too busy sneaking around with Billy Rob. She figured she'd get to it tomorrow. Only, before she knew it, all her tomorrows would be spent behind bars.

She tried to make up for it that night, the one that changed all of their lives. When she came back down to the café from her rooms upstairs and found Billy Rob, and realized what had happened, she did what any good mother would have done to protect her son. To make up for never knowing how to be the kind of mother Woody had deserved.

Now she'd taken one more act, which she'd already set in motion. The last thing she could do—that anyone could do—to make things right for her poor boy.

CHAPTER THIRTY-THREE

O nce the Clement twins understood that there might be some overlap between their interests and mine, they didn't seem to mind talking to me. They weren't dressed as eccentrically as they had been at Woody's memorial service. And they weren't nearly as wound up. But they still had the distracting habit of finishing each other's thoughts.

"Gramps didn't lose the caves in any poker game," Kitty said.

"There was a card game," Sean added. "And the guy who took the property from him did play with them."

It was Kitty's turn again. "But it was just a friendly, low-stakes game. Penny ante poker."

Then Sean's. "Anyway, Gramps was the big winner that night."

Being with them still made me feel like I was watching a tennis match, but it moved slower now than the frantic pace they'd maintained at the service.

We three gathered together in the clearing beside their tents. Drew was back in the RV, making coffee. We'd stopped at a grocery store earlier to stock up on some grub. Since we really didn't need to avoid detection, I hadn't bothered to buy a prepaid cell phone and just stuck with Woody's iPhone.

"So what did happen, guys?" I asked.

They exchanged anxious glances. I sensed they'd never shared this story with anyone outside of their family. Kitty's head hung low, staring at her hands in her lap, while Sean took the lead.

"After the poker game that night, 'the young thug' who sat in with the regular crowd—to use our grandfather's description—followed Gramps out to his truck. He threw Gramps against the fender and demanded that he sign the deed to the caves over to him."

That was it? The story their family had kept secret. "Surely, your grandfather didn't agree just like that."

"No, not even when this guy had threatened the rest of the family." The twins exchanged another pained look. "Gramps only agreed after the threat was carried out." He turned to his sister. "Show her, Kitty."

Kitty held up her left hand. She was the one with the shorter pinky. When I saw that at the service, I assumed one of them had been born that way. Now I felt my own breathing become shallow, as I sensed things were going to get way too real for my liking.

"The guy took Mom and Kitty hostage at gunpoint, and then he chopped off the end of Kitty's finger right in front of our mother. We were only babies at the time, so we don't really remember it."

Kitty's head hung even lower now. And she stared at the hands resting in her lap. I suspected she remembered it better than her twin thought, that she'd never forget it. I tried not to shudder.

"After that, Gramps gave in. Never even told the police. How can the cops protect you from someone who wouldn't even try to hide his identity when he cut off a baby's finger?" Sean looked around absently, almost as if merely talking about the man who had assaulted his sister so long ago frightened him even now. "That was one dangerous dude."

Did the dangerous dude have a sidekick? Had Woody been his cohort, or even just an onlooker to this extortion? He'd learned it somewhere.

Sean shrugged. "Gramps was never the same after that. None of us were."

Kitty finally spoke up. "The strange part was that the thug had Gramps transfer the deed to the caves to some other name, not his own."

"So?" I said. "Maybe he owned money to someone, and that was how he paid his debt."

"Could be," Sean said, though he sounded doubtful.

"Another funny thing...he told people he won it in a poker game, rather than mauling an infant for it," Kitty said with a bitter bite. "Later, the ownership of the caves passed to the California governor, and *he* told the same story, about winning it in a game."

"That doesn't surprise me. He is a politician." For the moment.

"Whoever sold him the property told a colorful story, and he appropriated it as his own."

"I guess it could have happened that way." Sean still sounded doubtful.

I was missing something here, something critical, but I couldn't put my finger on it. I set the question aside and turned the conversation toward another mystery.

"What is it you two have been doing in Tecos, with the Ferrari, and making offers on Woody's restaurant?" I looked at their old pickup. "You can't really afford it, can you?"

Sean snorted. "No way. The car, that was just to make it seem like we had money to burn. And the way we dressed—well, we did that so people would believe we were eccentric. Who else but a couple of wackos would want Woody's restaurant?"

I still didn't get it. "Why put on a charade at all?"

"It was just a smokescreen, Tracy." Kitty chewed her fingernail. "By continuing to hang around Woody's place and appear to check it out, we were able to watch the activity at the caves. We'd always hoped to approach the governor and ask him to give them back to us, not a couple of states that didn't deserve them. Not much chance of that, huh?"

They were sure dreamers. If they were telling the truth, that is. They could have been the people the governor heard shouting that day. They could even have been Philly's blackmailers. Just because they didn't like the idea of anyone extorting their family didn't mean they wouldn't do it to someone else. Then again, they might have been looking for a way to hold up the governor.

I remembered something I hadn't asked. "Let's go back to the story of the guy taking the property from your grandfather. What name was the deed transferred into?"

Sean said, "Tag Kowalski."

I gave my head an absent shake. "Never heard of him." There was still too much here that didn't make sense.

"But you do know the thug who made Gramps sign the property over to Kowalski, Tracy," Kitty said.

"I do?"

"You were only a kid, too, so maybe you don't remember. But his name was Terry Kennedy. Gramps said Terry was some guy who hung around Tecos, until your dad hired him and swept him out of town."

Terry? Dad's miserable assistant? There are no coincidences, I reminded myself, as I tried once again to make sense of the crazy happenings that kept coming at me on Route 66. My brain almost burst.

* * *

When I stepped back into the RV, I found Drew readying a tray filled with mugs. "Hey, the powwow broke up already? I was just about to bring over the coffee."

I grabbed one of the mugs on the tray and chugged the hot coffee. It wasn't up to Brewed Awakening standards, but maybe the caffeine would jumpstart my feeble brain. I slumped onto that built-in sofa, but the burlap bag still lay on the floor beside my feet. I jumped up and stomped on it, before collapsing back against the throw cushions.

"Soooo…the conversation with the Clement twins didn't go well," Drew said.

Slowly, I let it dribble out, the story the twins had shared. "I told Dad that Terry was a rat, but he never believed me. He cut off a baby's finger!" I hadn't considered him *that* rotten. "And for what? At best, to pay off a debt, or at worst, to give his booty away."

And even though I wanted to dismiss my suspicions about the twins themselves, because I had come to like them, they also raised their share of questions. But then, who didn't?

Drew sat beside me, and I let my head fall onto his shoulder. "I'm really starting to hate the revenge Route 66 is taking on me."

"It'll get better, babe." Drew gave me a comforting kiss on the temple. I sank into him.

Before I knew it, his lips had found my neck, and the kisses he was leaving there spoke more of lust than comfort. It occurred to me that we had been interrupted the last time we tried this. I threw my arms around him.

And *that* was the moment someone chose to rap heavily on the RV door.

I pulled away instantly. "Jeez, it's usually only my parents who can meet a cue like that."

Sean Clement began shouting through the door. "Tracy! Come quickly. We've just heard something awful on the radio."

Drew jumped up and yanked the door open.

"You've got to leave here now and find a place to hide out." Sean said, urgency making him breathless.

What? Again?

His voice dropped to a whisper. "The FBI is looking for you."

"For real?" I asked. Strangers don't *keep* making up the same goofy stories.

Sean's head bounced up and down like a bobble doll.

So it was actually true. I was a wanted woman. But that was absolutely crazy and, sadly, not as much fun as I'd hoped.

CHAPTER THIRTY-FOUR

W e went on the lam again, for real this time, but only after debating whether we should leave the safety of the campground at all.

"Drew, the woman who checked us in saw my face," I said. "For all we know my mug is being flashed on TV screens from coast-to-coast. She could be calling the Feds right now."

Was there a reward for me? Hey, maybe I could collect it.

"Honey, she thought I looked close enough to Woody's license photo to believe I was him. I don't think she'd recognize you if you walked up to her and bit her nose."

Nope, he wasn't cheating me of another fleeing-from-the law-excursion. Yet even after we made the decision to leave, we argued over which direction to go in. Drew insisted we should head west, going back the way we came.

"West? Are you nuts? Eventually, we'll hit our house. They might think to look for me there."

Drew tugged awkwardly at his earlobe. "I was kinda thinking we'd head to Albuquerque or somewhere that has a Bureau field office. Trace, you have to turn yourself in."

"No freakin' way. If they're so smart, let them find me." How smart could they be if they thought I was a criminal?

We glared at each other, Mr. I'm-not-anal-anymore and me.

After Sean dropped his bombshell, we all spent a little time huddled around their radio, until we caught another report. The Feds were definitely looking for me—or someone named Tracy Eaton—something I never thought I'd say. Unfortunately, the report didn't give any information about the charges hanging over my head. Cops often like to hold that information back.

"Drew, the universe provided us with this fine set of wheels—did you ever think of it that way? Why would we have this moving house if we weren't meant to use it?"

By that point, he'd nearly torn his earlobe off.

"I swear to you that I didn't do anything wrong." This had to be the first time I swore to something when it was absolutely true. Not surprisingly, he seemed reluctant to believe me. "Look, they'll figure it out and move onto whoever they're really looking for." In the meantime, I'd have more fun. I'd had so little lately, I was going into withdrawal.

We compromised. I agreed to head west, and he promised to think about not turning me in. Eventually, we got underway. This RV, unlike many that I'd seen, didn't have either a TV or a satellite receiver. Maybe that was why Woody never used it. As we drove along, we tried listening to the radio. But the trouble with moving through large stretches of open country is that radio stations are few and far between. The chance of catching them during national news broadcasts further reduced the odds.

For a while, that gave the whole jaunt a surreal quality. But eventually, reality, that pesky devil, broke in.

A snippet from one report we happened to catch advised their listeners, "Ms. Eaton is wanted in connection with a case associated with one of America's Ten Most Wanted."

Whoa! The FBI's Ten Most Wanted? Now I knew for sure that this had to be a case of mistaken identity. There had to be another Tracy Eaton out there, with a far more adventurous life than mine. Still, despite my determination to keep it light and fun, I felt my first shiver of panic.

Then the confusion set in. Other reports put me in places I'd actually been, like my home in Chatsworth, California, and Flagstaff, Arizona, and Tecos, New Mexico. But some reports placed me in Las Vegas and Laughlin, neither of which I'd seen in years, as well as Camp Verde and Prescott, Arizona, towns I'd never been in.

Now and then we also heard reports that Governor Tandy, with his parole officer's permission, had returned to California to face his critics. I remembered how tight Tandy and his parole officer had been. Getting time off from his community service and leaving his ankle-monitoring device behind must have been a snap. Though a California appearance schedule hadn't been announced, it was expected soon. While I felt vaguely sorry for Tandy, I didn't have enough energy to worry about him.

We pulled into a motel that claimed to provide WiFi. Drew carried his laptop into the motel coffee shop, hoping to find an online report. But the motel's Internet connection was down, so he trudged back to the RV in defeat.

He'd been driving since we set out, but I couldn't stand the passivity of the passenger role anymore. When he left again in search of a hot spot, I slipped into the driver's seat. I caught another radio report while he was gone—this one advised listeners that someone named Stuart Athers was also sought in connection with my unspecified crimes. That just proved how nuts this mix-up was. Who the hell was Stuart Athers?

I didn't tell Drew about the report he'd missed. I knew panic had to be pushing him toward outright hysteria. I didn't want him forcing me to drive to the next police station with my hands raised over my head. Besides, keeping secrets was my way, and it had never made more sense than now.

Proving how well I knew him, over the next mile or so, he said, "Trace, this is getting downright scary."

Drew Eaton, master of understatement.

"Do you realize every police department in the country has probably been alerted about you?"

Just when you think you've heard everything.

"What if some small town Barney Fife decides to plug you full of holes, rather than ask questions."

Before I could address that problem, Woody's iPhone rang. Dad's name showed on the Caller ID.

"Dad, what are you doing calling me?" I demanded when Drew put it on speaker. He was the one who told us to buy prepaid cells, something I hadn't been wise enough to do. "Some phones have GPS, you know."

"Gips?" Dad shouted, as he usually did when talking on the phone. "What in the name of Jiminy Cricket is a Gip?"

How could I expect a guy who thought that volume improved

transmission to know what GPS meant?

"Doesn't matter anyway." His voice broke in a sob. "It's Philly, honey. He's been kidnapped. Kidnapper wants ten million bucks in cash before he'll let Philly go."

"No!" I gasped in shock. This caper went from bad to crazy-worst.

Unable to make any sense of it, I reacted in the only way I could—I pressed harder on the accelerator. I cursed myself for having seized a self-indulgent excuse to leave in the first place. I didn't care now if it meant risking arrest—I *had* to be there. Nothing mattered but Dad and Philly, and finding some way to get us all out of this deepening mire.

"Hang on, Dad," I promised. "We're on our way."

Too bad I still didn't have a clue how to fix any of it.

* * *

The miles sped past unseen. During one particularly quiet stretch, I said, "In case you haven't noticed, the universe hasn't been dispensing anything but trash lately. Maybe if you just wait for whatever comes to you, you get what nobody else wanted." There! I said it. Now we'd have to see if Meditation Man got it.

Initially, Drew limited his response to a loud snort. But after some moments of dramatically pursing his lips, he added, "Who am I kidding? That stuff doesn't work for me. I'm not Chaz."

Chaz, our laid-back neighbor and handyman. He seemed part of another life now. Would we ever see my home again? Maybe I'd be condemned to living the rest of my life on Route 66. Wouldn't that be a bite on the ass?

"Why does that New Age stuff work for Chaz and not me?" Drew sounded perplexed.

"Because he's the river, and you're...not." Maybe Rock Guy would finally understand who he was meant to be, and things could go back to normal. I swore that if my stodgy ol' Drew returned, I would never again try to change him. Unless, you know, he really did turn me in.

We sank into silence once more. I hoped Drew was thinking about his place in the world, which was surely the probate department of some impossibly boring law firm. Eventually, though, the conversation returned to Philly.

"You should have beaten the truth out of him," Drew said, for about the tenth time. "Stupid old man. Games be damned. How much fun is it now?"

Drew still didn't appreciate how tenaciously Philly had hid whatever his blackmailer held over him, and how determined he'd been to protect us from whatever threats had been made. But I also wished I'd found a way to coax the truth out of him. My guilt throbbed like a corn on a pinky toe.

My thoughts turned instead to this unexpected kidnapping. There couldn't be two bad guys in one small town, both with unhealthy interests in Philly, right? The kidnapper must have been the blackmailer, trying a new tack. Maybe some of the extortionist's notes, which we hadn't seen, had ordered Philly to get the money from Dad. When Philly didn't, his angry extortionist took matters into his own hands.

The size of the ransom staggered me. Ten mill was a powerful lot of money. Dad reported that he, and Mother, as well as Drew's parents, were trying to raise it. They were all well off people, but nobody keeps that kind of cash lying around. That much money also takes up lots of space, even in large bills. How was the kidnapper planning on transporting his booty? Were we going to need the burlap bags I'd come across in the caves and Woody's RV to carry it?

The amount also struck me as significant. Ten million dollars. There was some connection I felt I should have made.

CHAPTER THIRTY-FIVE

We got smarter after that first call. Not a lot, but some. Dad started calling from a payphone he found near Brewed Awakening. But if anyone had been listening that first time, or if they remembered that old public phone, my goose was already well done.

We worked out a semblance of a plan for sneaking back to the Rest Ur Head. Dad told us to park the RV in the rear of a supermarket in a neighboring town, while he would trade cars with Duncan, the motel desk clerk. Then, while Duncan cruised the New Mexican arcades in a Bentley, we'd sneak back by squeezing into the back seat of the world's oldest Camaro. Eventually, we'd work out how to get the RV back to the motel. If we made it through all of that without a detour through Leavenworth, I wouldn't complain.

But when I slowly rolled into the rendezvous spot, under the cover of fast-dwindling twilight, I questioned Dad's meeting place choice. I thought it would be a back alley, a delivery route at best. But there was an actual entrance to the market from that back lot. That parking area wasn't well lit, and no more than a few vehicles had parked there, but neither was it as remote and abandoned as I expected. Maybe it was all he could think of on a moment's notice. Then again, he had paid for the RV—maybe he wanted to leave it somewhere safe. It would be good if I knew his priorities.

Drew was back in the bedroom part of the camper. He'd insisted he'd never be able to sleep, not with his uncle and me in such jeopardy. But our assault on his ethical code had left him so exhausted, within moments of his stretching out on the bed, soft snores filled the cabin of the motor home. Unless I wanted to deny him that much-needed rest—and deal with him getting even more uptight—I was on my own. I brought the RV to a stop in the darker part of the lot, near a block wall fence at the rear. But even well away from the market's rear door, I still felt exposed.

Where was Dad? I didn't see Duncan's car.

I felt so antsy waiting in that RV. I needed to be on the move. Since nobody came out of the market during the minutes I waited there, I decided to risk creeping out in search of another hiding place. Surely, there had to be a Dumpster somewhere that I could crouch behind, or even in. It wouldn't be my first time.

When would I learn to be circumspect? Not before I was jailed for life, that much was certain. Just as I was passing a nondescript sedan, also parked along the block wall, I heard voices from inside the market's automatic door.

"Congratulations, Roy. Big night, huh?" someone said.

"Howdy, Sam. Yup, I expect I'll still be celebrating till it's darker than midnight in a coal mine," another voice cried cheerfully.

Crap! Fricker. I didn't recognize his voice as much as the style of address.

Could I dive under the sedan? Race back to the RV?

Before I could decide, I heard the click of a car door being unlocked right beside me. A woman's voice said softly, "In here. *Now.*"

Not understanding anything beyond the need to hide, I yanked the car door open and hurled myself across the back seat. I scooted around hastily and quietly pulled the car door closed.

"Stay still," my benefactor hissed.

I twisted my neck to see who had been sitting quietly unseen in the driver's seat. Genevieve Cannon, the hanky-panky-making minister's wife.

Outside of the car, boots tapped against the pavement. I heard the click of a door remote somewhere nearby. I longed to see what kind of personal car Fricker drove, so I had time to escape the next time I spotted him headed my way. But my muscles had turned to stone.

"Evenin', Miz Cannon," the Chief shouted. "Lookin' quite peaceful there."

How could he tell? Thankfully, shadows were settling over the lot. I hadn't even noticed that she'd been sitting in the car when I crept past it.

"I feel it, too, Chief," Genevieve called at full voice.

I heard the slam of a heavy vehicle door, and then, the start-up roar of a powerful engine. Only after I heard tires pulling away did I risk a peek at the big sage green pickup moving out of the lot. I sank against the back seat of Genevieve's car in palpable relief.

"Tracy?" She cleared her throat. "Thank you for what you told Don. Whatever it was, it worked."

Thoroughly-wasted-Don remembered what I said to him? I thought for sure he was too drunk to process anything. But something didn't make sense. If their marriage was on the mend, what was she doing here? Waiting for Don to finish his shopping? Or avoiding him at home?

Not my business. She'd saved my butt—that was all I cared about. Though, despite her offering of thanks, she didn't seem all that grateful. She was way too standoffish. Maybe I knew too much about her for her comfort.

"But now we're square, right?" she asked.

Square? For what she did, I'd give her my first-born. Or even my mother. If my father didn't show up soon, I'd throw him in for free.

Just then I heard a car break the sound barrier with the boom of exhaust blown out its pipes. Duncan's Camaro—I'd heard that a few times at the motel.

Once it parked, I crawled from Genevieve's car and slinked over to it. Even in this light, I'd know it anywhere. That car had obviously received more than its share of dings. Duncan had primed those spots, but failed to smooth them down before slapping a streaky coat of banana yellow on with a paintbrush. Not only was the surface still lumpy, missed spots popped through the paint like zits through acne cover-up. Surely everyone in town knew this car. Couldn't Dad find someone who owned a nondescript vehicle who wanted the experience of driving a Bentley?

After I slipped into the backseat, I snapped to him, "Where were you?"

"Trying to convince a pair of Federal agents that I *really* didn't know where you were." Dad threw back his longish white hair with polished ease as always, but I noticed his hand trembled.

"Did they follow you here?" I twisted my neck for a quick view of the parking lot, but all I saw was Genevieve's sedan pulling out the exit.

"Tracy, give me a little credit. I have someone working on that."

Who? With Drew and me on the lam, and Philly a captive, who else was there? "Fricker was just here."

"Don't worry about Chief Fricker, either, honey. He's interested in you as well, but he'll be too busy tonight to get in our way."

Where was he getting this information?

"Has Fricker interviewed you any more? You know, for Woody's murder."

"Not lately. I think he's decided that if I were really guilty, I would have skedaddled, instead of you." Dad looked around. "Where did you leave Drew? You didn't dump him somewhere when he threatened to turn you in, did you?"

Dad knew us too well. "He did threaten to turn me in, but I talked him out of it."

After I told him where to find Drew, Dad went to the RV. Moments later, he led my sleep-dazed husband out and stuffed him into the Camaro's passenger seat.

"So, Dad, you think you can sneak us back into the Rest Ur Head without any trouble?"

"Sure thing, honey. But that's when our real troubles will start."

It was good to know we had just been taking it easy until this point.

* * *

We did slip back into the suite without incident, but we weren't there long enough to breathe when someone knocked on the door. It sounded like a code knock—three heavy and two light raps. Would the Feds or Fricker have thought to try that?

"You *were* followed," I said.

Drew just stared at the door like a rock that wasn't getting swept downstream no matter what. I wasn't that crazy about the idea of being taken into custody at the moment, either. Now that things were finally cooking, I needed to be here for Philly.

"Give it a rest, Tracy," Dad said with barely contained patience, pushing his way to the door. "Do you really think you're the only one who knows anything?"

Duh! I thought we'd established that long ago.

After a giving a quick look through the peephole, he threw the door open.

Elise, the chipper little barista of Brewed Awakening popped in, carrying a tray of coffee cups and a paper bag. "Brought you kids some eats."

She was so accommodating. Were we right to trust her? While she and Drew laid the grub out on the coffee table, I pulled Dad aside for a whispered talk.

"Dad, is there anyone you didn't share this with?"

"Don't you get smart with me, young lady. You have no idea what I've been dealing with here. All by myself, I might add. But this is how you always do it. You make total strangers into sidekicks."

Right—me. I knew how to pick 'em. Parents, don't try this at home.

With a sudden sigh, I quit trying to maintain the illusion that I knew what I was doing, either. "Dad, I've let everyone down. More than you know." Starting with Philly, of course, but Lucy, too.

Dad's sigh echoed my own. "Me too, honey. I've let everyone down myself. More than *you* know."

He pulled me into his arms, and we sank together into a silent funk. By contrast, across the room Elise seemed absolutely giddy.

"Well, gotta go," she said with outrageously good cheer. "It's party time. Tracy, it occurred to me that Chief Fricker's first anniversary with the town is next week, and I decided to throw parties for him tonight and tomorrow to keep him out of action. You know, supposedly so everyone in town can find a time to attend."

I looked at Dad. "So that's why Fricker will be too busy to worry about us." What a great idea. I felt sorry I doubted her. I asked Elise, "You'll be able to keep him occupied?"

With an emphatic nod, she said, "Even if I have to throw myself at him." She winked. "Not a bad idea anyway." With that, she was gone.

Her happy mood lifted my own bad one. We gathered around the coffee table and dove into the food Elise had brought. Once an exceptionally good BLT filled my empty stomach, I asked Dad to tell me about the Feds that had questioned him.

"Did they tell you why they want to talk to me?"

Dad shook his head no. "Not a word about the charges." He leaned back in his chair, sipping his coffee. "They were not what I expected. I figured they'd be indifferent locals, sent on a follow-up mission for another office. Instead, I sensed real excitement coming from those young fellas, as if they thought landing you would give them a big career-making boost."

Little ol' me? Little ol' *innocent* me? I had news for them— nobody's career was gonna be built on my neck. But why would they think so? If Philly hadn't needed me so desperately, I might actually have turned myself in, just so I could figure out what they thought I did.

We also talked about the ransom call that had come from the kidnapper. "It came during the night. I never even heard the phone ring." Dad flushed sheepishly. "If I had, I'd have been up like a shot. You know, in case it was you kids calling. But I never even noticed that Philly hadn't returned to the suite that night." He sent an apologetic nod Drew's way. "We hadn't been getting on too good lately."

Talk about understatements.

"That was Philly's choice, Alec." Drew snorted. "He should have let us in on whatever is causing him all this grief."

"That's not Philly's way, son." He glanced at me. "Not ours, either."

Once we cleared away the food debris, Dad put his cell phone on the table.

"It came in on your cell?" Drew asked. "The caller knew the number?"

"Or he got it from Philly," I said. "Drew, let's face it, your uncle is no tower of strength. It wouldn't have taken much to get Dad's number of out of him."

Dad played the voice mail message the kidnapper had left the night when Philly had been abducted.

"Philly Chase—I've got him. Go look in his room. You won't find him there," came through the speaker.

The whispered voice sounded low and brusque. Vaguely familiar, if my brain wasn't playing tricks on me. Who was that? Someone we'd already come across? We didn't know that many people in Tecos, and after having eliminated most of them, there weren't many left.

"Ten million—that's what it's gonna cost to get him back," the kidnapper went on. "As sure as shootin', I'll kill him if you alert the cops or the FBI."

Still, the quality of that whisper gnawed at me.

The kidnapper went on to give the deadline, and a promise to call before then with a place where the ransom would be left.

"Well, Tracy," Dad said with a tone desperation. "Do you know who it is?"

I hated to have to spill the truth. "Not a clue, Dad." I suddenly made one connection, though, and it was a good one. "I *do* know where that call was placed." I directed a meaningful look at both of them. "What do you say, guys? Are you as tired of taking it on the chin as I am? Let's turn things around on Kidnapper Man?"

CHAPTER THIRTY-SIX

We worked out a plan on the spot. Then, while I kept a low profile in the motel, the guys went out to buy supplies for our mission. They returned with three fancy little phones. The smallest, lightest cell phones I'd ever seen. Not only could they make ordinary calls and text, more importantly, they functioned as walkie-talkies, and also contained a light function that we could use to either illuminate our paths or flash soundlessly to signal each other.

They also bought large, rubbery yoga mats to muffle sound, a garden spade for me, and big backpacks for all of us. Not as large as the fictitious T.K. Mann had worn in my dream states, nor the one the real member of the T.K. Mann team had used to carry his booty when he jumped from the plane, but the biggest backpacks we three could carry, filled as they would be with the only weapons I figured we could manage.

As great as the new phones were, I'd already decided, when this was over, I was keeping Woody's iPhone, just on general principle, even if I had always objected to the idea of having a phone that was smarter than me. Now I saw that a genius phone made good sense. If I didn't learn to work it, I never again had to take a call. A smart phone could make my call-avoidance techniques soar to the next level.

While we thrashed out our plan, the kidnapper placed his final call.

"Listen good, cuz I won't repeat it," that low, rough voice said. "As soon as the banks open and you collect the money, pack it in a plastic garbage bag. Put that into a locker at the Albuquerque train station."

Knowing that Drew and Dad would pay attention to the instructions, I focused more on the velvety texture of the voice. He didn't say much, though. He ended by ordering us to place the locker's key in a small zippered cloth bag, which he said we'd find outside our suite door.

We all stared at each other in disbelief. Outside *our* suite? Drew and Dad raced to the door. Sure enough, a green plastic garbage bag and the promised cloth bag both rested on the sidewalk outside our door, held down by a stone.

He had been right there! While we were blathering on, trying to psych ourselves up, Philly's tormenter had stood on the opposite side of our door. Laughing at us, no doubt.

I reconsidered Duncan again. He had the best access. Could that high-pitched voice be part of an elaborate act? Or had the Clement twins followed us here? For that much money, they could *buy* back the family caves.

For his final instruction, the kidnapper ordered us to place the cloth bag holding the key in a trashcan he said we'd find outside the Tecos PD.

Ballsy. With such hubris, I couldn't make Duncan fit, unless he was a better actor than I thought. Nor Sean Clement. Nor Don Cannon.

What about Mark Baker, the mayor? His nerves were steelier than any of theirs, and he'd taken obvious pleasure toying with me that day I confronted him with evidence of his secret meeting, like the kidnapper was toying with us now. But nasty little land swindles seemed more his style than a caper this dangerous. Besides, didn't he have to spend some time at the Town Hall? How could he free up enough of it to guard his prisoner?

The kidnapper closed by saying that after we followed the ransom drop instructions, we'd get a call later in the day telling us where we'd find Philly.

Right. There would be no call. Once he had that money, he would be on the move. By the time we found Philly, he would be long dead.

The kidnapper's daring rattled Dad and Drew, to the extent that they considered paying the ransom and hoping for the best. Only trouble was that Dad's partners hadn't raised enough cash. When the bank opened in the morning, the wire transfer would be millions short.

I reminded them that our money had come up lacking. "Do you really think he seems the type to negotiate?" I didn't remind them that Philly's life was on the line—we all knew it.

That the bad guy had placed the bag outside our door made me feel outclassed, yet I remained the most upbeat of all of us. Our collective confidence didn't grow any stronger during the fitful hours that we tried to sleep. Our shared mood was even worse when we awoke well before dawn, and waited for the sky to brighten enough to set out.

Drew was so brittle and jumpy, I half-expected him to try to call the whole thing off. Dad, on the other hand, acted casual in the extreme, whistling the entire soundtracks of several films he'd appeared in, all off-key. *Denial*, not just a river in Egypt, but the sea on which the Grainger ship perpetually sailed.

Me, I was more jazzed, of course. There was nothing like a crazy caper to get my juices flowing. Yet I couldn't reach my usual escapade euphoria. Under my excitement was the knowledge that I had let Philly down consistently throughout this trip. Now we were down to the wire, and I was as clueless about what we were dealing with as I ever had been.

To escape Dad's atonal whistling, I hid in our room. After a quick knock, the whistler opened the door.

"Time?" I asked.

"Not quite." He sat at the end of the bed.

"Where's Drew?"

"Outside, making a phone call."

"A call?" Who could he be calling?

Before I could follow that thought, Dad said in a strangled voice, "Tracy, we need to talk."

Ooh! Nothing good ever started that way.

He cleared his throat. "Your mother told me you read my letters to Lucy."

So much for being a wise wife. Was there nothing the woman wouldn't blab?

"I would never have left you, Tracy. I want you to understand—"

"I know that," I said with ease. I also knew he would never have left Mother, even if he had entertained the thought. Sharing a life with Lucy had never been a serious goal. Lucy was an alternate universe. His safety valve when Mother got too high-maintenance. He'd wanted to believe he had a new life waiting for him out there on Route 66, where he could chuck Hollywood and live like a regular guy if he wanted to. I'd read enough of the letters to understand that. I also knew, even if he didn't, that it would never have worked. Even back then, it had been too long since he'd actually been a regular guy.

First Drew, and now Dad. Wasn't anyone besides me happy with the life they'd created? But then, how many people found what suited them like childish behavior suited me? Sure, I knew people *could* change, but they mostly didn't. Even when they seemed to, they usually just altered the packaging, while they were the same old person underneath the new face. Remember, leopards and spots?

Since we were letting it all hang out, I confessed that I'd seen him climbing down the ladder from Lucy's apartment the night we arrived. "What were you looking for?"

"The letters, of course," he said with feeling.

"Why? They haven't troubled you all these years."

He scratched his head sheepishly. "When Philly and me were talking about getting Lucy out, I didn't want her to come back and find them. To give her any false hope, I mean."

About her and Dad getting together? I suspected decades without men had cured Lucy of any need for them.

"And, you know, to make sure what I wrote in them never came out," he added. "Martha and me—we've created our share of scandals. I just want to live quietly now."

My parents really had no idea where they fit on the fame continuum now. Didn't they know that reality TV stars, stretching their fifteen minutes, had pushed actors off the tabloid covers? Younger, hotter actors, at that. Who cared whether some old fart had a fling with a rural luncheonette owner decades earlier?

There was still something I had to ask. The words had been stuck in my throat for so long, they threatened to choke me now if I didn't spit them out. "Were you Woody's father?"

"Jiminy Johosophat! What are you thinking, my girl? Look in the mirror—*that's* what a child of mine looks like!" His outraged bristling told me how much that had offended him. "Besides, Woody was already a toddler when I first met Lucy, when we filmed *Revenge on Route 66* here. You knew that, Tracy. I've told you many times."

Maybe he had. Once I realized how out-of-touch the loveable loonies who raised me were, I learned to listen to them only selectively. This wasn't the first time that had come back to bite me on the butt. But I would risk an occasional nip on the ass to hearing everything they said. That would have melted my brain.

"But just because he wasn't mine doesn't mean I didn't care for him. I tell you, honey, I miss that boy so much." Grief clouded his aqua eyes.

"Why?" I said before I could color the question with diplomacy.

"Oh, Woody was great fun when you got to know him. He knew things about everyone in this town."

This time I let discretion win. I didn't tell Dad what Woody did with all the dirt he'd gathered. "But all the money and stuff you gave him—why were you so generous?"

Dad's head fell forward. "That was for Lucy. Because of what I wasn't able to do for her after she confessed. It was a mistake, too. Fricker was right—I robbed Woody of his ambition."

I figured Woody had handed it over without a fight.

"Tracy, you're not jealous, are you? You've had everything, and poor Woody never had a chance."

My eyes stung. I did have everything, including a father who saw the best in everyone, even Woody. For the first time, I appreciated the extent of Dad's loss. I felt a new fire burning in me. We would not lose anyone else, I vowed. We would not lose Philly.

Drew popped his head in the door. "Ready? I've filled the backpacks."

That was what he was doing outside, filling the backpacks, not making cell phone calls. Dad just got confused. We followed Drew out to the sitting area, where he had placed the three backpacks on the scarlet couch. The contents of two of them bulged, while one looked only partially full. The three phones they'd bought were gathered on the coffee table.

While they took their phones and put on their backpacks, we reviewed the code we'd established for phone lights, as well as the shorthand we'd use in our texts.

Then Dad said, "Ready, Andrew, my boy?"

Drew gave a tight nod. With a sigh that did nothing to encourage me, Drew started for the door. But he stopped and turned my way. He grasped my shoulders and gave me a quick, hard kiss, while Dad looked discreetly away. Without a word, Drew opened the door, and he and Dad left.

Then it was my turn. I took my backpack and cell phone back to our room. In addition to using Duncan's Camaro again, which Dad and Drew had driven off in, Dad also borrowed a maid's uniform for me. To make it easier for me to slip out, in case the Feds were watching.

I put the uniform on over the stretchy workout clothes I wore underneath.

I started to lift the backpack that Drew had kept as light as he could for me. But it was still so heavy. Why shouldn't it be, considering he had stuffed it with rocks.

Rocks! Those were our weapons of choice. Like cavemen. My idea, too, I hated to admit, but only so I could stop my demented partners in crime from trolling for illegal guns, which would surely have brought the cops down on us. With as many charges as I seemed to be facing, I couldn't afford any more.

I pulled the backpack into position, and gathered up all the extra rolls of toilet paper we had in the suite. I figured if anyone was outside keeping watch, that would give me natural credibility.

I started for the door, but hesitated. The weight of that backpack was pulling me down, both literally and figuratively. Since I arrived in Tecos, I hadn't been *acting*, but *re*-acting. Jumping to someone else's tune, and I'd had enough of it. That was not my way.

I dropped the backpack on the bed, and started pulling things from it. I'd keep the yoga mat and the phone, but the rocks had to go. They might work for my cavemen—anything to keep them from shooting each other. But I needed to travel lighter. I grabbed the marble shooter I'd confiscated from Woody's things, which I'd hidden in the dresser, and stuffed it into the backpack, along with extra marbles. I spotted the keys for the Mustang and the RV and tossed those in, too, just in case we needed to make a fast getaway.

Now I was ready. My energy and excitement were soaring again. After all the hits I'd taken on Route 66, Tracy Eaton was finally back!

CHAPTER THIRTY-SEVEN

I slipped out the suite's door into the cool, charcoal dawn, and rested the backpack on the sidewalk in the darkened doorway. Dad and Drew had promised to check for watchers when they left, and they would have signaled me if they'd seen anyone.

Still, I'm nothing if not thorough. Some of the time. I strolled around the property, carrying those rolls of toilet paper, hoping that if the Feds were watching, they'd be dumb enough to believe maids began their rounds before daylight. Once I felt sure I was alone out there, I ditched the TP rolls in a darkened doorway, where someone would trip over a toilet paper bonanza in a few hours. Then I reclaimed my backpack and readied myself to put my part of the operation into effect.

After tiptoeing across the space separating the Rest Ur Head from the restaurant, I let myself in the front door. In the darkened hallway beside the kitchen where we'd found Woody's body, I peeled off the maid's uniform and headed for the back door.

In listening to the kidnapper's calls, I'd heard the rich, velvety sounds added to the caller's whispered voice that the Tecos Caves had always lent to mine. With Tandy in California planning his PR tour, it was a good hideout choice.

Drew and Dad had driven to the entrance. Once inside, they'd split up. When one of them figured out where the kidnapper might be holding Philly, he would text that information to the rest of us, and we'd come at that space from different directions.

I hoped that we'd find them in Y-274, the cavern where we believed they'd met before. Leopards and spots, remember? People don't change their habits. My way in would make it easy to reach that particular cave. But it didn't really matter. Wherever they were, we were going to find them. Deep inside, I promised Philly that.

I crept out the back of the restaurant and made my way to the openings to the caves behind Woody's property. When I was a kid, I'd used these openings into the caves plenty of times. The first time I disappeared into them, Dad had alerted the police. Fricker's predecessor mounted a manhunt for me. I'd heard them combing the caves for me, of course, and since I'd already discovered all the smaller openings between caverns that I could move through, I led them on a merry chase, until I got hungry enough to let them find me. I developed such a good internal sense of that rock maze, that on subsequent trips, I'd come and gone from the caves without anyone ever knowing it.

Despite having gone through part of the cavern system recently with Drew, and studying an old map Elise found, I wasn't sure I had such a clear sense of the place anymore. I'd never fit through some of the smaller openings now. I had to hope the really critical ones would still accommodate me.

I quietly closed in on the rear openings. Unless someone had been through them recently, it wasn't always obvious that there were openings there at all. After my first little escapade, the police filled them in with rocks and boulders, which I'd learned to roll aside when I needed to. Mountainous brush and years of wind-blown dust could make it all look like big, dirty piles of boulders.

But I saw that someone had been here recently, and lots of the rocks had been cleared from the openings. The Clement twins? Did they sneak in here after parking the rented Ferrari behind the restaurant? If they were the good guys, as I believed, I sent them a silent *thank you,* while I placed my gear on the ground.

Using the spade, I cleared some remaining dirt away to widen the opening. I placed the end of the yoga mat on the ground outside the mouth of one cave, and let it unroll into the cavern. Wanting to travel light, I shed my backpack after remembering to take the marble shooter from it.

I slid as quietly as possible along the yoga mat through an opening that only barely accommodated someone my size. If I hadn't lowered my head, I would have hit it on a low hanging stalagmite. It was dark in there. Even though my new phone would shed some light, I was afraid to use it without knowing where Philly and his abductor might be.

If they were there. If this wasn't all a giant waste of time.

I kept crawling. Quietly shifting the mat and sliding along it. Moving deeper and deeper within the maze. At first I didn't see or hear anything. Then, I came upon a cavern that gave off a faint flickering glow, such as a fire or a kerosene lamp might put out.

When I heard a voice—Philly's voice—my heart stopped.

"You've done okay for yourself, Tag," Philly said.

Tag? Wasn't that the name that Angus Clement was forced to sign the caves over to? Another voice, clearly some distance away from Philly, muttered something in response, but I couldn't distinguish anything beyond a low murmur.

"Yeah, you're right—you've done way better than just okay," Philly said. "You always were the clever boy. You'd take the wildest chances, and you got away with them. You've pulled the biggest con of them all this time."

I still couldn't hear the other person's response. Dammit, why couldn't he speak up? It occurred to me that I was right about something else—Philly wasn't intended to come out of this kidnapping alive. If he knew his abductor's identity, as he clearly did, and he also knew about some gynormous con that this guy, Tag, had pulled off, Philly would have to carry Tag's secrets to the grave.

How, oh how, was I going to fix this?

Philly choked on a little laugh. "Sure, pal, your nerve and criminal savvy, and the fact that there's absolutely *nothing* you won't do, has carried you far in this life. But you got that new face to thank for pulling off this gig. "

New face? He'd had his face altered? Who was he?

"Tag, did you ever think—" Philly began.

I never did hear the rest of Philly's sentence because another voice suddenly broke in. A too familiar voice—Dad's.

"Tag? His name's not Tag." Dad's voice bristled with outrage. "You might have gotten some surgeon to give you a new face, and your voice might sound quite different now. But I'd know your cocky stance anywhere. You're Terry Kennedy, my old assistant."

My mind went into a rapid-fire processing of new information.

On one hand, I wanted to scream because Dad was now in this abductor's hands, too. He and Drew were supposed to throw rocks at Philly's abductor from the mouth of the cave if they got the chance, and retreat fast if that didn't slow him down. Instead, he'd given the kidnapper another hostage.

At the same time, I reeled from this new information. This guy from Philly's past, Tag Kowalski, was the same person Dad hired to help us years ago. I'd tried to tell everyone that Route 66 is a vortex of coincidence, but nobody would listen to me. Another connection clicked into place. When Terry Kennedy made the Angus Clement sign the caves over to Tag Kowalski, he was actually taking possession of them himself. So how did the governor get them?

"Alec, what…how…?" Philly sputtered.

"I'm an actor. I watch people, watch their walks, their stances, the way they hold their heads. How else do you think actors come up with characters' movements?" Dad said. "Hey, Terry, I hear you picked on my kid."

He was sticking up for me *now?* Too bad it was thirty years too late, and it took putting himself in the hands of what I'd bet was a stone cold killer to do it.

"You shouldn't have come here, Alec," another voice, a raspy voice, said.

That voice I knew, but I couldn't place it. It wasn't Terry's, though, not what I remembered, anyway.

"You should have picked up my money at the bank and followed my instructions to the letter, King Buckaroo," the raspy voice went on. "You better hope your daughter is carrying out my wishes, or sure as the sun rises in the sky, you and your friend are not leaving this cave alive."

The shock of recognition hit me. But what I was thinking was crazy. Absolutely nuts, and absolutely impossible.

"Now sit—" Raspy Voice began.

I heard the scuffing of steps from someone not bothering to hide his approach.

Then another voice said, "Delay that order, Mr. Grainger, and you back out of this cave, nice and easy now."

Fricker. Him I'd know anywhere.

Terry must have made some threatening move because Fricker came back with, "You best drop your weapon, sir, or your hand won't be worth a sack o' rubber nickels. I warn you, I'm a damn good shot."

Relief warred with confusion in me. What was Fricker doing here? Shouldn't he have been asleep at this hour, or getting ready for today's ongoing anniversary party?

Understanding came in a flash. Drew must have alerted him—I remembered Dad telling me he'd made a call earlier. The old Drew would never have trusted us three to pull this off. I know I promised not to try to change him again—but really, couldn't he have waited one more day to complete his metamorphosis back to where he began?

I wondered briefly where Drew was. Hiding somewhere safe, I hoped. So I could kill him when I got the chance.

"Drop it," Fricker ordered again.

I heard the sound of something heavy being dropped.

"Good man," Fricker said. "Now kick it over here." He ordered his deputy Paulie to cuff him.

I had to learn whether my insane theory was right. I pulled myself forward, through a small opening that connected to the cave where all the action was taking place.

Despite what I thought I knew my jaw still dropped in shock. Tag Kowalski aka Terry Kennedy had kept the same initials for his latest metamorphous, though he flipped them around. He was now known as Kyle Tandy—and he was the freakin' governor of California!

Obviously, the news stories that indicated he'd returned to California to fight for his job were just cover so he could hold Philly hostage. Good thing he and his parole officer were so tight because this would have been tough to pull off in an ankle-monitoring device.

I marveled that Dad recognized his stance as Terry's, but had so little interest in politics, that he didn't recognize his own governor. Philly was right—Tag/Terry/Kyle had been one lucky guy. Dad could have blown his con at any time. But I had seen the governor on the news—hell, I'd sat across from him in this cave—and never recognized him as Terry. Throughout his term in office, nothing but his heartless eyes had ever troubled me.

Fricker spotted me lying at the mouth of that cavern on my belly. "Ms. Eaton! Tracy! Don't you be going anywhere." Paulie, the deputy, also turned my way.

In the moment when they turned their attention to me, Tandy reached down for the gun he hadn't kicked that far away. In a flash, he snatched it up in the hands cuffed in front of him and pointed in the direction of the police officers.

Without giving it a thought, I fired my marble shooter. Nailed him right in the forehead. Tandy produced a brief stunned expression before he began to fall backwards. As he fell, I fired another shot. This one caught him under the chin.

"Ms. Eaton, you stay right there," Fricker ordered again.

Drew stepped out from behind Dad. "Tracy, don't leave."

Screw them both. I slithered backwards down the path I'd crawled along, as skillfully as a snake. Along the way, I heard Fricker calling for me, but I ignored it.

Philly shouted, "Keep going, kid."

That instruction I followed. Once I backed out of the main opening, despite legs that had become cramped, I ran all the way back to the motel with every intention of grabbing the Mustang and hitting the open road. On the lam once more, for real at last.

CHAPTER THIRTY-EIGHT

At some point during my sprint to freedom, it occurred to me that fleeing in a bright red sports car might not be the wisest choice, even if it would provide the greatest charge. I decided the RV was still a better idea, especially since we hadn't removed our stuff from it. Besides, Fricker doubtless knew what kind of car Woody had driven, but Woody never used the camper. In the end, I grabbed my temporary moving house, and made my escape.

I hadn't gotten all that far before my new cell phone jingled.

Assuming it to be Drew, I said, "What do you want, you traitor?"

Drew plunged right in with, "Be fair, babe. I secured an agreement from Fricker. He promised to take you in unharmed, and to negotiate a safe surrender to the FBI."

Only marginally better than letting them shoot me on sight.

"Tracy, for all I knew we were going up against a psycho with nothing more lethal than rocks. I didn't even know you took Woody's marble shooter. I was trying to protect us all."

I grunted. "Governor Psycho."

He seized the change of subject. "Wasn't that a shock?"

I'd certainly see every politician differently from now on. Visualizing them in the prison jumpsuits they might actually wear someday, instead of just wishing for it.

I bit my lip. "Did I kill him?" Even knowing he was one super bad dude—who admittedly had stretched self-definition to an admirable degree—I wasn't sure I wanted that on my conscience.

"He's not dead," Drew said in a too-hearty voice. "Though he is in a coma. They've airlifted him to a hospital in Albuquerque."

Great. So he wasn't dead, but he'd be known as Governor Psycho-Veggie from now on. Would *I* end up in that prison jumpsuit? Lucy and me, side-by-side?

"…Trace?" Drew asked. "I need to know where you are."

So he could turn me in again? Not likely. Sure, I wanted him to revert to an earlier state, but why was it so hard for him to achieve a balance I could live with?

"Nope. You don't deserve to know that."

I abruptly ended the call, remembering to turn the phone off and pull the battery out, so his new BFF Chief Fricker wasn't able to trace the GPS. I stewed in anger, debating about where I'd go from here. It lightened my mood to know I could go anywhere, especially if I used elaborate disguises, which would make it more fun anyway. So it was a great surprise to me when, with a sigh, I took the turnoff to the hospital where Kyle Tandy lay in a coma.

* * *

The hospital where they'd brought Governor Psycho-Veggie was a pretty standard affair, eight stories of stucco and glass, with a couple of acres of parking. A big circular drive, which brought visitors to both the ER and main entrance, separated the heliport on one side and a small wooded area on the other. A helicopter waited there in the heliport for its next emergency. A pair of workers buzzed around the grounds in a golf cart, towing an open cart filled with gardening tools, which they parked here and there as they tended to the rustic landscaping.

I took the precaution of swapping the RV's old license plate for one on some out-of-state motor home that I found parked near the emergency room entrance. I did hate the thought of sending the Feds after some oldsters from Vermont who'd already had the bad luck of needing an ER in New Mexico, but Drew had seen the old plates we'd used when we first hit the road. By now he had doubtless shared that number with the entire law enforcement community. Besides, for all I knew, once the oldsters discovered their new plate, they might treasure the collectible Route 66 item.

Rationalization—without it I'd never survive.

I parked the RV in a section of the lot reserved for doctors, which I figured would draw the least scrutiny. As I started to leave, I spotted on the kitchenette counter the lunch pail Lucy had given me, which we'd brought along in the RV when we first went on the lam, because I never cruised Route 66 without it.

An overwhelming wave of sentiment hit me. That lunchbox, I grasped for the first time, was a touchstone for me. A lifeline to the normalcy I'd never had, but always yearned for. Now I understood that I'd had the best of all possible upbringings. But when I was little, I didn't want to be the girl immortalized with her parents in *People*, I wanted a normal life, like the kids on TV. Sure, as a show-biz brat, I should have known how fake TV-land was. I should also have realized Route 66 was, in its own way, as wacky as Hollyweird. But back then, that lunch pail was my link from the life I had to the one I thought I wanted. Who was I to criticize Dad's dream of another path on Route 66?

It was also tied into my very first secret—his, mine, and Lucy's. That was why I'd never spent the money. When I was younger, before I met Drew, working a day-job while trying to write my first book, sometimes I was dead broke. Yet I never touched it because that would mean breaking the circle we three shared. As Dad suggested then, when someone gives you something special, you should always treasure it.

I clutched the lunch pail to my chest now, trying to recapture my love for Route 66—a connection that had become frayed on this trip. Before that wave of sentiment washed me out the door, I put my lunch pail and the marble shooter into my backpack, and went in search of a place to hide.

I found a ideal roost. There was a block-wall fence behind the wooded area on a rise at the side of the parking lot. Though I probably hadn't climbed a tree since before I entered puberty, I shimmied up a tall pine without losing too much skin, and perched atop the fence. The only bad part was the gagging *eau-de-death* scent wafting up from a close-by trash Dumpster, which smelled like it must have been some squirrel's final resting place. But I couldn't sit too far away from it, either. While the tree offered me decent coverage, if anyone looked too closely in my direction, I'd just dive into the bed of pine needles that had fallen behind the Dumpster, and then, run like hell.

For the longest time, I didn't see anything, apart from the routine traffic of a busy hospital. With no warning, Fricker appeared, right in my line of sight, flaunting his "flashiarity," which was khaki-colored today with cream piping. This guy really had bought out an entire cowboy shop.

He stood in the driveway, aiming long looks in every direction. Before his gaze reached where I sat behind those tree limbs, I went into the dive I'd rehearsed so many times in my mind. Only I didn't exactly land *behind* the Dumpster, on the soft bed of pine needles, but *in* it. In the Dumpster, with garbage cushioning my fall. Breathing in that stench was so much worse up close. Exactly how many dead squirrels did that Dumpster hold?

Even worse, it was too prominently displayed, *near* tall trees but with no actual limbs to shield it. And I hadn't taken the precaution of finding a dark hat to cover my hair. If I popped my head up, my bright blonde hair would glow in the sun like the pot of gold some chintzy leprechaun was withholding from us.

Bummed, I sank back into the garbage, trying to find some distraction beyond counting the dead animals that shared my space. Suddenly, I heard the sound of shoes scuffing, first, against the pavement, and then, the ground surrounding my hiding place.

Fricker? It didn't sound like his determined stride, but I'd bet he could be sneaky if he wanted to. Once a whiff of sweet pipe tobacco drifted my way, momentarily relieving the Dumpster smell, I knew it wasn't Fricker.

"Trace?" a voice asked softly. Philly.

"Philly? How did you find me?"

"I know how you think."

Incredible. How could those closest to me simultaneously display so much and so little understanding of my mind's inner workings? On one hand they believed that I was one of the country's most wanted fugitives, yet they still knew I had a tendency to hide in garbage cans. How was that possible?

"Is Fricker still scoping out the parking lot from the hospital entrance?" I asked.

Puff, puff. "Don't see him there now."

With Philly propped against the outside wall of the Dumpster, and me the inside, we started talking.

"You doing okay?" I asked.

"Are you kidding? I'm great. I thought they'd be carrying my dead carcass from that cave, but here I am, out in the sunlight, free, while my old pal Tag is in a coma, thanks to you."

"Any word on that coma?"

"The docs drained a brain bleed, and now they think he might be moving closer to consciousness."

"Somebody's watching him, right?" "Slippery" didn't begin to describe his character.

"For sure. Fricker himself heard too much in that cave not to take him seriously."

We sat in silence for a while. Then I asked. "You ready to tell me now what this has all been about?"

With a sigh, he went into it. He started with his days in Chicago, and the young Tag Kowalski he knew, and how Tag killed a shopkeeper during a robbery.

"Even from Europe, I'd hear about Tag occasionally," Philly went on. "I heard he got into counterfeiting for a while, then went on to California. I guess that was with you and your pop. But he came back along Route 66 at some point, and got into an accident that really messed up his face and neck. He had some plastic surgery done on them."

So that was how he ended up with his new face and that strangled voice.

"Then he went back out to California again, and I guess that's when he got into the movie biz." Philly sighed. "I never heard any more about him after he reinvented himself that time. I always figured he was dead. I hoped he was."

Yeah. I could see that. When I asked why he schemed to get us there, only to warn us away from looking, he reluctantly confirmed that the notes he received had made a threat against Dad.

Philly's voice dropped low. "You know me, Trace. I'm a cut-and-run kinda guy. But I couldn't risk Alec's life by leaving. Tag's killed other people with just as little motivation."

Too true. "Why didn't you tell Dad what happened in Chicago?"

"Wasn't sure he could forgive me," Philly muttered under his breath.

Man, we were both getting too good at guilt. *"You* didn't do anything, Philly, except show bad judgment when choosing a friend. You've done a better job this time. Besides, I think Dad would do anything for his Main Buckaroo."

We both laughed at that.

"Hey, did Governor Psycho-Veggie ever tell you why he did all this, you know, with the blackmailing and the kidnapping?"

"Sure, he's broke. Do you believe that? With all he made as a studio exec and what he scammed as governor, he went through it all. And he picked up plenty in bribes, he told me that. The way he tried to blame the aide who committed suicide—that was all a lie. Tag…or Terry, or Kyle—he raked it all in himself."

I wondered if the aide really had committed suicide, or if Governor P-V had offed him to make the aide look like the guilty one. It wouldn't have been his first murder.

"Did he tell you why he wanted ten mill specifically?" I asked.

I heard knocking on the Dumpster, and I could picture Philly scratching his bristly hair. "He said something about some giant score that he never did collect on. Tell ya the truth, Trace, he was pretty obsessed with how that was owed him. 'Sure as shootin,' he kept saying. 'I want what's mine. Not a penny more, but not a penny less.' It made him sound crazy. He didn't care where replacement dough came from. He leaned on me to get it from Alec. But it seemed real important to him that it be the same amount."

The one that got away… A thought raced into my mind.

But just as fast, it raced out, thanks to the sound of footsteps approaching the Dumpster. A stylish, strutting sound this time. Dad's steps.

"She in there, Philly-my-man?" Dad asked.

"Where else does she hide?" Philly asked with good cheer.

Was I really that predictable? At least the old farts had patched up their differences. For good this time, I hoped.

Another set of steps. These sounded more like a march. Had to be Drew. "The Dumpster?" he asked.

"Tell the traitor this powwow doesn't require his presence," I said through the metal wall.

"Come on, Trace," Drew said in a huffy voice. "You know I had your best interest at heart. At times you have to trust me to know what's right. Sometimes you know, and other times, I do."

Wow, he'd never made that admission about me before. Might we have finally achieved a useful balance?

"He's got you there, honey," Dad said. "If you hadn't pulled out that marble gun, we'd have needed Fricker. Maybe we've all learned something here. You don't have to keep us in the dark all the time."

Keep your friends close, but keep your plans closer—that's my motto.

"Oh, no," Dad said suddenly

That didn't sound good.

"See those young fellas rushing into the hospital?" Dad said.

I inched up far enough to see two suited guys hurrying towards the entrance. Fricker came out and momentarily met them there for a brief exchange, before the newcomers went into the hospital, leaving Fricker outside.

"That's a coinkydink," Dad said. "Those are the same Feds who interviewed me."

"Coinkydinks!" I shouted, suddenly flashing on the thought that kept eluding me. Jeez, everyone's language was rubbing off on me. "I mean coincidence."

"Yeah, we know, Trace. Coincidences keep happening on Route 66," Philly said. "You tell us that all the time." After a little sniff, he muttered, "Boy, do you tell us."

"No. This is a different coincidence. The ransom Tandy demanded for you, Philly—ten million dollars—that's the exact amount that T.K. Mann jumped out of that plane with."

"Yeah? So?" Philly asked.

"You said Governor P-V felt gypped because he'd never gotten the payoff for some big job he pulled. What job was supposed to pay out ten mill?"

On the other side of the Dumpster wall, none of them said a

thing. Were they mulling it over?

"Don't you see? He was the third man in the T.K. Mann triumvirate. His was the body type the passengers described, right?"

Before they could react, another thought flashed into my head. I gasped.

"What?" Drew demanded. It sounded like dread.

"The money. The missing money. T.K. Mann's missing loot—I know where it is! I finally freakin' know where it is."

CHAPTER THIRTY-NINE

"Y ou know?" Drew asked. "So spill."

By now I'd popped my head out of the Dumpster and stood facing them all. They all took a step or two back. I guess the scent wafting off me was a tad ripe.

"It's in the time capsule. You know, the army trunk in that park with the plaque in California."

Dad frowned. "That's not possible. I filled that time capsule myself."

Jeez, being a master of denial obviously came in the genes. "No, you didn't! You got bored with the idea long before we reached the stage of actually filling it."

Dad flushed. "Tracy, you're making me sound like a dilettante."

Man, if that shoe fit any better, it would have been his actual foot.

Dad threw an anxious glance at Philly, but Philly rose to his defense. "Nah, Alec, you're just a busy guy."

Drew asked, "What really happened?"

"Things kinda disintegrated. Dad delegated it to Terry, and Terry assigned it to me and Woody, and Woody promptly lost interest."

Dad's chin jutted out defensively. "Woody was going through a lot then."

Yeah, becoming a sophomore in high school and a major airline hijacker kinda ruled out the petty stuff, like filling time capsules and getting your yearbook photo taken.

"Look, I was only a little kid. I didn't drive. It wasn't like I could go out and buy things to put in it. I seem to remember coming across a maid's passkey…" I hurried on past that before someone questioned *how* I came across it. "So…I took things from people's rooms." After a moment, I added in my own defense, "I contributed one of my own Barbie dolls, too."

"That's right, you did steal things," Dad said. "You took my Hang Ten jacket." He turned to the others. "I had a great jacket in burnished-russet."

Russet? Was that a creative way of saying it was the cloying color of a Creamsicle? That was the jacket that made its way into my T.K. Mann dream. Nothing in my brain ever gets lost.

"And you took my space pen that wrote upside-down." Dad frowned. "An astronaut gave me that pen, and you stole it, Tracy."

Actually, I kept that pen for myself. Payment for his sticking me with the time capsule. Even as a little kid, my motto had been—*Always get even.* That pen had been hidden in my room for years until the ink ran out.

"Enough of the trivia," Drew said. "What about the money."

I squinted into the distance. "That's where my memory gets a little fuzzy. I know people gave me stuff—I went around to all the rooms in the Rest Ur Head at first, begging for material to put in it. But when I didn't get enough stuff, I started…you know, gathering it in a more creative way. I remember putting loads of money into the trunk, but I can't recall whether Terry gave it to me, or I took it from his room."

Philly snorted. "Why would he give it to you? The Tag I remember didn't give nothin' to nobody."

I gasped.

"What?" Drew demanded. The sound of dread in his voice kept building.

"I just had an awful thought. What if *I* took the hijacking money, and when Terry found it gone, he blamed Billy Rob?"

Drew picked up the thread. "I see where you're headed, honey. You think that maybe Terry killed Billy Rob for stealing the stash they were supposed to split. But ten million is a huge amount of currency. Would a kid really have been able to carry that?"

I bit my lip. "I think I made multiple trips. I can't remember how many."

Philly scratched his head. "If Tag killed Billy Rob, why did Lucy confess? Why's she serving a life sentence for something he did?"

"I always thought she confessed to a crime she didn't commit to protect someone. You know, like she believed Woody did it, and she chose to do the time herself, instead of inflicting it on her son." Dad looked around at all of us.

We sank into silence.

One more connection fell into place. "Philly, you said Governor Psycho-Veggie was obsessed with his missing ten mill. Do you think he might have decided now that Woody had it after all?"

"You're saying that Governor Tandy killed Woody?" Drew seemed to roll that thought around in his head. "It fits. Woody clearly spent more than he made in the café. Maybe Tandy thought Woody had been living on the hijacking money for years." He avoided Dad's gaze. "If Tandy was that desperate for money to make another new life and that obsessed with his missing score, he might have snapped with Woody. Killing him when Woody couldn't or wouldn't give him the hijacking money he wanted."

"Yeah," Philly said. "When he demanded that I get replacement dough from Alec, he acted like he knew the original money was gone."

"What a mess," Dad said. "What a mess we all made."

Nope, I wasn't taking on his guilt. It was bad enough that I had to shoulder my own. So much death and destruction...Billy Rob, Woody...Lucy serving a life sentence for a crime she didn't commit. And it was *my* fault. Mine, not Dad's. If I hadn't taken Terry's stupid money, none of this would have happened.

"I have to make this right," I said with fierce intensity. "As much as I can at this stage. We have to find that money and turn it in. Then we can share our theory with the Feds, and get Lucy to open up."

"What about that other guy the Feds are looking for in connection with you. I forget his name. How does he fit in?" Philly asked.

"One problem at a time," I insisted. "Now we need to grab the RV or the Bentley, and hightail it back to California, and find that money."

Dad stared off into the distance. "Going by car will take too long."

Drew snapped, "Not if we don't stop at every kitschy little—"

"What I'm trying to say is that there's a faster way to get there." Dad pointed across the hospital parking lot to the helipad. "What if we take that helicopter?"

CHAPTER FORTY

66 "N ow you're talking, Dad. Let's go." I handed Philly my
backpack, before scrambling over the side of the Dumpster.
"Wait!" Drew shouted. "Alec, you're not really
suggesting we should *steal* a helicopter? One used to transport sick
and injured people."

"Borrow, Andrew. Why make it sound so nefarious?" Dad said.

Drew sputtered, "It *is* nefarious! You're talking about borrowing
without permission—that's stealing." A vein throbbed in his
forehead. It couldn't be good for him that he kept getting so upset
at us.

Still, he wasn't stopping me. "Let's go," I said to the others.

"Tracy…" Drew warned.

I whirled around to him. "Listen, bud. You're the one who said
I should trust you sometimes when you know what's best, and that
at other times you would trust me. This time, I need your trust.
I have to do this, Drew. I might be responsible for the death of
both Billy Rob and Woody, as well as Lucy's having spent her life
in the slammer." I looked deeply into his eyes, so he'd know how
important this was to me.

"The Feds will get to the bottom of it," he said.

"Really? You mean after they arrest me, they'll still consider
alternate suspects? Drew, you told me yourself—once cops decide
they've got the right person, they stop looking."

Drew took a deep breath, which he blew out slowly. When he
pounded his forehead with his fist, I knew I had him. "Okay, let's do
it. But fast—before I realize what a mistake I'm making."

We dashed across the big circular drive in front of the hospital.
The gardeners had left their tool cart near the helipad. "Someone
grab those shovels," I said. To my surprise, Drew took them, without
giving me an argument.

As we ran, Dad pulled a little pad from his back pocket and scribbled something on it. Once he handed it to me, I saw the note read, "Thanks for the loan of your whirlybird." It was signed, "Actor and pilot, Alec Grainger."

"Nice note, Dad."

"Well, a little politeness makes things go down sweeter," he said. "Put some money with it, honey, so they won't mind as much."

I stopped. "What money?"

"Tracy, I gave you a fistful of it," he said with a scowl.

Philly and Drew climbed into the helicopter, but Dad and I remained beside it.

"And you have millions waiting in a Tecos bank for you," I said.

"Which I haven't touched."

"Crap." Why was it always me? I'd stuffed Dad's stash into one of my jeans' pockets and Drew's money in another. I pulled out the last of Drew's bills, and placing them below Dad's note, I anchored it all with a rock I found on the ground beside the heliport.

Dad leaped into the cockpit. Despite his unfortunately dated terminology for helicopters, he actually had a license to fly them. He'd learned for some movie he'd made back when he still performed his own stunts. I hadn't understood why he agreed to a pilot's license when he refused one for drivers, but he insisted the FAA was stricter than the various cops that had stopped him for traffic violations over the years, since he'd never actually ended up with a ticket. I slipped into the seat beside Philly. Just as Dad fired it up, Fricker came charging out of the hospital.

"Hold it!" Fricker shouted. "If you think I'm going to let you take off like a snake that's slithered down someone's pants, you—"

"We're finding T.K. Mann's loot and giving it to the Feds," I shouted over the engine noise. "Come along, and you get credit. But you'll have to shoot us to stop us."

After only a moment's hesitation, he lowered his head and jumped on board. Dad took off an instant later. We had only barely cleared the hospital's airspace when I saw Fricker texting someone on his phone. The Feds, no doubt. Another fink ratting us out.

* * *

We had to refuel at a desert airstrip along the way, hoping the Feds hadn't sent out an alert about us, or if they had, that the attendant there hadn't read it. Given that a supermarket tabloid never left the guy's hands, he would probably only have noticed if we had Bigfoot on board. We finally landed back in California, in that gang-banger park, where we had buried an army trunk decades earlier. Drew, Fricker, and I dug up the trunk.

Since they hadn't buried it deeply, it didn't take long. Once Drew and Fricker wrestled the trunk onto the seedy grass, I flipped it open—they hadn't even padlocked it. I spotted some of the stacks of twenties and reached for one.

"Look!" I shouted, waving them around. "I told you T.K. Mann's money would be here, and it is."

Fricker snatched the stack from my hand. "This here is funny money, girl. Counterfeit. That's as easy to say as when a hoss-fly talks in your ear."

It gave me the creeps, but I was actually starting to understand this guy.

Philly took another stack and flipped it in his fingers. "Sure is. I told you Tag got into that briefly. Bad job, too. You can see why his career in counterfeiting went south."

Unsure now, I took another stack from the trunk. Even I could see it was a pretty approximate version of U.S. currency.

"I don't understand. I was so sure..." I'd never felt so disappointed.

Way off in the distance, I could hear the faint sound of sirens.

"Feds," Drew noted nervously. He looked to Fricker. "You contacted the Bureau, right?"

"That I did," Fricker admitted. "But they'd have followed the helicopter's GPS without it." He paused, reading another text on his phone. "They say the money was a dead giveaway."

Money? What money? Not *this* money, right? A glimmer of a thought sparked in my mind.

"Drew, do you still have Woody's iPhone?"

Drew took it from his pocket, while shifting uncomfortably from one foot to another. "Don't you hear those sirens? They're coming for us, and we don't have the money we promised to find."

"Yeah, yeah. The iPhone—can we surf the web on it?"

He sighed. "Trace, for all you know about smart phones, you really belong on Route 66."

Maybe I did at that. I told Drew to look up some of the video shot when T.K. Mann hijacked that plane. He handed the phone to me. I didn't know quite what I expected to find, but I hastily looked at one tape, only to close it and begin another.

Finally, one struck me. It was video some news camera had captured of the sick passenger T.K. Mann had let leave the plane, after the government delivered the ransom, and before the refueled plane took off again. I watched the back of the unknown man who made his way across the tarmac.

"Wait," I said. "I've never seen this tape before."

Drew glanced over my shoulder. "The TV special showed that when you went to the door for our burrito order."

I damned Loco Pepe and his devastatingly great Kitchen Sink Burritos. If I had seen this piece of film, instead of answering the door for the deliveryman, I might have ended this whole mess right on the spot.

I shoved the phone in Dad's face. "Dad, who is this?"

He didn't even have to think about it. "Why, that's Billy Rob."

I showed it to Drew. "You see. I told you one of his legs was shorter, and he walked with a lean to one side."

Drew gave the little screen a quick glance, then looked uneasily toward the sound of approaching sirens, though they still didn't sound that close. "Uh, Trace, the Feds…"

I pretended I hadn't heard him, while conflicting waves of emotions rolled through me. Excitement built the way it always did when I was zeroing in on the prize, but countering it was the fear that I wouldn't pull things together in time. And fear seemed to be winning.

"Why does Billy Rob look so fat?" Dad asked. "He appears to be a much sturdier man in this film."

"Because he was covered with bundles of money! I was right about the three of them being involved, Terry, Billy Rob, and

Woody—Terry was the main hijacker. But he didn't leap from that plane with the money in his backpack, as everyone surmised. Since he was the most identifiable one, if the cops caught him when he landed, I bet he didn't want the risk of having the money on him. Instead, Billy Rob posed as a sick passenger—he was the one Terry sent out to retrieve the cash, and then, Billy Rob carried out the money again packed in his clothes."

Drew nodded thoughtfully. "Remember what Elise told us, that Billy Rob wasn't able to pick up Woody at school at that time."

"And then the three of them created confusion on the ground," I continued. "By all dressing as T.K. Mann and riding around on identical bikes."

Billy Rob must have cheated Terry, hiding the loot somewhere other than where they planned for him to leave it, probably the caves. When he refused to divulge its location, Terry killed him. Then Lucy must have found Billy Rob's body and thought Woody did it, and she took the blame. So it wasn't my fault, after all. Knowing that made me feel a bit better, though frustration still choked me.

The vehicles with those sirens had entered our zip code now.

My gaze fell on the funny money tossed in the open trunk beside us. It occurred to me to wonder whether the money Lucy had given me in my lunch pail was counterfeit, too. Had I maintained a sacred trust, refusing to spend what was really just Monopoly money? I yanked the lunch pail from my backpack, handing the backpack to Philly. For the first time in decades, I opened the domed lid.

I stared into it shock. "Someone stole my money," I shrieked. "All the money Lucy gave me is gone!"

"Tracy, it was only five dollars," Dad said. "Five bucks doesn't go as far as it used to."

"It was five *thousand*, Dad. You can still get some mileage from that."

"Five thousand? Where would Lucy get...? Tracy, you let me think it was only five dollars," he said sternly.

"You leaped to that conclusion." He was the one who taught me about secrets and lies. It seemed only fair that I used that knowledge against him.

"Babe, I took the money before we left home," Drew said. "I thought you understood that. I used it to pay Chaz."

"But— but..." I sputtered. "I thought we were using your stash. You know, the money you tuck away around the house."

Drew choked. "I spent that within weeks of leaving my job. How much did you think I had?" He took the lunch pail from my hands. "I've always been curious about this lunchbox, but I never got around to asking you about it. When I saw it stacked with our luggage for the trip, I looked into it for the first time and found the cash. Naturally, when Chaz stopped by while I was gardening, I paid him from that. Then I put the rest in my wallet, and eventually, you took it." He shrugged. "What's the point of having money if you don't spend it?"

I could have told him why I didn't want to spend it, but those sirens *were* drawing closer. Besides, a thought tickled my brain. Chaz...? "Drew," I asked, "what's Chaz's real name?"

He shrugged. "I can never remember. Charles Something Something, the Third."

"Could it be *Stuart* Charles Barrington Athers, the Third?" I demanded. Not Charles Stuart Atherton Barrington, as I thought. Stuart Athers. "Stuart Athers!" I shouted.

Suddenly, I knew. I knew it all. Why the Feds thought Chaz was my partner in crime. Why Woody was killed. Why Woody's café had holes in the walls. Why the FBI thought I'd gone to towns that I'd never visited—towns that I'd bet contained casinos. And why Drew was never suspected of anything.

The sirens were almost upon us now.

"Everyone back in the helicopter," I shouted. *"Now.* This time I *really* know where the T.K. Mann money is."

"What about the time capsule?" Dad asked of the trunk still open on the ground.

"Oh, right. Dad, grab my Malibu Barbie, willya? I've missed her. Then we really need to get out of there. Hasn't anyone else heard how close those sirens are?"

Once again, we all piled back into the aircraft, and we lifted off, just as three black sedans screeched to a halt beside a dirty old Army trunk and a hole in the ground.

CHAPTER FORTY-ONE

Though Dad insisted he was flying on fumes, he got us back to Flagstaff, Arizona, bringing the copter down in the space in front of the bizarre little cottage in Hinky Dill's Biker Bunny Bin.

Once again, as soon as we landed, the sound of sirens filled the air, starting closer this time. Wasn't it great that there were so many Federal agents on the public payroll, they could tap new ones in whatever state we happened to pop into?

I leaped from the helicopter and headed for Dad's storage unit.

"Wait, honey," Dad said. "Shouldn't we stop by Hinky's cottage first?"

"Dad, as long as there are casinos, I don't think we'll find Hinky here except to refill his coffers," I said, finally understanding that middle of the night phone call about Hinky's intended casino crawl.

I found my key ring, and picked out the key to Dad's storage unit on it.

"You know, Hinky has an extra key to my unit," Dad said. "It seemed a good idea to leave one with him in case we ever lost ours."

Funny, it seemed like the worst idea I'd ever heard. As the sound of sirens grew nearer, I unlocked the pointless padlock on the storage unit door. I turned the knob, but before I could push the door open, several vehicles surrounded us. At least a dozen agents popped from their cars with guns drawn. They ordered us all to put our hands up.

Everyone did, including Fricker, although he also held his badge in his hand. Everyone obeyed but me.

"Sure, thing, agents," I said. "But first, you'll probably want to take a gander at what you'll find in here."

I was taking a chance, of course, since I hadn't looked in there myself. But this time I had to be right. I gave the door a little shove, and leaned in myself, even though I was risking going down in a hail of bullets, like Eliot Ness nailing some old-time Chicago bad guy. Instead of filling my poor body with lead, one of the agents cautiously came forward to look, though the others did keep their guns pointed at us.

On the other side of that door, there was cash everywhere. On the shelves, on the floor, bills sticking out of many of the hundreds of lunch pails that filled in that room. T.K. Mann's hijacked money, missing for thirty years. It looked as if someone had grabbed fistfuls of currency from those lunch pails, and left this behind. Not someone, Hinky. He must have discovered what they contained when he opened the one with the bunny painted on it the last time we were there, and asked if he could have it. Hinky probably figured he'd have enough for life here, even the way he gambled.

Another agent roughly pulled me aside and put my hands behind my back. As he cuffed me, Fricker said with a chuckle, "Agents, you might not want to jump on this young lady like a king snake on a rattler. She isn't America's Most Wanted. She solved the most infamous crime of the last two centuries."

Strangely, they arrested me anyway.

CHAPTER FORTY-TWO

Just as going on the lam had been a lifelong dream, so was getting arrested by Federal authorities, making this a win-win caper. I didn't even try to evade arrest this time. Not that I could have with all those guns pointed at me. But for an amateur sleuth, this was the ultimate. Loads of sleuths get warned off cases by local cops—I had been plenty of times. But by being thrown in Federal lockup, I rose above the lot of them. I had arrived.

Besides, since they initially put me in solitary, it gave me time to think. I found myself remembering little things that I hadn't noticed at the time. Such as that night at Hinky's Biker Bunny Bin, when I thought I saw the shadow of someone headed toward Dad's storage unit as we were leaving. If I had turned around then and caught Hinky breaking in, would I have solved it on the spot? Or if I'd seen him pulling cash out of those lunch pails, would I have assumed Lucy had been a lot more frugal than anyone suspected, and had shown a distrust of banks. I mean, if you find someone has been stuffing his mattress with money, do you leap to the conclusion that he'd accumulated those bills by robbing banks, rather than avoiding them?

Nah, I couldn't second-guess myself. If I did, I'd have to wonder how much would have been different in how many lives if I'd told Dad decades ago exactly how much money I'd found in the lunch pail Lucy had given me. If I had, that might have short-circuited a lifelong love affair with secrets. Where would I be today without them?

I also found myself thinking about the odd holes Woody had carved into the walls when he redecorated the café. He must have been looking for the money, too. Not the smartest move he'd ever made, since there was never any alteration to those walls thirty years ago. Woody hadn't been the sharpest knife in the drawer. Still, in

his own way, he desperately wanted that lost score as much as Tag/
Terry/Kyle had. Billy Rob had pulled a helluva joke on his T.K.
Mann partners, but he took the punch line to his grave.

I remembered what Woody had said that night we arrived. How
Lucy shouldn't have taken something from him. I assumed he meant
her killing Billy Rob. Woody must have thought she killed him for
the hijacked money. Where did he think she'd put it? Woody had to
have been the absolute dullest knife in the drawer.

I realized now that I should have known something was up
between the governor and Woody. Accounts of their relationship
were inconsistent. Starting with why they would have a relationship
at all. When we ran into Tandy in the caves, he told us he'd met
Woody once when he first came to town, and though he swore he
never ate Woody's waffles again, he made it sound as if they knew
each other better than a one-time encounter would presume. Dad
had told us Tandy honked his Jeep's Jaws-theme-horn when he
drove past for Woody, but he never stopped in. So when did they
see each other?

I'd bet they met regularly, probably in the café after hours. Just
as they had that night when Drew and I arrived in Tecos, when
Woody rushed us all out the door. They were probably friendlier
at first, with Tag/Terry/Kyle seemingly eager to reconnect with his
old partner. Besides, if the governor never came to the café, when
did he give Woody those blackmail notes for Philly? Woody might
have even been promised a piece of whatever sum they gouged out
of Philly or Dad. Then again, I could see Woody participating just
because extortion was his favorite activity. If you don't keep your
hand in, your skills get rusty.

But something must have happened the night Woody was killed.
Maybe Tag/Terry/Kyle grew tired of trying to charm his old friend. I
knew charm was always his first approach, but I also knew he could
discard it in a flash, in favor of something nastier. Had he snapped
again? You'd think he'd have learned that killing the victim first
meant the victim would never tell him what he wanted to know. But
he clearly found it so satisfying.

I also found myself thinking about that day that Dad had been so desperate to leave Tecos. The day we piled all the lunch pails in a trailer, and he, Terry, and I bugged out. They hadn't let me have any visitors at first, but once they did, during one of Dad's visits I asked him about it.

"It was an all-around terrible time," he said with a sigh. "Lucy being sent to prison, Woody shipped off to his grandmother's, and I couldn't do a thing to stop any of it. There was nothing left for me in Tecos, but no reason to leave, either."

With a sigh, his gaze drifted off to the past.

"But then someone shoved a note under the motel door, threatening your life if I didn't leave quickly. I thought about taking it to the cops, but when Terry told me you wanted to leave anyway, what was the point of staying?"

I stifled a sigh. "Let me guess—there was some nice square printing in that note." I visualized the blackmail notes sent to Philly.

"Right. How did you...?" Dad flushed sheepishly. "Oh, I get it—Terry wrote it, huh?"

"He probably wasn't too comfortable in Tecos. With Lucy's conviction, the cops had stopped looking for Billy Rob's killer, but T.K. Mann was still America's Most Wanted. He needed a good reason for leaving town, and you gave it to him."

"I can't get over how wrong I was about him. He wasn't really a nice guy, after all."

With that we crowned a new king of understatement. But I really shouldn't blame Dad. I'd seen Terry with his bonhomie mask stripped away, the way few people had. He had also fooled the electorate of California in a big way. And in that guise, he fooled me, too.

Twelve days after my arrest, when I'd about reached my quota for alone time, they let me out and dropped all the charges. I didn't know Drew and Fricker had been working behind the scenes on my behalf, taking the Feds through the hijacking, Billy Rob's murder, Woody's, along with how the hijacked money finally surfaced in my hands, Chaz's, and Hinky's. They didn't even charge us with stealing a helicopter, though I suspected Dad ended up paying a hefty rental for it.

While I was in the clink, I missed the opening salvo of the

media circus the governor's guilt had generated, but fortunately the
hoopla continued. There's nothing I love quite as much as a circus,
especially since this one contained some payback that was long
overdue.

Governor Psycho-Veggie came out of his coma and was once
again a changed man, but this time, one eager to talk about a life
of crime. Eager? Hah! They couldn't stop his bragging. Nobody
knew whether he'd suffered brain damage when the marble hit his
head or from the brain bleed or what the docs had to do to release
the pressure, but Tag/Terry/Kyle started confessing to everything,
including shooting that shopkeeper in Chicago, and moving on to
crimes spread over decades and clear across the map. States and
cities lined up to charge him, though the Feds claimed first place.

Maybe nothing happened to his brain, maybe the Ultimate
Buckaroo had simply grown tired of reinventing himself. Even a cat
only has nine lives.

He confirmed for the FBI much of what I'd surmised about the
hijacking, apparently proud of what had been a foolproof plan, apart
from Billy Rob's wrinkle. Billy Rob had walked off that plane with
the money packed into his clothes. He presumed that Billy Rob had
taken the money to the caves, as they planned, since he'd found a
couple of burlap bags there. But that was when Billy Rob changed
the arrangement, not *leaving* the money there as they'd agreed.

When Terry cornered him at the café, Billy Rob refused to tell
him where he'd put it. Anger made Terry kill his partner in crime. In
the short time he had to search the café, he never found the money.
It didn't occur to him to look in those lunch pails that had always
lined the walls. He also said he never expected Lucy to confess to
his crime, and he considered that just another lucky break in a life
that proved to be full of them.

His brags became almost too preposterous to believe, and people
started doubting all of it. After all, people expect governors of
California to have a weaker-than-usual hold on reality, and everyone
wondered whether he was making this stuff up. For a while it looked
as if he might not be prosecuted for some of his crimes. Only it
turned out the hospital that worked on his face after his Route 66

accident had kept a sample of his blood, so a lab was easily able to connect Terry Kennedy and Kyle Tandy with the same DNA, so the history he related started, once again, to look truer and truer.

The Clement twins came forward to tell their story. They couldn't prove their grandfather's account, but the fact that Terry Kennedy made their grandfather sign the deed to the mines over to Tag Kowalski also linked those identifies.

And as the media storm built, more and more people contributed their tales. Bits of evidence built together until it was only a question of how many life sentences he could serve during the remainder of his one life.

The Feds also tracked down Hinky. Because of his burned skin, Hinky hadn't left fingerprints on the money—just as Drew hadn't because he handled it while wearing gardening gloves. Still, it wasn't hard to find Hinky. They simply combed casinos, following the trail of marked bills. The sad thing was that he was on the greatest winning streak of his life. I'd heard he sobbed when they confiscated his winnings. Easy come, easy go—another lesson he should learn. I didn't know why I kept feeling the impulse to fix that guy.

As the evidence against Tag/Terry/Kyle kept mounting, what Philly knew about the shopkeeper's murder made him antsy.

"With so many people lining up to testify against him, Philly, there's no need for you to admit to anything," I'd told him when he came to see me at the jail. "He's going to spend the rest of his life behind bars no matter what you do."

"No, kid, I gotta own up to I what I know about Tag killing that shopkeeper. I've wanted to tell someone for a long time."

Philly told me later that he felt scared when he and Drew went to Chicago to talk to the DA there. Fortunately, they gave him immunity in exchange for his promised testimony, assuming that case against Tag/Terry/Kyle ever came to trial. Philly walked a little taller after that.

When they finally let me go, Drew wanted to head straight home. He felt great pressure to make things right with Chaz, who had spent even more time in jail than I had. I hadn't actually heard about his arrest—it must have happened during one of my self-imposed news blackouts. Sure, I also wanted to apologize to Chaz, but I had another debt to pay, and it was one we were geographically closer to.

I went to see Lucy again. She seemed much as she had the first time, both sensual and serene. But some of the burden of grief seemed to have lifted. I wasn't sure how much she knew about what had happened, and I hated to have to tell her that Woody's darkest secrets had all come out. But she surprised me when she started to talk.

"Tracy, honey, I don't know how to thank you for what you did for my poor boy, the way you got justice not only for him, but also for his daddy, after all these years."

I didn't know what to make of that change of heart. "But, Lucy, you told me *not* to look into Woody's death. I thought you'd be angry or—"

She started laughing. "Oh, honey, I've known you most of your life. I know the best way to get you to do anything is to tell you not to do it."

That wasn't me.

"You're exactly like Martha in that way."

Now she was just being insulting.

* * *

While the Feds eventually came to accept everything we contended about Tag/Terry/Kyle, somehow that didn't translate into an instant release for Lucy. In the weeks that followed, Dad and I traveled to New Mexico several times and met with the governor and the Federal authorities there. Eventually, the governor of New Mexico pardoned Lucy, and after thirty years away, she finally came home.

The town of Tecos threw a party a few days after her release, which they held in Woody's café. We were all there for it.

Among the guests, I saw a more subdued Mark Baker, still hopping around as if to music, but slower than before. It seems the Feds were already onto Cary Chandler, the Department of the Interior guy and Mark's partner in crime. When Elise shared the photo that

Woody had taken of them meeting in that motel room, Mark agreed to roll on Chandler, and for that they gave him immunity. He didn't get to carry out his little land swap swindle, but he did keep his job as mayor. Apparently, nobody else wanted it.

Don and Genevieve Cannon were also there, looking as happy as newlyweds. Genevieve told me they were really talking for the first time, shedding all their secrets, and things had never been better between them. I still couldn't explain why she hid out in the supermarket parking lot that night, though I had a good feeling they would make it. But married people sharing secrets? That was just wrong.

I also spotted another couple at the party that I never expected when Chief Fricker draped his large arm around Elise's tiny shoulders and pulled her close to him. The little cinnamon-colored freckles across Elise's nose glowed, and he looked happier and more animated than ever. I hadn't seen that one coming, but I liked it.

The person who made the biggest splash at Lucy's coming home party was someone who wasn't even there—Mother. I tried to make her come with us, but she feared she might steal the show, when Lucy was supposed to be the star. Not only had she convinced one of her friends who owned a high-end clothing company to bring out lines of Lucy's designs over the next several seasons, which was going to make Lucy wealthier than she ever dreamed, Mother told Dad to stay in Tecos as long as he wanted. I guessed she finally understood that Lucy was no threat to her marriage.

At the center of it all, Lucy, wearing one of her own dresses, did look like a star. In the days following her release, before the party, Dad had arranged for a top oncologist to examine her. The specialist concluded that she'd been getting better care in prison than we thought she would, and her breast cancer prognosis was excellent.

So, it had all come together so perfectly...apart from a few little threads that I needed to tie up. When I saw Lucy climb the stairs to her old apartment, I followed her. I found her seated on one of the chrome chairs from her luncheonette, holding the stocking that had been draped over it.

"Pretty great day, huh, Tracy?" Lucy asked.

I nodded. It was a great day. Still, there were things I needed to know. "Lucy, did you know all that money was stuffed into your lunch pails?"

"Lord, no! I like to think if I had known, I'd have been honest enough to turn it in." She shrugged. "But who knows? When I saw Billy Rob dead, and knowing what I thought—maybe I would have grabbed Woody and the money, and run."

"So none of the money was visible?"

"Tracy, there was nothing there but Billy Rob and lots of burlap bags."

I tried to keep my face neutral at the mention of the bags.

Lucy shrugged again. "Sure, I know *now* what those bags meant, but not then. Woody kept some of them, and I used the rest to make toys in the days leading up to my incarceration, which I passed out to the kids in the hospital."

I'd missed that clue. I remembered seeing burlap toys in a basket with other sewing projects she'd left unfinished.

"I didn't even know about the hijacking," Lucy added. "Everyone was talking about something, but I never watched the news back then. Unless Alec or Martha was on it, of course."

Good to know that Dad's friends were as uninformed as he was.

"So why did you confess?" I asked at last.

"Honey, you have to understand about the days leading up to the murder. First, Billy Rob got a job painting the town hall, and he asked me if he could take Woody out of school to help him."

That was her idea of Woody making history? Maybe in the Crier family it was.

"Billy Rob never had any interest in Woody, so it made me feel good to know they were working together. But Woody was awful in those days. Nasty, edgy. And every time I saw them together, they seemed to be arguing."

Lucy stared out the window, her eyes momentarily welling with tears.

"After we found Billy Rob's body, Woody became even more difficult. He hadn't always told me the truth, you know. I can't think where he would have gotten that tendency to fib."

Where indeed?

"But I always knew when he was hiding something. I asked him right out if he'd killed Billy Rob. He said he hadn't, but he acted so guilty, I thought he was lying. I didn't know he was hiding something else, something every bit as bad."

"So…you confessed to what you thought was his crime."

Lucy nodded. "To make up for…oh, so many things I wasn't very good at." Dismissing the past with a wave of the stocking, Lucy brightened again. "You know, I don't think I'll come back to this apartment to live." Right now she was bunking down in Woody's old room at the Rest Ur Head. "It's too big. I'm not used to this much space," she said with a self-deprecating laugh.

Knowing how much the clothing manufacturer had paid her for her designs, I said, "Lucy, you could live anywhere now."

"Why would I want to? Tracy, this is Route 66—the best place in the world."

Despite everything that had happened to us there, I understood how she felt.

* * *

I thought things would quiet down for us once we went home, but they didn't. Chaz, our former handyman, wouldn't have anything to do with us. For a guy who was so one with the universe, he could sure hold a grudge.

And that town at the start of Route 66 took away Dad's plaque. They said we didn't respect the time capsule. That much was true. It was good to have my Malibu Barbie back, though—I kept her on a shelf in my office now, right next to Woody's marble shooter. Dad even reclaimed his Hang Ten jacket. It was still there in the trunk that we left open in the park. Weeks later and nobody had taken it. Go figure. Nobody wanted free duds from the eighties. Unlike all the funny money the cops were still trying to round up. Apparently, everyone who walked through that park helped themselves to bundles of counterfeit bills until there were none left.

But hey, one day, months later, a check arrived in the mail from

Washington, D.C. The government had offered a reward for anyone giving information that led to the conviction of T.K. Mann and the recovery of the money. And that sure fit us. It amounted to two hundred and fifty thousand bucks!

Drew whistled when he saw that check and said, "What do you know? Chaz was right. The universe did provide. I don't need a job, after all. I have lots of time to decide what I want to do next."

I'd never hear the end of that one. There was an upside, though. Now, at least, I didn't have to write that stupid travel article about Route 66. I mean, really, who would believe it?

THE END

Kris Neri

Kris Neri is the author of the Agatha, Anthony, Macavity, and Lefty Award-nominated Tracy Eaton mysteries, *Revenge of the Gypsy Queen, Dem Bones' Revenge, Revenge for Old Times' Sake,* and *Revenge on Route 66.*

Her other books include *Never Say Die, The Rose in the Snow* and the Lefty Award-nominated Magical Mystery series: *High Crimes on the Magical Plane* and *Magical Alienation.*

She is a two-time Derringer Award winner and a two-time Push-cart Prize nominee for her short fiction.

And with her husband, she owns The Well Red Coyote bookstore in Sedona, Arizona.

Readers can reach her through her website: www.KrisNeri.com

Acknowledgements

My deepest gratitude goes to:

- Betsy Lampe and Betty Wright who gave me the idea for this mystery. Betsy told me the idea of using Route 66 in a Tracy Eaton mystery came to her in a dream. I always liked the concept, but Route 66 had no real meaning to me until I moved into its shadow and discovered what a perfect place it would be for Tracy and the gang.

- Mark Baker and Don Cannon, old friends. Both Mark and Don secured the right to have a character named for them in one of my books. Since this book was in the works, I told them I could easily re-name existing characters after them. Mark and Don, knowing how I poke fun at characters in this series, thanks for being such good sports and letting me have my way with your names. I hope you like what I did with them.

- Lisa Kline, my editor. Thanks to the issues and questions Lisa raised, this is a better book than it would have been without them. I also want to send special thanks to Greg Lilly, Cherokee McGhee publisher, for his continued support of Tracy and her family and friends, and for giving them such a comfy home.

- To friends Sherry Shively and Ada Wright, to whom this book is dedicated, for their friendship and support.

- And especially to Joe — husband and best friend, partner in business and partner in life: Without you, none of it would mean as much.

TRACY EATON MYSTERIES

Revenge of the Gypsy Queen

" ... a hilarious debut mystery... Neri's sleuth offers a sharp eye, a smart mouth, and an irrepressible sense of humor...in an intricately plotted, surprise-in-your-face, don't-put-it-down mystery."
— Carolyn Hart, author of the *Death on Demand* series

Dem Bones' Revenge

"Kris Neri has written another winner. Fasten your seatbelts and enjoy this sly, smart Hollywood roller coaster, which should appeal to mystery and movie buffs alike."
— Laura Lippman, author of *And When She Was Good*

Revenge for Old Times' Sake

"Kris Neri's cool-under-pressure protagonist and her witty narrative voice are the reasons this series is an award winner. The clever plot twists and vivid characters bring to mind what might result from the unholy coupling of Mel Brooks and Janet Evanovich."
— Bill Fitzhugh, author of *Pest Control* and *Highway 61 Resurfaced*

Revenge on Route 66

"Kris Neri's Lefty Award-nominated Tracy Eaton is back, this time on a wild ride along Route 66. If you're looking for laughs, hairpin turns, and whiplash plot twists, you won't want to miss this madcap adventure. Buckle up!"
— Julie Hyzy, *New York Times* Bestselling author the White House Chef Mysteries and the Manor House Mystery series

From **Cherokee McGhee** Publishing
& available from fine bookstores everywhere.

CPSIA information can be obtained at www.ICGtesting.com
Printed in the USA
LVOW121808260613

340373LV00007B/822/P